HIDING OUT

CAROLINE SPRINGS CHARTER

LILA ROSE

Lindsey Lawson
The woman who has been supporting me
from the start and who has always had my back!

CHAPTER ONE

WILLOW

"Come on, Low, you need a night out. When was the last time you got laid?" my co-worker, from the small supermarket we worked at together, questioned as she stood at her empty register. Thank God I was also free of customers in the run-down, rarely busy supermarket because Lucia went on. "You need a good shag, woman. Everyone can see how tense your arse is."

I giggled and shook my head at her. "Babe, why're you so worried about my arse? *I'm* fine with not getting any, so *you* shouldn't worry about it, either." I sent her an eye roll before picking up a new magazine to read.

"You work too hard, always askin' for extra shifts. You

LILA ROSE

have no fun, and a no-fun Willow is a dull bitch. I want, just one day, to come to work and you tell me about a good poundin' you got the night before."

"Pfft! Aren't your own adventures enough to keep you occupied?" I asked, thumbing through the 'Who's Wearing What' section.

"I don't have enough goin' on in my life since bein' with Alex. I need to live through you now, girl, unless I cheat on my man. You wouldn't want that, would you? It'd be your fault if I cheated."

Snorting, I said, "You're so full of it. As if you would cheat on Alex. He dotes on you like you're a queen. Why'd you want to ruin that? Plus, like you said, he's magical in bed. Now *that's* something I've never experienced." Sighing, I put the magazine back and grabbed another. My sex life was, and always had been, non-existent. I was a twenty-two-year-old, born-again virgin. 'Born again' because I'd only had one lover, which lasted long enough for him to take my V-card and leave, never to be seen again. Not that Lucia knew that. I shuddered at the thought if she found out my snatch hadn't any visitors for the last six years. She'd probably organise a 'losing your V-card second time around' party, lining up several men to knock out that pesky grown-over-again hymen.

I glanced up at her and then back down before continuing. "And you know why I have to work my arse

2

off. I need out of my cousin's house. I need to make a life for myself."

Living with a cousin I hardly knew, despite being there for two years, was something I never thought I'd do. There were so many contributing factors to why I was still there.

Like two years ago, the first time I tried to leave my high-on-ice parents' house only to find I couldn't because they'd stolen from me. After saving my arse off, I'd decided it was NL day, as in New Life day. I went to the bank to collect the hard-earned money, only to discover my account was dry. My parents had stolen my money so they could get high and invest in their own little pharmacy. An ignorant error on my behalf, having them added to my account in case they needed extra money for food and such. I'd left school at the age of sixteen so I could work and get out of my parents' house. It took me until I was twenty to have enough cash to make the escape. I didn't hate them for it, though.

I couldn't. They were my parents.

I was annoyed. No, that wasn't right. I was pissed. I wanted to string them up by their toes on the clothesline and beat them senseless, but I didn't.

They were neglectful parents, but they weren't so bad. They didn't beat me. They weren't mean to me nor did they abuse me. They simply didn't care enough about their child.

Ever since my younger sister drowned when I was six, ice became more important than anything to my parents. I cooked, cleaned, and did my own homework without any help. I raised myself. So even though I didn't hate them, I'd felt nothing when they died two months after I'd turned twenty. Unsurprisingly, they'd OD'd from an experimental batch gone wrong. I'd lost both my parents in one night, yet I spilled no tears to grieve for them.

I felt nothing.

My apathy wasn't because they'd left me with nothing; I had no money and no place to stay, so I was evicted. I was sure my lack of concern was because they didn't care enough about their only living daughter which caused me, in turn, to not care about them.

I still wasn't sure if that made me a bad person. The only saving grace at the time was the fact that my cousin, Colton, had turned up the day after their deaths and offered me some help. Not having many friends I could rely on, or any other family, I had no choice but to take him up on his offer. I didn't want to live on the streets and fend for myself. So even though Colton was practically a stranger, I had limited options but to trust him.

At least it worked out. Colton kept to himself. We shared the house, but honestly, we hardly saw each other. I was always busy working and he was busy...doing whatever he did. I'd asked questions about him, but it seemed he wasn't willing to share too much. I prayed every night I hadn't moved in with a serial killer. He never gave off the vibe he'd like to hack me up into tiny pieces, thankfully. He *was* my cousin, after all, and he was kind enough to look out for me. Still, I bought a lock for my bedroom door. However, what helped was that over the two years, he was more like a weird reclusive housemate than a family member. He'd moved me into the house he inherited from his father. My uncle had been rich, *very* rich, and left everything to Colton. I never really knew my uncle. He disowned my family, his drugged-up brother. I couldn't blame him, really; I'd been ashamed, as well.

Despite a pretty peaceful two years, I was ready to move out and stand on my own two feet. Excitement thrummed through me every time I thought about having a place of my own, followed by a giddy feeling in my stomach. Even though Fate had thrown me a crappy deck by bringing me into a world where the people who *were* my family didn't care an ounce about me, I was proud of the person I'd become. I strived to be better each day, to be nothing like my parents, where through the struggles of life, I didn't turn to alcohol or drugs and things were looking up. Finally, I was escaping the deep doo-doo that'd been thrown my way.

It was a new beginning for me, and I couldn't wait.

Shrugging the thoughts away, I continued talking to Lucia and flipping through the pages. "You never know, when I'm finally on my own two feet and in my own place, maybe I could find my own Alex. Or even start to have some fun by getting down and dirty with some stranger who would cause my girly parts to sing a hymn…" I stopped because I got the eerie feeling Lucia and I weren't alone. I looked up from the magazine to find a fine specimen of man standing in the doorway of the supermarket. Gorgeous, blondish-brown messy hair, ocean-blue eyes, and a large frame, which I guessed was popping with toned muscles, he wore dark jeans that hugged his firm thighs. I found myself wishing he would turn around to give us a show of his butt while shaking it. Combining that with a tight black tee and leather jacket, I was losing grip on reality and wondered if I'd somehow knocked myself out.

Then it all came back to me, the last words said from my mouth. I blushed and prayed that the sinful man hadn't heard. Yet his smirk and wink as he walked past told me he had. I wanted to curl into a ball under my counter and pretend I wasn't there.

"Willow," Lucia said.

"Yes?" I sighed.

"Can you get me a mop?"

Dragging my reluctant eyes away from a *sweet* tush, I looked to her to see she was still watching the walking sin. "Why?" I asked.

She grinned wickedly before saying, "Because I just

creamed my panties and made a puddle on the floor while watchin' that damn fine man walk in here."

"Lucia." I gasped and quickly looked down the aisle where my fantasy man had walked. He was no longer in sight. "You can't say that stuff out loud."

"Oh, girl, I can and I will." Then she laughed. "At least it wasn't me who said I was gonna get down and dirty and have my girly parts sing as he walked in."

"Snap, he heard?"

"Sure did." She grinned.

Standing up straight, I looked to the clock. It was past seven at night which meant... "At least I don't have to embarrass myself more. It's time for me to go." I smiled, grabbed my bag from under the counter and walked over to Lucia for a quick hug goodbye.

"Sure you don't wanna stay? He may offer himself up for your dirty ride."

Snorting, I said, "No. I think I'll keep him in my fantasy drawer."

"Have smokin' dreams tonight, girl."

Waving over my shoulder, I said, "Oh, I will." I turned to wink, but didn't get there. Instead, I squeaked when I spotted Mr Sin himself standing at her counter. Lucia burst out laughing as I practically ran from the shop.

The bus ride home seemed to take longer than any other day. It didn't help that I was sweltering and the man next to me was enjoying being in my personal space, making me hot and uncomfortable. I contemplated if the air-conditioning on the bus was even working. I felt the beast of a man beside me look down at me once again. I didn't want to meet his gaze in case he wanted to start up a conversation.

Oh. Snap. He shifted and a whiff of BO caught my nose, nearly making me gag.

Gripping my bag closer to my chest, I closed my eyes and rested my head against the window. *Come on, stop, come on.* The whole ride threatened to put a dampener on my good mood. Yet, I still couldn't wait to get home and tell my cousin I was moving out. I'd even found a small apartment in the paper that morning. I rang the realtor on my break and I would head there the next day to take a look. Everything appeared promising, though. A couple of weeks and I'd be on my own.

A smile lit my face. Yes, even with the scent of BO in my nose, I could still smile. It was as though nothing could take away my happiness.

Finally, my stop came. I squeezed past Stinky and felt a pinch on my arse.

Turning quickly, I pointed in his pudgy face and snapped, "Would you like to have babies one day?"

His eyes widened, but he nodded.

"Then don't ever do that again to any female or one day, your balls will be sliced off by some pissed-off woman. You're just lucky I'm in a good mood or it would be me."

I made my way down the aisle and off the bus. Heck, the small breeze in the humid air was better than that rubbish bus trip.

Around the corner of the bus stop was Colton's house. Walking up the path, I reached the house and unlocked the door. Thick heat greeted me, letting me know my cousin wasn't home. Once I turned the air-conditioner on, I made my way down to my room and dropped my bag. After a quick shower in the bathroom at the end of the hall, I dressed in a sleeveless tee and denim shorts. Feeling more comfortable out of my work gear, I walked into Colton's study munching on an apple.

I needed access to his computer to transfer some money from my chequing account to my savings account.

His laptop was already open on his desk and with a quick wiggle of the mouse, it came to life. I logged in and smiled to myself. After today's wages, there would be exactly what I needed to make the move.

My apple slipped from my hand to the floor.

No.

Not again.

It was empty, except for fifty cents.

Where was my money?

My heart tightened in my chest. Tears formed in my eyes, but I wiped them away.

I searched through the transfer information and discovered Colton's name as recipient. There had to be an explanation. There had to be. He wouldn't do it to me, not after knowing what my parents did. He wouldn't. He couldn't be that heartless.

The one person I had left in my life I couldn't trust, either.

No. Hold out hope. Something could have happened. There had to be a good explanation on why my goddamn money was gone. There had to be.

He wouldn't need my measly savings. He had an inheritance worth hundreds of thousands.

I searched through the help information, trying to see if there was a way to stop the transfer. Confused by the small print swimming before my eyes, I took the time to frantically search through his document files. I lucked out when I found his own bank sign-in details in a Word document.

A moment later, I stared at the screen and his bank balance. His account sat at zero.

God. I really, *really* was stupid.

It was then I heard the front door open. I pushed the chair back and strode from the office, down the hall and into the living room where Colton was shouldering his bag off.

"Where is it?" I asked, ashamed my voice quivered.

"What?" he asked with a smile.

"My money. Your money."

His face darkened. "You been in my study, woman, my account? What the fuck you think you doing in there? In my fucking business?" He stalked towards me.

For a second, fear clawed its way through me. "Colton, my account is empty, transferred to you. Your account is fucking empty." I kept my voice strong. "My money, where has it gone?"

Abruptly, just before he got to me, he stopped and smiled. "Don't you worry about a thing now. I have it all figured out. Everything will be fine, cuz." The gleam in his eyes told me everything would not be fine.

"I-I need my money, Colton. I'm moving out." My hands restlessly played with the bottom of my shorts to keep from picking the bastard up and throwing him out the window.

He laughed, shaking his head like I had said the funniest thing. "Sorry, cuz."

That didn't sound good. "About what?"

His head cocked to the side and he smirked over at me. I watched as his hand went behind him and he pulled a gun free, pointing it at me.

"What? No!" I took a step back. My hands out and up in front of me, my heart beat erratically in my chest. I didn't even know he owned a gun, or if he was smart enough to use it. "Colton, what's this about?"

Even when my heart was going haywire with panic, I wanted to wrap my hands around his throat and squeeze the life out of him. Better yet, I wanted to take that gun from him and shoot him in the balls. However, I did nothing but freeze.

"You see, I lost a bit of money. I like to gamble, and I gambled with the wrong people. I had to do something to save myself."

My stomach dropped. "What?" I whispered.

"I gave them all the money we had."

My arms went around my stomach. I gripped my sides as the hurt and betrayal bombarded me.

The only family member left on Earth turned on me for his own benefit.

Like my parents had.

I'd trusted him when he said he would support me.

He'd lied.

Like all my family seemed to do.

My money was gone. Colton's money was gone, and his fear was what brought my own fear on. Even though he looked smug, I could see the terror in his wide, twitching eyes. The people he'd played with were bad people.

"S-so, I'll, um, I'll just work harder and get some

money back in." Like hell I would. I was out of there as soon as I could.

He sighed and shook his head. "My money and yours wasn't enough. I had to give them something else."

God. I closed my eyes and my head dipped forward. I was too scared to ask.

It seemed I didn't need to though because Colton supplied it. "You."

I was going to be sick. I was going to throw up all over the carpet. My body shook with shock. Had I heard him right?

Lifting my head, opening my eyes, I asked in a quiet voice, "Me?"

"Yeah, cuz. Found a good buyer through some mates. They deal in slavery themselves, but when I showed them a picture of you, the biker wanted you for himself. Said he needed a good black bitch in his house taking care of shit." The sick shine in Colton's eyes when he explained he'd sold me was enough to know my owner would bring new, darker times with him. "He'll be coming by in a couple of hours. You just have to be a good girl 'til then."

He gestured with the gun for me to walk down the hall. I started and he followed, still talking, "There ain't no use running and going to the cops. He's in with them. Pays them off. I didn't want to do it. I was happy to help you out after your 'rents died, but I have to look out for myself over anything. You just happened to be staying here when things went down for me."

He reached out, grabbed the back of my hair and yanked it. I screamed in surprise and stumbled back before he shoved me sideways into his bedroom. I gripped his wrist, digging my fingernails in as he kept pushing me forward with force. I then stumbled into his en suite. He slammed the door behind me. A lock was snapped into place before I heard Colton say through the door, "Don't worry, cuz, it'll all work out." He laughed. "Though, even if it don't, I'll be a happy rich guy once again. I'd do fucking anything to have money under my belt, always."

I banged and kicked the door, screaming, "Let me out, Colton!"

"Now, stay quiet and I'll keep you breathin' until he gets here. Oh, and in case you get a hair-brained idea, there's no escaping through that window. Your fat arse wouldn't fit." I listened as he walked off chuckling.

My life, my pitiful life, would no longer be my own.

I refused to let that happen. I just didn't know how to make it possible.

I wanted to live, to be free and be who I was inside and out. No one had the right to own me.

For a little while, I sat on the cold floor and cried. Never once had I cried when my parents passed or when my uncle died. Never until then. Sobs racked my body.

They came hard and I shook from the force. My head thumped painfully at my temples.

My life seemed doomed and I let myself wallow in self-pity, let the turmoil in my stomach take over and fill me with dread. How could it happen? How could my cousin be involved with people who sold women? Had I been a trusting fool from the start? Regardless, I never saw the signs. How could I when we hardly kept each other's company.

I wasn't sure how long I sat on the cold floor, but it was long enough to shake my stupid self and do something about my life *once again*.

I had to take the control back.

I had to try something, anything.

Fighting for my life was worth it. I'd done it many times. It was time to do it again.

With renewed energy, I stood from the floor and looked around and through cabinets but found nothing; he'd cleared everything out except for towels. I wasn't strong enough to take my cousin down forcibly when he would come for me, and no doubt, my *owner* would be there to back him up.

Instead, I looked to the small window again, and decided I had to try it at least. Turning on the shower to cover some noise, I quickly picked up the bath towel, wrapped it around my fist and punched the window. At first, I thought Colton would rush back in once he'd heard the glass shatter. However, my cousin, being the stupid fool he was, was probably sitting in front of the TV, drinking a beer with the surround sound up loud.

Moving quickly, so I could get as far away as I could before he noticed, I first placed my arms through the small window and wiggled my body against each corner, grazing it against the sides and shards that remained. Still, I didn't care. I needed out.

Standing on the toilet, I forced my body forward until my top half was out. Panic seized me as my hips got stuck. I prayed Colton wasn't right, that my arse wasn't too big.

I couldn't give up, though. Shifting around, slicing more grooves into my skin, I managed to wiggle free. My body sank quickly to the rocky garden below the window, and I bit my lip to stop myself from crying out. I didn't have the time to take in the pain. I sprung up with determination and ran.

CHAPTER TWO

DODGE

EIGHT HOURS LATER

hree months I'd been at the Hawks' Caroline Springs charter and shit had hit the fan. Not only were the Venom MC fuckers causing hell, but we had our own problem within our own club. Nothing we could prove, but we had our suspicions of someone within the club working against us and helping out the Venom MC instead. If that was the case and we found the dickhead in our own goddamn club backstabbing us and telling the Venom our every move, then whoever it was had better disappear before Dallas or I found them.

We were sick of our boss's nightclubs being ransacked, and wished to fuck Warden had already installed the cameras in the compound and garage. Then we could catch the bastards. But he was stuck in Ballarat dealing with his own shit. The Venom knew when one of Talon's nightclubs was unprotected. Or they'd draw brothers out from one club to another with false shit like the women being threatened, hold-ups or bomb threats.

Plans had to change. Brothers from the mechanical business were being over-worked while working backup at night at the clubs around our territory.

Things were in chaos. It was time to change it and take the control back.

It had been early when I walked into the compound. The mechanical business on the side of the building wasn't even open yet, which was good. Tired of fucking waiting on Warden, I was doing my own little installing. We needed to catch the snitch before the Venom cunts ruined everything.

Memphis had given me the go-ahead and those we trusted—Dallas, Saxon, Pick, Billy and Dive—knew I was setting up cameras that morning in the compound and then the garage.

It sucked that it'd come to not trusting a brother of

Hawks, but we needed to weasel out the prick running his mouth off to someone in the Venom club.

At least things had settled down for Pick and Billy. They'd been back in Melbourne for a month. They'd moved into their own place with Josie. She was back at uni and they were enjoying each other. Fucking strange to me, the three of them together, but each to their own. I guessed it was whatever floated their boat and, if the three of them together was it, then so be it.

How in the fuck did it work, though?

My imagination would provide me enough pictures to go through if they only starred Josie. She was fucking hot. But shit, I'd shut my brain down if it tried to get me to picture shit with her *and* my brothers. That crap was just not happening.

Switching on the last camera in the compound, I jumped down from the chair and placed it back where it belonged. It'd been a fucked-up day when Richard passed. It hurt people deep, and still so many were grieving for him. What made it worse was Talon had enough crap on his plate with his family's sorrow, and now he had all the shit in Melbourne on top of it. Which was why I was taking some slack off him and Memphis.

Memphis was a great president for the charter. He was a mean motherfucker when he had to be.

But I was ruthless.

If I wanted something, I saw to it and, if anyone got in my way, they'd better look the fuck out.

First on my agenda was to find the dick who thought he was man enough to play with the big boys and stab his brotherhood in the back.

Then I'd be dealing with some members of Venom. They needed to get the message that Hawks weren't to be fucked with. I'd relay that message any way I could—fists, knives or guns, I wasn't picky.

Dallas was keen to have my back and I was glad to have him there. He was just as merciless as I was. Together, with the help of our brothers who moved from Ballarat to Melbourne, we'd have the shit sorted and things would finally fucking calm down.

At least, I goddamn hoped.

After looking up at the hidden camera, I moved into the business side. Unlocking the door from inside of the compound to the mechanical area, I swung it open wide. It hit the wall with a bang.

That was when I heard it.

A small whimper.

"Hello?" I barked gruffly. Nothing but silence greeted me back. Hell, had I heard it? Shrugging, I moved over to the long metal table and dropped my shit down. Opening the bag, I took out the camera and turned, only to kick over a fucking stool and have it crash to the ground.

Another whimper.

"All right, who's there?" I called and quickly turned back to the table to put the camera away in the bag. Then I scanned the area.

Nothing looked out of place. Had a cat or some damned animal got in somehow before a brother had locked up?

A scuffle came from the left, and my eyes landed on a dark bare foot being dragged backward. Someone was hiding in the fucking corner of the room. The spot was small. It was between two benches, so whoever was in there was small in frame. Couldn't be a large motherfucker about to get his arse handed to him.

Slowly, I started forward. "You better come the fuck out," I demanded before peering around the corner of the bench. My eyes widened and I took a step back when scared, mossy-coloured eyes blinked up at me through a thick veil of curly black, scruffy hair.

"What the fuck?" I whispered.

The small woman pedalled her feet back on the ground, her hands holding her frame up as she tried to push herself against the wall more.

If she didn't have the look of some dirty, homeless woman, she'd be a stunner. Her skin looked silky smooth. It was the colour of milk chocolate and caused my eyes to stay glued to her. My gaze flicked to her legs, her body and her face. Never had I had an urge for a taste of chocolate until that moment. Well, except for the woman at the store I'd seen the previous day. My eyes widened again. Holy mother fucking shit, it *was* her. The cowering woman on the floor was the same woman as the one at the bloody store. I'd had an urge to go up and talk to her in the shop, but she'd quickly disappeared, embarrassed from what I'd caught her saying. Even when her words, soulful eyes and body intrigued me to want to know her more.

Composing my shock, I stepped forward. She squealed and closed her eyes tightly.

"Hey, hey. I won't hurt you," I said calmly with my hands out in front of me. She stopped moving and glanced up at me quickly, only to avert her eyes back to the floor in the next second.

Christ, how was I supposed to deal with this? Why was she here?

"What're you doin' here?" I asked as my eyes raked over her body. That was when I saw the blood. Her arms and legs were scraped to shit. The material of her tee and jean shorts didn't cover much of her body. How in the fuck did she get scraped up like that?

She must have felt me shift as I reached for my phone in the back pocket of my jeans because she shifted around restlessly and panic flashed across her features.

"I'm just gettin' my phone," I said and waved it out in front of myself. "I'll call the cops and—"

"No!" she screamed. She tried to stand, but her bare

feet wouldn't support her. She cried out in pain and fell to her arse.

"S'okay, it's all right. Calm, little bird."

Little bird?

Maybe because she reminded me of an injured bird, all flighty and scared.

"Look," I reassured and sat on the ground in front of her, placing my phone on the filthy, concrete ground. "I won't call the cops, okay." She eyed the phone then gave me a small nod, her body sagging in relief. Did she recognise me, as well? "Is there anyone I can call for you?" I asked.

She shook her head once.

"Little bird, you can't—"

The door to the garage burst open and laughter reached our ears. The woman squealed, her arms winding around her knees. She buried her head in her arms, muttering and whimpering to herself about something I couldn't catch.

Jumping up, I started for the door as Slit, Muff and Handle stepped through. They were brothers to the Caroline Springs charter, brothers I was just getting to know, so I wasn't sure if I could trust them.

"Get the fuck out," I growled. They paused and eyed me.

"We've got work to do, arsehole," Muff said with a glare.

"Yeah, just because you think your shit don't stink and the boss man has a hard-on for you, don't mean you can tell us what to do," Slit barked.

"Slit," Handle was kind enough to warn.

Too late, though.

I was up in his face, pushing the dick backward and out of the room before he registered to fight back. The other brothers followed. "I don't give a fuck what you think 'bout me, but I have enough say to order you fuckers around. You do as I fuckin' well say. If you don't, I'll come see you in your dreams, and it won't be pretty." Glaring at the wanker in front of me, I finished with, "The shop is closed until I say further."

"Fuck off," Slit spat and stupidly added, "I could have you knocked out in seconds."

"Slit," Muff snarled. "Watch who you say shit to. Your brain ain't registerin' who your mouth is runnin' off to, dickhead." He shook his head at his friend. "That's Dodge."

Still close, with our chests touching, Slit stiffened. Now he knew the deep shit he just dug for himself. I had the highest kill count in Hawks. All charters included.

No one fucked with me.

I protected all.

"You get me now, pencil dick?" I asked with a smirk.

He nodded. I stepped back and ordered, "Shop is closed.

You need to tell Memphis? Do it. Have him ring me, or when he gets here, he can come see me. For now, you two,"—I pointed to Muff and Handle—"guard the doors, inside and out. No one comes in there except brothers who came from Ballarat." I thumbed towards the garage and then turned to Slit. "And you, get the fuck outta my sight."

"What's goin' on in there?" Handle asked.

"Not your business until I know I can trust you," I stated, and then walked back into the garage, slamming the door behind me.

Thinking of the scared woman caused me to sigh, my head falling forward, and I shook it.

Fuck. I'd just gone against brothers for a woman.

What in the hell was I thinking?

Even though I hardly knew the guys, they were still brothers. Slit, I couldn't give a fuck about, but I'd just admitted I wasn't trusting anyone around there. Which meant no fucker would think to open up to me and share shit.

And all for a fucking woman.

I swore, after seeing the shit boss man and my brothers in Ballarat went through for their women, I wouldn't get pussy-whipped like them.

Fuck it. I won't let it happen.

No woman comes between me and my brothers.

Tilting my head to the side, I glared down at the little

bird who cringed and shivered on the ground. No woman was worth any trouble.

But Christ.

Maybe I'd been around the Ballarat brothers and their misses too long and had gotten soft-hearted, because something deep inside me knew I couldn't leave the woman like her on the floor. I couldn't turn my back on her. She needed help, and I had to give it.

Didn't mean I had to give her anything else.

I was too hard for that shit.

I didn't feel.

All I liked was to fuck a tight, wet pussy and do it hard.

What I needed to do was get her the fuck out of there and let someone else deal with her before my heart got caught in the trap like all the other bastards.

I strode over towards her. She whimpered when I bent down for my phone. "I won't fuckin' hurt you," I barked. "I'm not callin' the pigs, okay. Just someone who can help you. Someone I trust." After pressing a couple of buttons, I held my phone to my ear.

"Brother?" Pick answered.

"Bring Josie to the garage. I'm gonna need some help with a little bird."

"What the fuck you talkin' about?" he growled.

"Just do it," I snapped and hung up.

CHAPTER THREE

WILLOW

SEVEN HOURS EARLIER

*R*un, run, run, run. It was all I could do. The thought burned inside of me. *Run* so I could get to safety. *Run* so he couldn't catch me and I would be safe. *Run* to live. *Run* to survive.

Looking behind me for the millionth time, there was no shadow following me. My heart lurched in relief, even though my chest ached from the panting and exhaustion. Sweat trickled down my back from the heat of the night, and I cried in pain as my bare feet took to the road, the street and grass, rubbing themselves raw.

My arms and legs were finally numb, and tears brimmed in my eyes in appreciation. The way my limbs had been damaged after I crawled out the small bathroom window, cutting my arms and legs with the shards of glass leftover, and then scraping them when I fell to the sharp stones below, was horrendous.

It was hard to see, but it was as if the night knew it had to be darker to cover my tracks. Was God looking down on me, wanting me to escape?

Whatever the reason, gratitude filled my heavy heart.

A gate banging shut caused me to jump and whimper. I bolted behind a large warehouse-type place. Leaning against the rough wall, I inhaled ragged breaths, trying but failing to ignore the wave of pain burning through my body since stopping. I needed a place to rest, a place that would keep me hidden for the night at least.

So Colton and my owner couldn't find me.

My cousin had fooled me, or rather, I'd been the fool in believing Colton wouldn't betray me like the rest of my family. God, my family was all fucked up. My parents were druggies, my cousin a gambler…heck, was my uncle a drunken cross-dresser?

A crazy laugh escaped me, and my hand flew to cover my mouth. Exhaustion and pain filled my head with stupid thoughts.

Rest. I had to rest. Crawling on all fours, I looked through the darkened night for a place to catch my breath.

Something shone from a window up on the building. I stood and cringed from the pain shooting through my feet. Great, another bloody window. At least it was open. I was be thankful for that. I waited and listened. When I heard nothing coming from inside, I opened the window further and jumped up, my bottom to the edge. Never known for my grace, especially when bleeding and in agony, I slipped and fell in a heap to the concrete ground below.

Rest. I just needed to rest. Just for a moment.

I found a corner, blocked off with benches on each side of me. From the smell of it, I worked out I was in a garage.

Rest. Even for a little while.

I never thought I would be able to sleep, considering my distress and the burning pain inching its way around my body, but exhaustion won out. I closed my eyes.

MY GAZE GLANCED over the man in front of me, the one who had woken me with a start when he'd banged the door open earlier. It was the same man I'd seen in the supermarket the previous day—the man with a sinful body, who now had a hard glare and words as he barked into his phone.

Trust no one.

I couldn't risk it.

My heart beat stupidly at the thought of him seeming to want to protect me. He'd driven those men out of the room because I was scared, and spoke to someone on the phone to seek help for me.

My heart was foolish to want to trust someone so soon.

My head was smarter.

I eyed him with a curious glance, keeping my distance.

The man turned to me with a glare in his eyes, only the glare didn't frighten me. If anything, my personality wanted to share my own scowl back, but it wasn't the time. I needed to know what the new situation just brought me.

"My name's Dodge," he snapped.

Dodge. What a funny name.

"Someone's coming who'll help you. For now, you're safe... Do you remember me?"

I nodded.

He sighed when I wasn't forthcoming with more information. "Do you know where you are?" he asked.

I shook my head slightly.

"This is a mechanical business owned by the biker club I'm a part of."

My eye widened. A sharp gasp filled the air as my chest rose and fell in a jerky motion. A biker club? My owner was a part of a biker club. "No," I whispered and shifted into the wall more. "No!" I screamed.

"Hey," he started, his brows furrowed. "What the fuck? Little bird, what's this about? I'm tryin' to help you. What's goin' on in that head of yours?"

"Y-you're one of them," I stuttered in terror and annoyance. I hated how weak I seemed.

"Woman, what're you talkin' about?"

"H-he was selling me, m-my cousin." Even I thought it sounded insane. In this day and age, people were still sold into slavery? I couldn't fathom it. "I was to become a slave." Judging by Dodge's eyes darkening, he seemed to believe it far too easily, which scared the crap out of me. "I was...my...I was sold. My owner...he's a biker."

His jaw clenched tight, his nostrils flared and I watched as his hand fisted his phone tightly. Then, all of a sudden, he took a deep breath and closed his eyes for a second. When they opened, the storm that had grown inside of them calmed.

He sat on the floor, keeping a short distance between us. "I can tell you now, little bird, no one I know would want to buy a woman to be a slave. That shit is fucked up, and I'll take a fucker out, even in this club, who thinks of startin' that crap up." He sighed. "The Hawks MC is clean. We don't run in shady stuff like sellin' women or drugs. No one fucks that up for us. If they try, *I* take them out, and when that happens, there's nothin' left to find of the fucker tryin' to bring a bad name to Hawks." He licked his lips like they were dry. "You *are* safe here."

How was I safe when he'd admitted to killing people who tried to cause trouble with the Hawks club?

He *killed* people.

He had death on his hands.

So, why *did* I feel safe around him? Why wasn't I scared of him any longer? My body relaxed as much as it could with my feet and skin still aching.

"What in the fuck is goin' on around here?" bellowed from the room Dodge had walked the men out to.

"Shit." Dodge sighed.

The door came open, and I peered around the corner of the bench to see who had walked in. It was an older man with a wiry beard, around the age of fifty. His eyes were angry, and he wore similar clothes to Dodge—jeans, a tee and leather jacket.

Dodge quickly stood from the floor and faced the man. "Memphis—"

"Explain to me why in the hell the shop isn't open. We have fuckin' customers comin' soon to pick up their cars, and some of the boys need to fuckin' finish."

"Memphis—"

"This had better be good."

"Jesus, old man, if you let me finish, I'd bloody tell you," Dodge said, and then gestured with his hand towards me. I cringed back into the wall as I felt the man named Memphis look my way.

"The fuck?"

The door opened again. Curious, I glanced around to see two large men and a woman walk in. The red-haired woman closed the door behind her.

"Dodge, you dick, next time don't hang up on me, and explain the cryptic shit you spew from your mouth. If there ain't a good reason to have our woman here while the guys outside ogle her arse, I'm gonna kick the crap outta you," said the man wearing a baseball cap.

"Let's kick it anyway for fuckin' up our mornin'," said the other man as he flicked his hair from his glaring eyes that were trained on Dodge.

Dodge was getting into a lot of trouble just for me.

For someone he didn't know.

Why, I didn't have a clue. Suddenly, I cleared my throat, and all eyes—except Memphis's, because his were still staring down at me—turned to me.

CHAPTER FOUR

DODGE

*I*f it were a western movie, a tumbleweed would have floated across the ground in front of our still forms while the silence built around us as we all stared at…fuck, I still didn't even have her name.

"Dodge," Josie said quietly, and she stepped up beside me.

Turning my gaze from the woman, I met the serious eyes of my brothers. "We protect her as one. She's club business now."

"What do you mean, son?" Memphis asked.

"Hi," Josie calmly said to the woman. "I'm Josie. You're okay here. No one will hurt you. That there is Caden, and that one is Eli, otherwise known as Pick and Billy to everyone else. They're my men." Her eyes widened. "They can seem like grumpy guys, but deep down, they're sweet." She smiled.

"Precious." Pick smirked.

"Sweetheart, we got street creed we gotta keep." Billy winked.

Josie rolled her eyes and turned back to the woman. She crouched down in front of the stranger. "What's your name, honey?"

We waited and watched as she licked her dry lips and then uttered, "Willow."

Jesus.

Willow.

See, my little bird *did* belong free, outside in a tree, a willow tree, not scared on the ground.

Shut the fuck up, you dickhead. My little bird? Outside in a tree? You pansy arse. Man the fuck up and harden your goddamn heart.

"What's she doin' here, Dodge?" Memphis asked.

Shrugging, I said, "I found her in here this mornin'." I ran a hand over my face before looking to my brothers, Pick and Billy. "Her motherfuckin' cousin was gonna sell her as a slave," I growled out low. A gasp behind me told me Josie had heard.

"This true, darlin'?" Memphis asked Willow. Again, we all looked to her. She raised her chin and I was fucking proud when she nodded. The look in her eyes was like she was daring anyone to question her.

Where the tough front was coming from, I hadn't a clue, but it looked good on her. Hell, she'd been shy as shit in the supermarket when she realised I'd heard her words.

"Why are you...?" Josie waved her hand at Willow's arms and legs.

"Hang the fuck on, I want to—" Pick started to snarl, causing Willow to cringe and her gaze to drop to the floor.

"Ease up, arsehole," I interrupted, my voice cold and then, *fuck me*, all eyes swung my way.

Pick and Billy were the first to smile wide. Memphis was smart enough to hide his behind his hand.

Glaring, I snapped, "Don't even fuckin' think it. Not gonna happen." To show it in some fucking way, because there was no way in hell my balls were going to be around some chick's neck, I took a step back. "Let's get this shit organised so I can get crap done." I huffed. "Willow's cousin's obviously a fuckhead, tryin' to sell his own flesh and blood. No doubt it's over money." I looked to Willow. Her nod confirmed it. "What's worse is that he was gonna sell her to some motherfuckin' local biker guy."

"The fuck?" Memphis snarled.

"Not *going to*." Willow shook her head. "I was sold. He

was supposed to collect me last night." Her cute nose screwed up in disgust. Her jaw clenched and she fisted her hands over and over, as if the whole situation pissed her off.

Christ. Fuckin' Christ.

The sick cunts were gonna die.

"S'all good, darlin', we'll keep you safe. No biker in this club would dare deal with the shit your fuckhead cousin's in," Memphis reassured, backing me up.

"We bloody hope," Billy muttered. He was right, though. We weren't sure a Hawks member in the Caroline Springs charter wasn't dealing in that shit. Someone was definitely fucking things up for us by going to Venom scum and, if it led to slavery, I would fuck them up good and proper by going slow and painful.

"What we *need* to do now is help Willow settle and get her cleaned up. Then we can go on from there," Josie said.

I couldn't help but smirk hearing the once timid girl now giving orders. Pick and Billy were good for her. She knew she was safe with them, so she could be herself. The grinning fools beside me were obviously thinking the same thing.

Or that they'd wished they were banging her right then.

Couldn't blame them. She had a rocking body.

My head flinched forward when a palm connected to

the back of it and then Pick growled, "Don't fuckin' *think* what you're thinkin.'"

Shaking my head, I walked over to the women. Stretching my hand out and down to Willow, she looked at it. For a moment, I didn't think she'd take it, but she did. Her small hand slid into my bigger one. I closed my hand around hers and I couldn't help but stare at the difference in skin tone, hers a lot darker than mine.

Christ.

I fucking liked the way her skin looked against mine.

Slowly and gently, in case she was hurt more than I thought, I pulled her up to stand. She winced and shifted from one foot to the other.

"What is it?" Josie asked before I had the chance.

"Nothing," Willow said in a small voice.

"Darlin', you gotta tell us if anythin' is wrong. We don't wanna move you in case it does more damage," Memphis said in a papa bear tone.

"My feet hurt," she said and looked down at her feet with a glare.

Billy walked up to her and picked up one leg. I didn't fucking like the way his hand slid down her calf then lifted her leg higher. "Billy," I growled out.

From his crouch, he looked up smiling. "Got somethin' to say, Dodge?"

Grinding my teeth, I shook my head and barked, "Nothin.'"

He chuckled. "Didn't think so. Now, let's take a look here." He lifted her leg again to the side and eyed her foot. His jaw clenched and unclenched again and again. I couldn't see from my angle as I supported Willow's weight, but from the look on Billy's face, I knew it was bad.

Hell, I found myself admiring her courage and strength. She got to her feet when they were obviously cut up, and she did it without complaint.

Will of damn steel. Amazing.

"You're gonna have to carry her," Billy said with a scowl as he stood beside us.

"You do it," I ordered.

Shit, fuck, shit. Everyone looked to me, even Willow.

"I-I've gotta get the place cleared out. Don't want anyone to see her," I suggested, and hell, it was a fucking brilliant suggestion.

And it saved having Willow in my arms. Having her small frame tight against mine, having her scent take over…Christ, I was fucked.

Get out. Get out and away as fast as you can.

With a head gesture, I motioned Memphis over. He gave me a look that said I was a piece of shit as he stalked up and took my spot, supporting Willow. Even though her hand tightened on my arm, as if she didn't want me to step away from her, I still did. And then I bolted from the room like a little girl with a goddamn disgusting crush.

IT DIDN'T TAKE LONG to clear the garage's car park and compound. Most dicks were glad to have the morning off. I told them all to come back after lunch. It was only Muff and Handle who eyed me suspiciously before they followed through with my orders and got the fuck out of there. They knew I wouldn't be happy if they didn't comply.

I walked back into the garage and asked, "What's the plan?" hoping to Christ someone had worked something out.

"Just workin' on where to put her for now, until we can get this shit off her back," Pick said.

"What about your old place, Josie?" I suggested, crossing my arms over my chest.

"She can't. Nary moves in there soon." She smiled, excited to have her friend move to Melbourne for uni from Ballarat.

"Here at the compound?" Memphis said.

"Not safe enough," I replied.

"I'm sorry to be a nuisance," Willow uttered. Her face was strained. She looked exhausted and in pain.

"You're not," I barked. "Look, we need somewhere just for now to get her patched up quick."

"Dive's?" Billy shrugged.

"Fuck no," I growled. That shithead would be in her panties in fucking seconds. There was no way I would put Willow even an inch from the fucker. He was too goddamn good-looking for his own sake, and all women were useless when it came to saying no to the dick.

"What about our place?" Josie offered.

"Precious."

"Sweetheart," Billy and Pick said at the same time, and the way Willow's eyes widened, she didn't like the idea, either. Was she scared of them?

"No," she suddenly said. Her cute cheeks reddened from her outburst. "Please, I'm sorry. I'm a nuisance bringing all this here."

"Do you want to go to the cops?" Memphis asked.

"No!" she screamed and tried to take a step back, crying out in pain when she placed her feet hard on the floor. "No, please, no police. My cousin said that the guy, the person who bought me, has people in the force. They'll find me."

That explained her reaction before about the cops. Stupid dirty pigs.

"What about Lan?" I suggested then regretted the words, because he was another man who thought with his dick.

Okay, we were all like that, but I didn't want Willow to be at risk with them.

Why?

Yeah, let's not go there, brain.

"Please," Willow begged. "Can I stay with you?" She blushed as she looked up at me. I actually turned to look over my shoulder, thinking she was talking to someone else. Only...no one was there. *Fuck.*

Looking back to her, I asked, "Me?" and pointed at my chest. She nodded, her eyes pleading. Her tiny hand fisted at her side as though she was scared I'd say no. Of fucking course I had to say no.

Billy spun and choked on a burst of laughter.

"It's the best solution," Josie said with a smile. "You've just moved into your own place and it's not far from us. So you'll have help close, especially with Dive—"

"Whoa," I interrupted, hands waving out in front of me, eyes wide. "No, ah, no. Sorry." There was no way in hell *I'd* be safe at my house with her. Sure, *she'd* be safe, but fuck, having her small body walking around my house, whether clothed or not, was temptation I didn't fucking need. What about when I hooked up with other chicks? I wouldn't be able to bring them home and bang the shit out of them with her in the goddamn house.

Jesus. My balls would shrivel up to prunes and drop off my body if I didn't get any pussy. They were already cringing from the thought.

For the love of God, I sounded like a real jackarse.

And you're worried about that for the first time because...?

Motherfucking Christ, I hardly knew the woman and already I was looking to change myself.

Can't fuckin' let that happen. I will not be pussy-whipped.

There was also another reason, another big bloody reason I couldn't have her at my place. Dive, the pussy muncher, lived right next door and he liked to pop over whenever he felt like it. Hell, he could do it when she was getting out of the shower, with all her glorious dark skin on show or...best not think about anything like that.

"Dodge," Josie scolded.

"I can't. I have... The place, it's a mess and..." Fuck me drunk. I had nothing of good value to say.

"Brother, a word." Pick smirked. He stepped over a few paces, just enough to be out of earshot. I followed, frowning the whole way.

"What?" I barked.

"Dodge, it's obvious she feels safe around you. Can't you just let—"

"No," I stated with a 'don't fuck with me' look.

Pick stood tall, crossed his arms over his chest and asked, "Why the fuck not?"

"Just...fuck!" For the life of me, I couldn't think of shit. Well, nothing he'd believe. Maybe a plastic surgery appointment? I'd be too busy because I'd be delivering meals to the elderly? I had to help in an animal shelter? Yeah, I had fucking nothing.

"Deal with it, dickhead. You're it for once." He grinned, slapped me on the shoulder and added, "I wish you all the luck in the world, brother."

"What you talkin' about?" I glared.

"Nothin', nothin' at all." He smirked and walked back over to the group. "Let's get out of here. Willow, you must be buggered."

"Are we going to Dodge's?" Josie asked.

Pick chuckled. "Sure are." He turned to me and said, "We came in the car, so we'll take her and meet you there." Pick gave a head bob to Billy, who swept Willow into his arms and started for the door.

It took everything in me to not run over there and knock my brother out when he winked.

CHAPTER FIVE

WILLOW

I was pissed and frustrated I'd put those people in the situation they were in. But I wasn't stupid enough to go out on my own, not when my cousin had warned me there'd be no help from the police. I looked to Dodge's retreating back and a pang of hurt filled me, but I fought it back. It seemed Dodge hated the idea of me being in his house. Still, I couldn't really blame him. I had dribbled some strange stuff when I'd first seen him at the supermarket, and I'd just dumped trouble into their lives without any notice at all...but I had no choice.

Dodge was the only one I felt safe with.

Despite speaking gruffly, looking sinfully hot, with a

certain amount of menace pouring off him, the way he'd been with me when he first found me in that room showed me he wouldn't harm me. Besides, he'd had many chances to hurt me before anyone turned up. He also had the chance to get rid of me when his co-workers arrived at the garage, but he didn't. Instead, he got them away from me and called for help from people *he* trusted.

I was safe.

Dodge killed people. The fact made me nervous and sick. Yet, the way he reacted with his biker friends and even Josie, I found myself thinking it wasn't like he went off on a killing spree. He would do it to protect his people, which meant he had the power to protect me, and that calmed those nerves down.

Nothing would get through him.

Finally, as Billy settled my body in the car, I could breathe again without the fear it would be my last breath.

In my quiet state, I watched out the window as Dodge said something to Memphis and then, after a curt nod, he climbed on his motorcycle. It roared to life after one kick. Josie climbed in next to me and then the car started. We began to move but in the direction that I couldn't see Dodge any longer, and I didn't like that.

My heart jumped into my throat as my body shivered and I cried out, "Stop!"

The brakes screeched and the car came to an abrupt

halt. We all jerked forward in our seats. My cheeks heated because I felt so stupid.

"What's wrong?" Josie asked.

"I..." I shifted in the seat, looking out all of the windows, wincing when I banged my cuts and scrapes.

"Um, Caden, how about we wait for Dodge. Let him go first," the sweet Josie said, and I could have kissed her. She knew what I wanted. I hated if they thought or it showed that I couldn't trust them, but with Dodge in sight, I was able to relax.

God, did that sound obsessed? Probably, which I was with my safety anyway. *And obsessed with his body.* It wasn't the time for that, though. It was obvious my mind was still supplying me with crazy thoughts when my life was torn to shreds once again—by another damned family member.

I sent Josie a grateful smile. When she took my hand, I looked down to them. No one had cared enough to want to reassure me about anything. Yet this woman cared and I didn't even know her.

Dodge cared and I didn't know him.

Who were these people?

The rumble of Dodge's bike slid past us. I saw him give a curious look to Pick who was driving. Pick only shook his head, but because I was on his side of the car, I saw his smile. It was the biggest I'd seen on his face. Dodge shrugged then took off in front of us. We followed quickly behind and my heart settled once again in my chest.

"Willow," Josie said. I gave her a glance to show I was listening and then my eyes went back to Dodge as she continued. "I guess you were living with your cousin?"

"Yes," I said quietly.

"Babe, whatever you say will stay between us and a few others we trust with our lives," Billy said. He turned in his seat as his friend drove and said, "You can trust us, Low. We want to help you out and get this fucker off your back. But we'll need the information from you." His new nickname for me showed he wanted me to feel relaxed and welcomed around them.

However, I remained hesitant to tell them anything. I didn't want them to think I was foolish for continuing to live with my parents after they stole from me, or after they find out my parents were druggies.

"Maybe we should wait for any information until we're around Dodge," Pick suggested.

My hand convulsed around Josie's and she said, "Good idea, Caden." It *was* a good idea, and it also saved me repeating myself.

How was I so lucky to find people willing to help me?

Was Fate finally being kind to me?

It was about time, honestly.

I could only hope her sister, Luck, would shine upon me while I told my unfortunate story about my sad life.

Even if Luck wasn't there, I would pick myself up once again and strive towards making it so. Some help wouldn't go astray, though.

IT WASN'T A LENGTHY DRIVE. Before long, we pulled in behind Dodge in a small driveway and up to a brick home that had seen better days. The garden was appalling and needed some help to brighten it up. Gardening was something I'd always enjoyed. It also got me out of the house when my parents had been in. I'd been too busy settling in, finding a job and then working when I'd moved in with Colton to even start on his garden.

My door opening caused me to jump. My hand went to my chest, but then I saw Dodge there. "You okay?" he asked gruffly, as though he didn't really want to ask, but still did it anyway. When I nodded, he slid his hands under my legs and behind my back and lifted me effortlessly out of the car.

"What do we have here?" asked a new, large man from the neighbouring yard. Tattooed arms poked out from his tank top. He jumped the fence and stalked towards us with a bright smile, only it looked fake, as if something were troubling him. I'd been given many to know one when I saw one. I felt Dodge's chest heave a long and loud sigh.

"Dive, fuck off," was growled low as he walked us towards the front door. "Fuck," he hissed. "Someone reach in my pocket and grab my keys."

"Dude, I ain't in the mood to feel you up," the man named Dive joked, his demeanour now true. "Unless you buy me dinner first."

"Don't—"

"Shut it, you two," Pick snapped. Honestly, I was finding the interaction amusing and comforting. If only Lucia could see me. "Stop movin'," Pick ordered as he reached out to place his hand in Dodge's front pocket.

"You move your hand closer to the front and we're gonna have problems." Dodge glared at Pick next to him.

"Don't let Billy see you get hard for his guy, Dodge." Dive laughed.

They were gay? But I thought Josie said... Oh, wow, she was actually with the both of them.

A slap sounded behind us. I glanced over Dodge's big shoulder to see Dive rubbing the back of his head and Billy scowling at him. "What?" Dive asked.

"Can we please just go inside?" Josie said with humour in her voice.

Finally, I heard the jangle of keys, then Pick unlocked the door and swung it open. He moved out of the way so Dodge and I could enter first.

At least the inside was better than the outside. It was

tidy, only bare, a real bachelor pad. Minimal furniture scattered around the first room we walked into, which was the living room. We had to step down into it. Dodge took me over to the large corner couch and sat me on it while he quickly shuffled back. I looked up at him, and with the light shining through the floor-to-ceiling windows behind him, he appeared like an avenging angel.

Josie came and sat next to me, with Pick positioning himself beside her while the other men stood around. That was until Dive dragged in a chair for himself to sit across from Josie and me.

"Now, you wanna tell me why you're carryin' a beautiful injured woman into your house?" Dive asked. He smiled and winked at me then said, "By the way, name's Dive, as in, I would dive into your pussy any day, baby."

Did he seriously just say that to me? I would have laughed and said something crude back, if I wasn't shocked from him just blurting it out like it was an everyday thing to say.

"Dive," Josie gasped. "Don't be crude."

"It's in my nature, babe." He winked. I rolled my eyes.

"I wouldn't go there, brother," Billy said.

"Not like he'd have a chance," Pick added.

"Women can't resist my charm," Dive stated while running his hand down over his chest. That was when I heard a growl fill the room.

Wide-eyed, I looked at Dodge, realising the sound had

been made by him. "Enough of this shit," he barked. He crossed his arms over his chest. "Willow, stay the fuck away from this guy. He's nothin' but trouble."

Dive gasped, his hand going over his heart. "You wound me, brother."

"Can we please just sort this stuff out so Willow can clean up and then rest," Josie demanded. Pick placed his arm around her shoulders and looked at her with a sweet smile. I caught Billy doing the same.

A pang of sadness filled me.

Never had I had that look from a male.

"Willow, babe, you wanna fill us in on what's goin' on?" Pick asked.

Nodding, I looked to the floor and started, "My parents were drug addicts…"

"Fuck," Pick hissed. He leaned forward, resting his arms on his knees. Josie's hand went to his back, rubbing it up and down.

"Go on," Dodge said.

"They weren't until I was around six, after they lost my younger sister. She drowned in the bath. My mother blamed herself and never got over it. My dad didn't help by blaming her, as well." Taking a breath, I continued talking with my eyes on the floor. "I guess they found that ice dulled the pain. From then on, I brought myself up. They were either too high or they just didn't care.

"I ate what I could get my hands on and cleaned the

house so I wouldn't get taken away from them." I shrugged. "I was scared that if I went anywhere else, it would be worse somehow, and really...it wasn't that bad. They didn't beat me or anything like that. It was like they forgot I was even there. I would have been out of that house when I was twenty if they hadn't stolen the money I'd saved. They OD'd a few months after, leaving me with nothing. I was scared, and the only person I knew of was my cousin. He took me under his wing."

Scoffing and then smiling sadly, I said, "I was going home to tell him last night I was moving out. I'd saved enough to stand on my own two feet...but then I discovered he'd stolen my money. I guess he had it planned all along. Gain my trust until I was useful in some way for him. That was when he'd..." I paused before I stumbled over the next words, still in disbelief. "S-sold me into slavery." I shook my head in disgust. "He'd blown his inheritance and stole from me to begin paying off his gambling debt." Licking my dry lips, I added with resolution, "He threw me under the bus. Pretty much told me he didn't want to use me, but he had no choice because he needed the money. I thought he cared about me, but I was wrong." Shaking my head, I said to myself, "Maybe it's just me. I'm a magnet for letting people stuff me around..."

"Bullshit," Pick growled. I looked up at him with wide eyes. "You were handed a shit card from a young age.

None of it's your fault." He stood suddenly and walked out of the room.

Glancing at Josie, I asked, "Did I…?"

"No." Josie smiled sadly. "We've all had something terrible to deal with in our lives." She took my hand as I watched Billy walk off to find Pick. "I'm just glad you turned up at the business so we can help you."

"Do you know who he was gonna sell you to?" Dive snarled, his teasing smile no longer in sight.

Shaking my head, I said, "No. All I do know was the money had already crossed hands and that I was bought by someone in some biker gang, who also had his hold on the law enforcement, as well. It's why I can't go to the police."

Dive looked over to Dodge who nodded. "Hawks' business now," Dodge said then walked off the way Pick and Billy went, with Dive following.

"W-what does that mean?" I asked Josie.

She smiled. "It means we're going to help you. No one will touch you unless they want war with the Hawks MC."

"I don't get it," I mumbled.

She asked, "What, honey?"

"Why are you all willing to help me? You don't know me."

"No, but we see ourselves in you. Like I said, we've all had issues in our past and we helped each other through them. That's what we're offering, honey, help. We want to help you, so you can finally live the life you're supposed to."

Luck was definitely looking out for me.

"Now. Let's get you all cleaned up." Josie grinned and that time, I actually smiled with her.

CHAPTER SIX

DODGE

*M*y blood pumped hard in my body. I wanted to go out and hurt some fucker. No, I wanted to kill Willow's cousin, and if her parents were still alive, I'd take them down, as well. Like so many I knew, she didn't deserve to be treated the way she was. Hell, she'd had no one since being a kid. How could a person like her turn out so normal after having fucked-up parents?

"You all right?" Pick asked as I walked into the kitchen at the back of the house.

Was I okay? Sure, it wasn't as if it had happened to me, so why was he even asking if I was okay?

His next sentence explained why. "You look like you wanna kill someone."

"I do," I barked.

"She seems so…together, even after the shit hand she was dealt," Dive commented as he sat at the table with Pick and Billy.

"Which is strange," Billy said. We all looked to him. "It's not that I don't trust her story, but come on, how does she not freak the fuck out bein' around us bikers and people if all she's known is heartache from her family?"

"She's strong, that's how," Dive said. "Anyone can see it, the light in her eyes. She holds out hope for a new life. From what she said, she's tried a few times to get away from her crap family, but they kept fuckin' her over. She wants a better life, and I reckon she's willin' to fight for it."

"There's still so much we need to know, but fuck, she needs help. No one, not in this day and age, should be sold to some cockhead as a goddamn slave," I growled.

"She gonna stay here? We gonna help her out?" Dive asked, resting back into his chair more.

Pick was the first to nod and say, "Yes, she's under Hawks' protection now." I couldn't blame the guy. He'd also had a fucked-up upbringing.

"So, she's stayin' here?" Dive said again.

"What're you gettin' at, fool?" I asked, leaning against the wall, my arms crossed over my chest.

"It's just, you ain't the nicest person to a woman, only when you fuck 'em. Maybe she'd be more comfortable at my place. At least I'm nice."

No fucking way. Not happening.

Billy snorted. "She won't go anywhere else."

"Why not?" Dive asked.

"She feels safe with Dodge. He found her, and now she doesn't want anyone else to protect her," Billy said.

"I don't think that's—" I started.

"Brother," Pick interrupted, shaking his head. "She screamed out to stop the car because she couldn't *see you.* That's why we had to pull over until you were in front of us. Her eyes were glued to you the whole fuckin' way here."

Holy motherfucking shit.

"Serious?" I asked, just in case he was pulling my leg.

"Dead set, brother."

Rubbing a hand over my face, I asked, "How am I supposed to deal with that?"

"I don't know, but she's drawn a connection with you, sees you as her hero or some shit. And if you think to even fuck her over in any way, you need to put your foot down now and tell her where your head is."

"That's the problem." I sighed. "I don't know."

"You need to find out, and soon," Pick said and stood from the table as Josie walked into the room.

"Can someone help me get Willow to the bathroom? I don't want her walking on her feet just yet."

Dive stood quickly. Without thinking, I pushed the fucker back into his chair.

"Precious…"

"I'm okay, Caden." She smiled sadly. "Are you?" she asked, and Pick nodded as he and Billy moved to her side.

"We'll help her," Billy offered. Josie nodded and rested her head against his chest. Anything like what Willow's been through would cut a person up, but it'd be harder for Pick and Josie because of their fucked-up pasts. You could already see the bond Josie had formed with Willow. Josie wasn't one to touch a person, wasn't even one to talk really, even though the guys had brought her out of her shell more. She was great with people she'd known for a long time. Not strangers, though. Never strangers… except Willow.

There was just something about the woman in the living room that bloody touched us all.

Shaking my thoughts away, I walked out of the kitchen down the hall, past the bedrooms and bathroom and into the living room to find Willow still sitting on the couch. Her eyes were on the hallway, waiting, watching for someone to come back. I couldn't help but see her shoulders sag in…relief, maybe, when she saw it was me.

Christ.

Her soulful eyes did something to me, to my heart, making it beat faster, making it want to take a chance.

Fuck, you can't, dickhead. Look at what happened last time.

My hand went to the back of my neck and I rubbed it, trying to erase the sudden thoughts from my head.

"You, ah, need a hand to the bathroom?" I asked Willow, distracting myself. She nodded and gave me a small smile that somehow sent a message to my dick to harden.

Fuck.

Walking up to her without words, I slid one hand under her legs as the other went to her back. I picked her small body up with ease and made my way down the hall while my cock thought it was party time and grew even harder.

Control your fuckin' self.

The bathroom door in the hall was already open and I could hear water running. I took a step in to see Josie leaning in, fixing the water pressure on the shower.

She glanced over her shoulder and smiled before saying, "Thanks, Dodge. Please set Willow on the toilet and I'll help her from here."

I paused for a moment, because I liked the thought of me being the one to help her naked body in the shower, to wash away her troubles, but then my dick jerked under my jeans. I quickly placed her on the toilet. She looked up at me and uttered, "Thank you…for everything."

"Uh-huh," was my awesome reply. *Stupid idiot.*

Turning, I found Dive leaning against the doorframe. "If you ladies need any help in here, I'm totally up for it." He smiled but then the grin faded a little when he saw my glare. I started for him, and he quickly backed out and yelled, "Or not! Nope, I'm not helpin' at all, so don't ask."

Before leaving, I spun around and eyed Willow, who was already looking at me. "I need a favour," I said.

"Yes, anything."

"I want your cousin's address."

Her eyes widened, and her hand went to her throat. "But…"

"Little bird, don't protect that scum. Give it to me."

"No,"—she shook her head—"I would never protect him, not after…but you could get hurt." She nervously looked to the floor. My eyes glanced over at Josie to see her smiling then looked back at Willow.

Her words shocked the fuck out of me. She was worried I'd be hurt.

"Willow," Josie began. "Dodge will be fine. He'll have brothers at his back. He won't go in it alone. It's not how they work." She reassured the worried Willow, who still looked unsure as she bit her bottom lip and furrowed her brow.

"Promise, things will go smoothly," I offered.

She looked up at me and nodded, then rattled off the address. My blood pumped hard in my body, causing my heart to tick faster; I was excited to hurt her fucking cousin, and hoped it would lead me to the cunt who wanted to buy her.

With a chin lift, I said, "You'll be safe here. Billy and Dive are stayin'."

"Pick's going with you?" Josie asked.

"Yeah, and he's ringin' in Dallas." She gave me a nod and I walked out of the room, listening to the door close behind me.

WE STOPPED our Harleys a block away, just in case the dick did have friends with him. We wanted to go in quiet to see what we'd be in for—before I blew his brains out. Dallas went left, Pick went right, and I went head-on. There was a car in the drive, but other than that, there was nothing else. It was hard to tell if anyone was home; all the blinds were shut tight.

It crossed my mind it was a trap, but I wasn't backing away. I knew Pick and Dallas would be close by, so I went for the front door and knocked.

Nothing.

I knocked again and then I heard footsteps.

The door opened and in the doorway stood a skinny black fucker. His eyes widened as he took in my club vest. "Fuck," he hissed.

"You got that right." I smiled and shoved him backward. I walked in, closed the door, and turned on the light to see Pick and Dallas already standing in the living room. Her cousin turned, spotted them and screamed like a bitch.

"Look, I don't know where the bitch got to!" he yelled. "I'm lookin' for her as fast as I can, but you fuckers keep turnin' up and wastin' my time."

So there were more hounding him.

We watched him study us. "Wait...fuck, fuck, fuck. You got nothin' to do with the deal, do youse?"

"No, but we wanna know who you *are* dealin' with."

He backed up into the wall. "No, no. I can't say or they'll kill me." I got close and drew out my knife from my belt at the back of my pants.

"And you think we won't?" I snarled.

He shook his head. "No." The dick actually smiled. His eyes flicked to my patch and then back to my face. "I've heard about the Hawks MC. Youse don't deal in trouble."

"Wrong." It was my turn to smile before I forced my blade into his wrist against the wall. His scream was blocked off by Dallas's hand over his mouth. "Most of the members don't feel the need to deal in trouble because they have us to do it for them. You heard of the enforcers for the club?"

He shook his head. Tears fell down his cheeks and dripped onto Dallas's hand. "No?" I asked. "A pity, because that's who we are." I gave a chin lift to Dallas. He removed his hand and supported the guy's weight against the wall with an arm across his chest. I held the knife in place while blood dripped from his wrist and pooled on the floor .

"W-why're you gettin' involved?" the dick asked, sweat coating his forehead.

"We don't like cunts sellin' women."

"I needed the money!" he yelled. "She fuckin' deserved it. She had to pay me back for takin' her in in some way."

"So you *sold* her?" I boomed.

"Dodge," Pick warned.

Taking a deep breath, I moved the knife up slowly, cutting through muscle, skin and tendons. The guy whimpered in agony. "Stop, stop. I'll tell you." His eyes closed, his breath came hard, but then he opened his eyes. "Wait, you know where she is."

"Tell us who bought her," I demanded through clenched teeth.

Pain laced his words, but he was still cocky. "You do, you have her," he said.

Removing the knife, I quickly placed it back in, only in his shoulder, causing him to scream once again.

"Tell me," I hissed.

"The Venom MC, someone from there."

Fuck, we'd guessed they'd been involved already.

"His name?" Pick asked.

"I don't know. He wouldn't give it. I was happy I paid off my debts. I didn't care about anything else."

"See," I started then shook my head before stepping back, removing my knife and pulling my gun with added silencer from my jeans. "That's where you should have cared. No one ought to sell a member of their fuckin' family out, no matter what," I said calmly before aiming and shooting him right between the eyes.

"Fuck," Dallas growled. "Next time, give me notice before you shoot a fucker." He turned to face me, I quickly hid my smirk. He was covered in brains and blood. "So I can get out of the goddamn way."

"Sorry, brother," I offered.

"Sorry, my arse. You'll pay for that, dickhead," Dallas grumbled as he picked up the bottom of his tee and wiped his face with it. "How we gonna find the guy from Venom?"

"We'll figure something out. We always do. We'll need to update Saxon and Lan with what's gone down. Don't want blowback for this shit," Pick said, jutting his chin out towards the dead fucker slumped on the ground. "For now, let's get outta here and back to the women."

"Gotta meet this bird if it's causin' Dodge to act like a crazy man." Dallas commented.

"What the fuck you talkin' about? I'm always crazy."

He rolled his eyes. "Yeah, true that. Lucky you like violence as much as me or I'd have to wonder about you." He started for the back door. "I'm going home for a shower. Meet at your house, brother. Gather the others."

"Done," I said.

Yeah, violence was what I enjoyed, especially if it kept the trouble from touching my brothers and family.

So what was Willow?

Fucked if I knew.

CHAPTER SEVEN

WILLOW

*W*hen Josie helped me into the shower, embarrassment heated my cheeks. I hated feeling so vulnerable, but I also knew better than to refuse help when I needed it the most. My reality was I was unable to handle washing away my own blood. My feet were raw, so I ended up sitting in the bottom of the shower and let the water run over my sore body. Josie, the beautiful, sweet woman I'd just met, hopped in the shower and took care of my feet. Dirt, rocks and glass clanged to the bottom of the shower floor as I grimaced, whimpered and cried when the pain got too much. Still, I knew I had to get them clean to heal.

While she took care of me, she talked, offering me comfort and distraction. She told me about her horrid story in life, and all I could think of was my sad excuse of a story in comparison. Hers was gut-wrenching and devastating. Yet, I was complaining about mine. I wasn't abused or beaten. I was simply forgotten. I wanted to cry for her. I had the urge to get up and get out of their lives because they'd suffered enough. Yet there I was, bringing more crap onto their doorstep just when it had changed dramatically, and in a very good way.

When her two men took hold of her, the love she had for them was written on her face, smiling dreamily when she spoke of them both. She didn't even deviate to one or the other... No, she loved them both with everything she had.

I wanted that.

I'd wished for it many times, but it never happened. Nor had I ever felt the urge to open my heart to anyone.

Even with that, though, my mind kept one name present: Dodge. I could see myself falling for him; it would be easy to. He'd helped me, and he was willing to keep me safe. Not only that, but he was as hot as hell.

But, I couldn't trust it, not after my own family taught me trust was a fantasy.

Trust would leave me damaged.

And I knew Dodge could hurt me in a way I would stay broken forever.

After the shower, she wrapped my feet in bandages and placed a towel around me. Then she called to Billy to carry me from the room to a bedroom where he placed me on the bed.

"Dive, get her a drink, something strong. She needs sleep," Billy ordered. I looked around him to see Dive standing in the doorway. He gave a chin lift to Billy and disappeared from sight.

When Dive returned, I drank greedily, enjoying the burn down my throat and the warmth in my belly while Josie found me boxers and a tee to wear. After finishing my drink, I dressed and then curled up in the bed with the blanket over me, closing my eyes.

Only, I couldn't sleep.

I faked it. I relaxed my body so Josie, who sat next to me on the bed, would think I was asleep. Eventually, she did.

"Sweetheart?" Billy's voice said to the room.

God. *God,* I liked that, the softness in his voice when he spoke to his woman.

"Coming," Josie whispered. The bed shifted and a moment later, the door shut. I opened my eyes and stared at the cracks in the blinds, thinking I wanted to be out there, in the sun, soaking up the rays.

Warmth to my chilled body sounded good. Even though it was a hot day, even though the house was set to a nice temperature, I was chilled to the bone.

Why? I regretted hiding in the garage of Dodge's work. I regretted him finding me, and more than anything, I regretted bringing trouble to them.

I wished I had the courage to sneak out of the house, had the courage to run and take the world on with my own hands.

The courage to fight back.

The whole fucked-up, unrealistic situation was vile and it made me feel sick to my stomach.

A sob caught in my throat. I planted my face into the pillow so no one would hear my anguish at how pathetic I had become. My inability to take control, to have the life I thought I deserved all rolled into that. Pathetic. And I despised myself for feeling it.

If it wasn't my family wrecking my life... I paused with that thought, even more frustrated. It was what I was doing to others, to the people trying to help me.

It wasn't fair, none of it, yet there I was, too scared to do anything about it.

I was weak.

Nothing.

Not sure how long I cried for, I just kept going. Eventually, too exhausted to do anything, I fell into a deep sleep. I knew when I woke, I had to do something to fix what'd I'd done, to take their new crap—*my* crap—out of their lives.

DODGE

As soon as I walked through my front door, my eyes sought out Willow. She wasn't in the living room where Billy, Josie, and Dive were sitting. Josie's wide eyes were on my hands that were covered in blood.

"Dodge?" she questioned.

"S'okay, not mine."

The tough woman nodded. When her eyes landed on her other man behind me, she was off the couch in seconds and in his arms. "She's in the spare room, sleeping," Josie offered the answer to the question on my mind.

Moving away from the entrance, I made my way down the hall and into the bathroom. I should have thought. I should have fucking thought before coming into the house with blood still on my hands. If Willow had been out there, it would have freaked her the fuck out.

Once clean, I walked back into the living room, fighting with my mind the whole damned time not to go searching for Low.

As soon as I entered, Pick said, "Called in Saxon, Memphis and Lan. They'll be here soon."

"Good," I said with a chin lift.

"Brother," Dive caught my attention and offered a bottle of beer.

"'Preciate it," I said then walked to the couch, planting my arse on it before taking a long swig of the cool beer.

"Done?" Billy was the first to ask.

"Yep. Call Cracker, can you? He needs to get a team together and to that address, clean-up is needed."

Josie cleared her throat. Maybe I shouldn't have said that shit with her in the room, but from the look on her face, she wasn't fazed I'd just taken a fucker out. Instead, she looked worried about something.

"I think...I'm not sure, but I think I stuffed up with Willow."

Sitting up, I rested my elbows on my knees and asked, "How?"

"Um..." she started, still standing in Pick's arms just inside the door.

Billy butted in, seeing his woman looking uncomfortable. "She told Willow about her past and she reckons Willow took it in the wrong way."

"She did," Josie said. "I saw it in her eyes, the guilt. She probably thinks her stuff isn't as bad as what I went through, and I think now...I think she's regretting showing up at the garage." Her arms wound around Pick's waist. "She'll try to leave so her situation doesn't touch us for long."

"Babe," Billy started.

"No. I know, Eli. I saw it in her eyes, she feels guilty for throwing this on all of us, but she doesn't get that we'd want to help her regardless of our pasts." Her eyes came to me. "You'll need to keep an eye on her so she doesn't run and get caught by them."

With a stiff nod, I said, "I will."

A phone rang. Pick pulled it out of his back pocket and touched a button before putting it to his ear. "Yo." His eyes went wide for a second before narrowing. "Be there." He hissed and shut the phone down. "Dive and I'll stay here with the women. But brothers, you got a situation at the compound. Before Memphis and Sax could leave, a fucker from Venom turned up. He's trying to get some business from us."

"Stupid fuck," Billy growled.

"Let's get gone," I barked. "Pick, call Dallas and redirect him to the compound."

"Done."

THANK FUCK the compound wasn't far. As soon as we pulled in on our rides, we saw the stand-off out front. Memphis, with Sax, Handle, Beast and Pride, all stood in front of the garage looking tense and pissed while they faced Blackie, an older member of Venom. He had some of his brothers with him. What in the hell was going on?

We climbed off our bikes and walked over, standing at the side of the situation. "What's goin' down?" I asked.

Blackie smirked at Memphis, then turned his eyes to me. "You call in your enforcer on us, old man? Can't take care of your own business?"

"I've already said no a million fuckin' times over. You ain't listenin' with your ears, you little shit," Memphis snarled.

Billy made a noise beside me. I chanced a quick glance and saw his eyes were on one of Blackie's brothers, but he quickly moved them away.

"What do you want, dickie?"

"Blackie," he bit out.

"Sorry, forgot." I smirked.

"Youse are the only good mechanics here. We just want someone lookin' and fixin' our bikes." Like fuck he did. Total bullshit.

"Get stuffed, dickhead," Billy said with a chuckle. "This's our turf. The rules fuckin' state you don't come this side of town unless you want war. Now why in the fuck are you really here?"

Blackie laughed. "Okay, you got me. I wouldn't want any of you bitches workin' on my girl." He gave a chin lift in Memphis's direction, but his eyes were on me. "Heard you were in a friend's business earlier today. He asked me to deliver a message. Keep out of it or things will get ugly."

My body froze solid.

Willow.

I got a step at him before Saxon stepped in front of me. I warned, "You better fuckin' not be involved in that sick shit, Blackie, or your life will be mine to take out."

"Oh, I'm not." He smiled. "However, someone I know and respect is. He ain't happy you ruined his plans for the black bitch."

Shoving Saxon out of the way, two steps and I was in his face, his tee and cut in my fisted hands. I hissed the next words nose to nose. "Leave her the fuck alone. You get me?"

Guns were pulled and cocked all around us, brothers on both sides shouted at each other, but my eyes stayed trained on Blackie. He caught my gaze and whispered, "He paid a lotta money for her. He owns her and Dodge, he'll come callin' for her."

"Who?" I snapped.

"I ain't stupid enough to tell you. My debt with him is over. I came here, I told you the message, so I'm free of that shit." He pushed at my chest. "Keep a close eye on her."

"Why're you warnin' me?"

"I don't like the shit that's happenin'. It's fucked up, even for me. Those women…fuck, man, they're screwed."

"He find out you sayin' this shit to me, he'll be all over your arse."

"He won't know." He grinned like a maniac.

"You trust your brothers?" I queried.

"Some. Still, I knew you'd go at me and your brothers would keep mine occupied."

"Tell me where the other girls are."

"Don't know where he takes them."

"Tell me who then."

"Not happenin'," he said. "Gotta keep *my* family safe."

"Your prez?" I pressed.

He scoffed. "No way, he ain't smart enough."

"How'd you know she's with us?"

"Someone was in the house when you and your brothers showed."

Fuck. Stupid move not checking the whole fucking house while we were there.

Christ. Amateur fucking move, which meant they knew she was with me.

"Dodge," Billy barked.

"Jesus," I snarled, annoyed I didn't get the answers I wanted, yet shocked he was giving me something at all. I shoved Blackie back hard. He fell to the ground. "Stay the fuck outta our territory. You come callin' again, I'll take you out."

He got to his feet, brushed himself off and said, "Fine by me." With a flick of his wrist, he and his brothers left our property.

We all watched them go before Memphis turned to

Handle, Beast and Pride, then yelled, "Get back to work. Party's over." Once they were gone, he looked to me. "What is it?"

"You don't trust those three you just sent away?"

"Beast, yeah, not sure about the other two yet."

"We're gonna need some help, maybe get Beast into our fold. Sucks we have to watch what we say and do in our own fuckin' brotherhood," I growled, shaking my head. "Meet at my place in ten," I added before heading to my Harley with Sax and Billy. We were just riding through the gates as Dallas pulled in. "My place," I bit out.

"Fuck, I missed the fun." He glared before turning his ride around and following us.

Too much shit was going on. Fucking straight-up weird shit, with Blackie warning me to keep an eye on Willow. Though, he knew the guy, whoever the fuck he was, and I saw the fright in Blackie's eyes over the sick fucker. It must be worse than we thought. Church was definitely called for. We needed to shoot the shit off each other and see what we were missing. I also didn't like the look Billy gave that other dude from Blackie's crew.

I hated, fuckin' *hated* not knowing all the facts so I could fix it by killing whoever I needed to.

Whatever was to happen with Blackie's warning, I knew one thing for certain... Willow wasn't going anywhere.

CHAPTER EIGHT

DODGE

illow was still crashed out when we got back to mine, but I found a new person sitting in the living room. Lan sent me a chin lift as I walked through the front door.

"Kitchen, now," I said with my own chin lift as I strode down the hall, knowing my brothers would follow. Lan, being a brother by default, had our backs, but he just didn't wear the patch.

I sat at the end of the table, and Pick took the other end. Sax, Dallas and Billy were on one side, Dive and Lan on the other, and that left room for Memphis and Beast when they arrived. Thank fuck my kitchen was big. Josie must have stayed in the living room. She knew when it was time for church that it was no place for a woman. Didn't mean her men wouldn't tell her what was going down. Like I knew our prez in Ballarat, Talon, would confide in Wildcat with all business he saw to. Which was how it should be in this day and age... unless it was something violent as fuck. Then they were better off not knowing, and their men were better off protecting them from sleepless nights.

"Somethin' you should all know," Lan started. He met my eyes, and I gave him the nod to go ahead just as Beast and Memphis walked in the back door off the kitchen. Once they sat, Lan went to continue but I interrupted.

"Memphis, you should sit here." I stood.

Memphis shook his head. "Don't be fuckin' stupid. I'm too old and tired, so you're runnin' the show for now, fucker, until I talk to Talon."

"Memph—"

"No, shut the fuck up. Let's talk."

With a stiff, shocked nod, I put his words aside and went on. "Beast, Memphis has given you the go-ahead to be here. Means he trusts you. I don't yet. Earn that trust from us here and we'll always have your back. But we can't trust yet. Not when we know there's a traitor among the Caroline Springs charter."

All I got was a nod in return. I glanced to Memphis, he shrugged. "He's a good guy. He just don't talk."

Shit. That'd make things hard, but like I'd said I trusted Memphis's word.

"Okay." I nodded and turned back to Beast. "Whatever you hear today stays in this room. If I find someone knows somethin' that's been talked about today, I'll know it's you because the others at this table have my full trust. They're true brothers who have my heart and soul."

He eyed us all then gave me a chin lift. He understood. If he fucked up then we'd fuck *him* up.

"Now, Lan, what were—"

The back door banged open and in walked one of Blackie's brothers. I stood quickly, my gun drawn and under his chin in seconds.

"Started without me, I see." The punk smiled.

"*Parker?*" Pick hissed.

Lan cleared his throat. "As I was going to say, I have a new partner who's deep undercover in the Venom MC."

"What the fuck?" Pick barked.

I stepped back, lowered my gun and sat back down, seeing the guy wasn't a threat. Parker pulled out the chair next to me, turned it around and straddled it. He grinned at Pick then Billy and asked, "How's sweet Josie?"

"Don't fuckin' ask about her. Tell us what in the fuck's goin' on," Pick bellowed.

"Calm down," Parker said. "Like Lan said, I'm a detective who's undercover in the hell of fuckdom with the Venom club."

"Parker?" Josie stood in the doorway, no doubt hearing her man yell his damn head off.

Parker's smile was wide. He stood and approached Josie, but Billy moved quickly and stepped in front of him with a hand to his chest. "Not another step," he warned.

Parker rolled his eyes and said over Billy, "Good to see you, honey."

"What're you doing here?"

"Meeting, little girl." He smiled.

"Precious, head back into the living room. We'll talk soon," Pick said.

She looked to her man and took note of his serious expression. She nodded once, waved to the room, and headed back down the hall.

"Pick, Billy, wanna tell the rest of us how you know this guy?" I asked.

But it was Parker who said, "I own and still live, sometimes, in the place Josie used to live at."

Well, fuck me.

"All right, how about we all sit the hell down and get some shit sorted," I said. Once Billy and Parker sat their arses down, I asked, "Got anythin' to tell us?"

"Got shit all. Only been within their walls for six months. Since I'm new, they don't tell me shit. All I do know is that the guy who's dealing with the slave business used to be a member of Venom. He'd left just before

I got in. What you do have to worry about is Venom fuckin' shit up for you Hawks guys. They want your turf, your businesses and they're willin' to play dirty to get it."

"Fuck, just like we thought."

"You got a rat. Overheard the sergeant in arms talkin' on the phone to someone from your club. He was gettin' nice information on who's where and shit."

"Tell us somethin' we don't know. Just installed cameras at the compound. Missed the garage because we found Willow."

"So, you do have her?"

"Yeah," I snarled. "And she's under Hawks' protection now. Nothin' will happen to her." I took a breath and told them what Blackie said to me.

"He actually said that shit?" Parker asked.

"Why in the fuck would I lie?"

"Hmm, he could be an ally then."

"He said he's got family he wants to protect."

"Yeah, a sister, a wife and two kids."

Dallas banged his fist on the table and growled, "Where in the fuck does all this get us? We still have jack-shit. What's the next plan?"

"You're right." I sighed. "I'll finish settin' up the cameras in the garage. We need to eliminate the snitch fast. Memphis, send out men you trust to the streets, see if anyone can find out who the sick fucker is and his whereabouts. For now, Willow stays here. I'll have round-the-clock protection for her." I looked to Parker. "Need you to talk to Blackie. He was willin' to give me what he gave me. See if you can get more. He knows the fucker, but he ain't willin' to talk. Tell him we'll have his back in protectin' him and his family."

Glancing at Lan to make sure I got his attention, I said, "Willow said the cocksucker who bought her is in with the cops, so you both need to watch your backs. Venom has a hard-on to fuck us up, and Willow's *owner* has a hard-on for her. Don't know if the two are mixed. We'll need to set up a meetin' with the Venom prez."

There was so much shit to do, but it had to be done. The need to have it all finalised so everyone would be safe was high.

"Fuck. Knew someone on the force was dirty," Lan said, "which is why I'm willin' to help you out with anythin'."

Looking to Parker, he nodded. "I'll do what I can while Lan finds the cunt betrayin' his brothers in the force. Detectives, cops, we're all the same and if someone's bein' a bitch, we all go in to sort it out."

"Looks like our club ain't the only one dealin' in deceivin' shits," Sax said. "The Venom don't know who I am. Let me go under, as well. I'll get in and get the information you need."

Saxon was a good kid. Just out of his prospect time, but always willing to do what he can, even if he ended up hurting himself in the process. Fucking lucky Stoke found him when he did. Lucky also, because he protected Stoke's daughter fiercely. Saxon took an interest in Nary, not that he'd man up and say shit about it. He kept his distance from her for a reason none of us knew.

"You think I can't get it." Parker glared.

Saxon leaned forward in his chair and growled, "You been there six months and you have nothin', so yeah, I reckon I can get it faster than you."

"No," I ordered.

Saxon turned to me, face blank.

"You were there behind Memphis today. One of those Venom fuckers would have taken notice of you."

"Yeah, you're a pretty boy," Dive teased. Saxon gave him the finger.

I wondered if Saxon knew Nary was moving down our way yet. It could explain the reason he was so willing to take himself out of the situation and into a dangerous one. Everyone felt guilty when Nary took a bullet to the face when that obsessed Cameron cunt took Josie. He shot Nary when she'd screamed to warn the others. Maybe Saxon was feeling it more because Nary looked up to him. She also had a major crush on him, like he did her. They needed to work their shit out. Mind games were fucking tiresome.

Not that I could talk relationships and manning-up.

I was afraid, like a pissy little boy, when it came to commitment.

A knock sounded on the front door. I was out of my seat, nearing the kitchen door, when I froze and turned back to my brothers. A pained look appeared on my face when we all heard, "Hellooo, beautiful. Tell me where the hot, bad-boy biker men are."

"Fuck," I groaned.

"Christ," Pick mirrored my tone.

"Hell's now upon us." Dive sighed.

"God-motherfuckin'-dammit," Billy said.

"I'm outta here." Dallas tried, but didn't move when my hard stare met his. Memphis's head was in his hands, shaking it.

"Who the fuck is that?" Parker asked.

I jumped when a voice behind me screamed, "I found them. Oh, my!" Julian's hand went over his heart. "This just reminded me of the first time I was dragged into Zara's house and delivered upon a house full of spunk-rats." He beamed. "Who's gonna give this momma a kiss hello?" His arms spread wide and he made a kissy face at us all. I quickly shifted back into the kitchen and moved far away from Julian at the entrance of it. "Come on now, I need some biker sugar. I know you all missed my gorgeous arse." He wiggled his fingers.

If there was one, he wouldn't be here without the

other. "Matthew, get the fuck in here and rein your fella in," I bellowed.

Julian rolled his eyes. "It's okay, my men. I know you all love me, no need to show it." His eyes glanced over us and landed on Parker. Julian moved into the kitchen and started for him. "Oooh, you're a new and sparkly toy. Hey there, handsome. I'm Julian, your next wet—"

"Julian," Mattie snapped in the doorway. "Hey, everyone, just popped in to see my sister while driving through. Sorry to interrupt." Josie appeared next to Mattie and wound her arm around his waist. He placed his around her shoulders.

"You're her brother and *his* partner?" Parker gaped.

Yeah, we're a unique fuckin' bunch for a family.

"Sure am." Mattie smiled. "Name's Matthew, but people call me Mattie."

"How'd you find out we were all here?" I asked.

Julian grinned. "I used my charm at the compound… though, I think they gave up your information just to get rid of me." His eyes went big and he shook his head. "No taste, some people. Sooo, what's going on in the bad-boy world?" he asked.

"Nothin' you need to know about, Julian," I said.

Parker stood from the table. "I'm outta here. Josie, always a pleasure. Lan, I'll go through you for any messages. Be in touch, fellas." Then he walked quickly out the back door. He was probably worried, like most of us, that Julian was going to take a huge chunk out of him.

"Can I get anyone a drink?" Josie offered.

Guess the fucking meeting was over for now.

"I'd love one." Julian smiled and took Parker's vacated seat. Josie found her way around my kitchen while Mattie stood against the wall with an apologetic look on his face.

"Dodge, you should call Talon and give him an update," Memphis suggested.

Julian tapped the table with his knuckles and said, "Oh, don't need to worry about that."

CHAPTER NINE

WILLOW

The room dark and unfamiliar, I wiped my bleary eyes. I wasn't sure how long I'd slept, but I felt better for it. Surprise fluttered through my mind when I realised how rested I felt, a miracle considering the last twenty-four hours or so.

Guilt remained heavy in my mind. I needed to seek out someone else's help—a bodyguard, anyone who could deal with it professionally without causing their family hardship. I had to find someone I could trust. A detective, maybe? There was always a risk they could be in with the dick-muncher who bought me and his evil plan, but I had to take that risk to get my overflowing crap from the Hawks' doorstep.

Stretching my sore body, I pushed the sheet back and shifted my legs to the side to sit. Looking down at my bandaged feet, I moved them up and down, side to side. They still ached, but the real test was if I could stand on them. Carefully, I touched them to the grey carpeted floor. They were tender, but not too bad. Standing, the ache in them doubled. Still, it was something I could handle for small periods.

Brushing my hair from my face, I made my way to the door and slowly opened it. The room I'd been in was just about in the middle of the hall. What I guessed was the kitchen, at the end, held a lot of voices. My heart beat double-time. Too nervous to walk in there, I went in the other direction to the living room, hoping I'd find Josie.

She wasn't there, so I had a choice to either wait out the people in the kitchen or go in and see what was going on.

Just when the thought to hide in the room again crossed my mind, there was an assertive knock on the front door. With the noise going on in the kitchen, I knew no one would have heard it. I bit my bottom lip, contemplating whether to answer it or not. It wasn't my place to answer the door. I should've gone and got someone, but another knock came, that one louder and impatient.

Nothing bad could happen with opening the door...right?

Walking to it, I reached out and unlocked the deadbolt with a shaky hand. Then slowly, I opened it a little. My eyes widened, a scream came out of me before I could catch it and I quickly slammed the door closed again, resting my back against it, my chest heaving.

There was a man.

A good-looking man.

But the scowl upon his face could cut anyone down, and I didn't want to be in the path of it. I shouldn't have opened the door.

Footsteps pounded down the hall. Dodge was first. I saw no one else but him and the panicked look on his face. His eyes grazed over me before he asked, "Willow?"

"T-t-there's—"

"Dodge, open the motherfuckin' door, right the fuck now," the scary man bellowed from outside.

"Honey, language," was snapped by a female voice seconds later.

Dodge smirked. He actually smirked, then it turned into a wide grin and then...then he laughed, while others joined in with him. Josie came to me first, her arm wound around my waist. She moved me from the front door to the couch while Dodge went to the door with a smile lighting his face and opened it wide. That sexy smile—one I'd hopefully have a naughty dream about—

reassured me everything was okay. The scary man didn't mean harm.

"Yo, boss, looks like you not only scare us, but the females, as well." Dodge stepped aside and the scowling man stepped in, followed by a beautiful pregnant woman with warm eyes, a wide smile and a head full of wild, dark hair.

My eyes quickly went back to the man Dodge called boss. He glared and growled, "I ain't gonna hurt you."

"I promise he won't. He's a big teddy bear under all that." The pregnant woman gestured with her hand over the man's body.

"Kitten," he growled to the woman.

"Oh, quit it." She came forward, her hand outstretched. I slowly took it. "Hi, I'm Zara and that's Talon, the president of all of the Hawks charters."

He...yes, I could understand why he was president.

"W-Willow," I uttered.

Zara smiled, winked then turned to Josie. "Sister, give me some loving." She stood tall, arms wide and Josie, with a sweet, kind smile, stood up from next to me and embraced her...sister?

Josie pulled back, her hand resting on Zara's belly, and then asked, "Where are my nieces and nephews?"

Zara smiled sadly. "With Mum." They sighed together. "We popped in because Talon wanted to talk to Memphis and Dodge."

I looked around her to see Dodge had disappeared with Talon.

"There's my baby!" was yelled. I jumped, stood, took a few steps back when I saw a man in his late thirties run across the floor only to stop at Zara, who rolled her eyes. He fell to his knees in front of her. His hands went to her melon belly. "How's my little pea? Nice and warm in there? Your daddy's just here, sweet'ums, no need to worry."

What. The. Hedge?

Daddy?

He was the daddy?

And scary man let that happen to his woman?

A new man appeared who looked similar to Zara. He came up, laid a hand on the man's shoulder who was still on his knees, and said to me, "Hi, I'm Matthew, Zara's brother. And the crazy one is Julian, my—"

"Fiancé," Julian supplied and then bounded up and over to me. "Aren't you just golly-gosh-gorgeous. I love the relaxed look in Dodge's clothes, like you just got out of bed. Looks good on you."

"Julian—" Josie started.

"Are you Dodge's woman?" He laughed. "Oh, I guess you are, being in his clothes and all. Don't worry about us, we'll head off soon so you can get back to your man… hey, why are your feet like—"

"Julian," Josie snapped.

"H-how are you still alive?" I stupidly asked without thinking.

His head jerked back. "What do you mean?"

"You…and Zara, a baby… How has *that man* not killed you?"

Everyone burst out laughing.

Had I woken up in a different universe?

"No, sugarplum, he won't kill me. I'm too handsome for that." Julian smiled.

"There's also the fact that Matthew is my brother, making Julian my brother-in-law. And if Talon tried anything, he would be sleeping on the couch for the rest of his life," Zara said.

Rubbing my hand against my forehead, I uttered, "This is all so strange."

"The best way a family should be," Julian said.

"Willow," Josie said to catch my attention. I looked to her. "Come sit down and I'll explain a few things." I did just that, thinking maybe more information would help my brain from exploding. "Zara and Matthew are biological brother and sister. I was adopted by Mum and Dad," —a small wince when she'd said Dad made me believe something had happened to him—"after my situation. Zara's having a baby for Matthew and Julian. It was their gift to them when they got engaged. Our family is…a little different to most. It's big and includes all members from the Hawks Motorcycle Club. That's how I met Eli and Caden, as well. We have a lot of love and a lot of desire to help each other out in any way we can. Since you became Hawks—"

"Oh, has Dodge claimed her?" Zara asked.

Josie shook her head. "Well, not in that way. Willow has had some trouble, and the men have taken it on. She's now under the protection of Hawks."

"What happened?" Zara demanded.

"Kitten," Talon barked when he appeared out of nowhere... Okay, he walked from the hallway with the other men following him. His deep gaze stopped on me. I held my breath when he said, "Dodge has told me of your situation. You stay here. You think of goin' to anyone, we'll bring you right back. We *will* fuckin' help with what's goin' down in our own goddamn backyard. No one is gonna deal with it like we can."

"B-but, I could, um, I could find, like a detective or something, who isn't under the thumb of my owner—"

"Owner?" Julian gasped.

"No," Talon growled. "Besides, we have one in our fold." He thumbed to the guy behind him who offered a charming smile.

"So, I could go with you?" I asked

"Not fuckin' happenin'," Dodge bit out.

Getting up the nerve, I stood and crossed my arms over my chest. I couldn't and wouldn't bring the nice people into it when I had a detective who could help me and keep me away from any trouble, even the troubles that could harm my heart. Lifting my chin, I said, "I appreciate the help so far, but I'm going with…"

"Lan," the detective supplied.

"Lan." I nodded. "I've brought enough trouble and I don't want any of this to sink into *your* lives."

Dodge took a step forward, glared down at me and said, "No. You stay here."

Leaning forward, I glowered and snapped, "I go with him."

"Low," Talon said with humour in his voice. I looked to him. It was the first time a smile—well, more like smirk—appeared on his face. "Dodge's right. You stay here. Lan has his own crap to deal with and can't keep an eye on you all the time."

"I'm a pain." I sighed and then said in a snippety tone, "No matter what, I'm a pain and I don't want to be. I'm tired of it, so if I can find another way to get out of your lives…lives that were just starting to look up, then I will."

Holy fudgetruck. I just said that to the scary dude.

Thank God, he was still smiling at my outburst. "Ain't happenin', girl, so get the fuck over it and let us help you. Look, we're in this no matter what anyway 'cause we have our own shit to handle with the Venom MC. So this is nothin' extra really, and it's a situation we can handle. So don't sweat it."

The whole event was so frustrating, I wanted to growl

to the room, stomp my foot and leap at Lan, to cry and beg him to carry me out of there.

"Let's get back to the owner part," Zara said.

"Kitten," Talon warned.

"Do I need to call my posse in?"

Posse? She had a posse? Wow.

"You call your muffkateers and we're gonna have words." His hands went to his waist.

Muffkateers...now *that* was laughable; however, I didn't. I guessed not many people laughed at Talon and lived to tell the tale.

"Oh, we'll have words no matter what, Talon Marcus."

I think I had a girl crush. Zara was...amazing!

"Babe." Talon groaned and looked to the ceiling, as if he were trying to stop himself from strangling her. "Dodge is handlin' it."

"Yes, why *is* Dodge handling it?" she demanded.

"Zara," Josie put in then shook her head. I could have kissed that woman again because she didn't want to embarrass me over my obvious obsession with Dodge and him keeping me safe. But Dodge came with Josie and her men, and she didn't need any more trouble.

Stuff it. From the determined look in Dodge's eyes earlier, I knew I had no choice but to play along. They wanted to protect me? Fine. It didn't mean I couldn't help with the protection part, and my help would be in the way of keeping who I could safe.

I was strong. I had balls when I had to. I just happened to be dazed, confused and very scared yesterday. No longer, though.

"He's the new president of this charter," Talon announced to the room.

"Oh, yay!" Julian cried.

Wow, again. Dodge...Mr Sinful himself, was the president of an MC.

"Okay, well, okay," Zara said. Talon smirked at her. "Keep that smile off your face. If he can't deal with the protection Willow obviously needs...if I'm getting this right, from her *owner*," she snarled, and a look of disgust had her nose scrunching up. "Then I'm calling in the girls and we'll come back here to help deal with keeping her safe."

A sniff sounded in the room.

I realised it came from me when all eyes landed on me.

"A woman's cryin', I'm outta here," a large mountain man hissed.

"Dallas," Dodge growled.

"Hell no, brother. I'll call in later. Tonight, I'll take care of the cameras in the garage," he said then quickly walked out the front door like his pants were on fire.

Besides, I wasn't exactly crying. Only a few tears rolled down my cheeks.

"Dumpling," Julian cooed at me like a little child,

which would usually annoy me, but coming from Julian it didn't. So instead of punching him in the throat, I let him wrap his arms around me. "Don't cry about it. You'll see, once you get into this club, you'll want to stay forever. Our group is awesome and now you're in it so…I officially welcome you to the pussy posse."

Numbly, I nodded. Never had I felt so much love and friendship in my life.

"Kitten," Talon growled, which he seemed to do a lot. "We better get back to the kids."

Zara rolled her eyes at him. She turned and stepped towards me, taking me in her arms for a long hug. "We'll talk soon. I'll call you and I'll call Josie for all the information I need to know about what the heck is going on."

"Zara," Talon warned, again.

She ignored him, smiled and added, "You're in good hands. It's Dive you need to stay away from."

"Hey!" Dive yelled.

"Though, Dodge has been known to have—"

"Wildcat," Dodge snapped.

Wildcat…I liked that for Zara.

"Anyway, I'll be in touch, and one day you *so* have to come to Ballarat to meet everyone." She hugged me again, then hugged Josie, Julian, Matthew, Dodge, Pick, Billy, Dive, Lan, Memphis and a young man whose name I didn't know.

"Kitten," Talon groaned.

"Coming," she sang then walked to her man, who placed his arm around her shoulders. He sent a chin lift to the room, which seemed to be normal for these men, and walked out the front door.

"Right," Memphis started. "Church tomorrow, announce the changes, see if that'll scare any snitch out of hiding. For now, I'm out." He turned to the youngest in the room. "You comin', kid?"

"Yep," was his reply. He shook Dodge's hand then gave him a manly hug and loud pat to the back, which Dodge replicated, and left after Memphis.

"Gonna get gone, as well," Lan said. He walked up to me, leaning in.

"Lan," Dodge said with a tone of warning.

Lan kissed my cheek, causing me to blush. He then handed me a card. "If you ever need anythin', even time away from this guy, I'll make it happen."

"Goddammit, brother."

"Catch ya." He smiled. Before I could get my brain to fire, he turned, stalked to the door in his tight jeans, and patted Dodge on the arm. Dodge just glared back. "Talk soon," were his parting words.

Dodge slammed the door closed and turned to me scowling. My eyes widened for a second and then I met his scowl with my own, placing my hands on my hips. Maybe the fire under my belt, which had me standing up to the scary bikers, was the fact that…I felt safe. In fact, I felt very safe for the first time in my life. I also felt as though I *could* be myself, which was a wonderful feeling. So even though I was glaring at Mr Sin, I fought the smile of glee wanting to spread across my face.

"This is all so exciting," Julian chimed in.

"Ah, you guys staying for dinner?" Josie asked.

"No, sorry, we should get back home," Mattie replied.

"But it's just getting good. I can see the storm brewing. How long have those two known each other?"

Was Julian talking about me and Dodge?

"Not long," Pick said.

Julian snorted. "No joke. Wow, I can see the sexual—"

"Julian, we're going," Matthew snapped.

"Poppet, you ruin my fun, but I still love you."

They broke mine and Dodge's staring competition by hugging me goodbye. All of a sudden, I wanted to cry again. I'd never been hugged so much; it was like I was already a part of their family.

Once they left, Josie announced, "I'm going to get dinner started, then my guys and I will leave."

"I'll help," I said and followed her to the hallway.

Halfway down, I heard Dive say, "Hell, I'm stayin' for the show."

"You eat, you leave, fucker," Dodge growled.

Yikes. Alone with Dodge was a recipe for disaster.

CHAPTER TEN

DODGE

*S*he'd changed. No longer was she the timid woman in the garage. This one had a backbone, and fuck, it made my cock sing. Especially since she was wearing my goddamn clothes and she looked fucking superb in them, made even better if I could've removed them. Christ, when she stood tall, her chin jutted out as *she* told Talon what *she* wanted to do? I could have fucking clapped.

Hell, I liked how she was before. But now, I was in deep shit and it was rising with every glare she sent me as we sat and ate with my brothers and Josie.

Her fight was back, and I liked it a shitload.

My dick happily agreed.

Talon mentioned round-the-clock protection for Willow. It seemed the fuckhead knew she was under Hawks' protection, something I'd told my brothers earlier.

Which meant brothers of mine, brothers who had dicks of their own, would be around Willow—when I wasn't.

I didn't like that idea, but I had no choice.

Hell, I still couldn't believe I was president of the Caroline Springs Charter. Apparently, there was no vote needed when the big boss, Talon, made the ruling. I thought he'd go for Pick or Billy, but being the enforcer already, Talon knew I'd be the biggest hardarse out there, and I was getting a good team at my back. Memphis didn't want any position, so I had Pick as my second, Dive my third. Dallas was the main enforcer and Billy, the sergeant in arms. Saxon, a kid good with numbers, was the secretary.

All I could think was that I hoped Memphis was right, that with the change of commandment the snitch would get scared and show himself. Though, I doubted it. I'd been the main enforcer and if that didn't scare the snitch, then I didn't know what would.

A need to find the fucker and have my hand wrapped around his throat was eating me up inside. It made it goddamn hard to trust the rest of the brothers in the club, and that sucked hairy monkey balls.

Thank Christ, Dallas was going to take my job and install the camera in the garage for me. He was also going to be the one to watch the feed. Well, between him and Saxon, hopefully we could find the pussy and get rid of him. Then that'd be one less thing to worry about.

Willow shifting her arse back in her seat caught my attention, which made me wonder how her arse would feel shifting over my lap, which in turn made me get hard.

My attention span was shot with her around. She caused my brain to function from my dick.

I couldn't fall for her, though.

Just couldn't.

Not happening. Never.

And especially not after what went down with the last serious bitch ten years ago. She chewed me up, spat me out and left me like roadkill on the side of the road.

Literally.

Sophie was banging hot. I'd been twenty-two when I met her, and as soon as my eyes landed on her perky tits and arse, I was a goner. Too blind to see past the big tits, tight pussy and big bank account, I didn't see the cold-hearted viper she really was.

I'd fallen and hard. Worked my arse off to prove I could support her and her money-hungry spending hands. So I didn't know that when I worked, she was out filling her pouch with my stepdad's cock, who was climbing his way higher in the accountant firm. Luckily, my ma wasn't alive to see it. Not only that, she was also banging my best friend, just for the fun of it.

We'd been out driving one day when she decided to come clean. I wrapped my hand around her neck and threatened her life for fucking mine up for two years, which may have been the reason she kicked my arse out, landing me in the middle of nowhere.

Two years I'd wasted on that bitch. Two years I'd wasted having a fuckhead of a friend and stepdad. That was when I moved and Talon found me when I was involved in backyard fights to get some extra cash on the side. He took me under his wing and told me I was born to be a brother.

Never looked back.

And I never trusted another bitch again.

They were nothing but trouble.

I'd had my fair share of pussy, and that was all I needed. Just some hot, wet, tight hole to slip my condom-covered dick in, and then they'd fucking leave.

Except now, I had a woman living under my roof. A woman who'd caught my attention right from the start. A woman who caused my body to react in every fucking way she moved, when she spoke, even when she bloody ate, for fuck's sake.

Yep, I was fucked.

Dinner wound down. Josie and Low were at the sink whispering to each other as they did the dishes. I wasn't so sexist that I didn't offer to help, but I was waved away by Willow, saying I was already doing enough for her.

"Dude," Dive whispered. "The way you're starin' at her arse and lickin' your lips is kinda perverted, and that's sayin' somethin' comin' from me."

Shaking my head and chuckling, I rolled my eyes and looked to see my brothers smiling at me. "Not happenin'," I said.

"A week," Pick said as he laid a fifty on the table.

"Three nights." Billy smirked and placed his own fifty on the table.

"Tonight, and don't let me down, brother." Dive glared and coughed up his own fifty.

"Never," I stupidly said and dug out a fifty to put on the pile.

"You twat." Dive shook his head. "You just lost big time."

A throat was cleared. "What are you guys betting on?" Josie asked. Our eyes went up to see both women facing us and leaning their butts against the counter.

"Nothin'," I said quickly. I went to swipe the money from the table, but Billy got it first.

"I'll keep it and give it to the winner."

"Winner for what?" Low's sing-song voice asked.

Looking everywhere but at her, I ignored the question and prayed my fuckhead brothers didn't dish out the answer.

"We better get going," Josie announced. "I've got a class in the morning and some things to do tonight."

"Yeah, two of them," Billy mumbled, causing us to laugh. Willow hid her giggle behind the back of her hand while Josie blushed.

"Idiot," Pick uttered, shaking his head. He stood first, claimed Josie with an arm around her shoulders and started them to the doorway while we all followed them out. In the living room, Josie gave Low a hug. She said something into her ear and I watched Willow nod. I did a quick slap to the back and a chin lift to Pick and Billy before they walked out, closing the door behind them. I would have kissed Josie on the cheek, but I knew I'd have two men breathing down my neck for even touching her. Even though she was like a hot stepsister to me.

"Sooo," Dive began, rocking back and forth on his feet. "I'm sure you guys are tired. You both look buggered." He stretched and yawned. "Yep, I'm just as tired. You both should get some sleep and, look at that, Low's already dressed for bed. And in your clothes to boot." Dive smirked and winked at Low, who then looked down at her clothes like she'd forgotten she was in my boxers and tee. *Fuck, she looks amazing in my clothes.* She blushed, her hand going to her heated cheek.

The prick had done that on purpose. I went to grab for him, but he danced out of the way and went to the front door. "I'll just let myself out. Have a good night, *girls*. Oh, and Low, I do mean *girls*, because I'm sure you'll soon find out that Dodge is lackin' in the man area—"

Grabbing the first thing I could find, which was a DVD case, I flung it at his head. The bastard was quick. He shut the front door and we could both hear him whistling as he walked to his place next door.

A giggle had me turning my glare and head from the door to Willow, who stood just in front of the couch.

"He's an idiot," I offered.

She smiled and nodded.

"You tired?" I asked.

"Um, not really because of that nap I had." She sat on the edge of the couch.

"How's the feet?" They seemed to get the brunt of the ordeal; the rest were cuts and scrapes, nothing too bad.

She shrugged and looked to her feet. "They're okay. Good enough to walk on, at least."

"You should still rest them," I said as I made my way over to the couch and sat down at the other end from her. Leaning back, I met her gaze.

"I will," she said and then—fuck me sideways—she licked her lips. My eyes, like laser beams, followed her pink tongue. She cleared her throat before she continued.

"I want to thank you...um, for letting me stay here and, ah, making me feel safe."

My heart beat hard in my chest. She seemed nervous now instead of the firecracker I witnessed earlier. Was it because we were alone in the house together? Where I could take her right here on the couch, have her naked under me as I slowly slid my cock inside her wet pussy.

Jesus. Abort all thoughts of Low naked now, you fool.

Shifting on the couch, so she couldn't see my growing need for her, I said, "It's not a problem."

"I'm sorry I've put you in this predicament, Dodge."

"Trey," I growled.

Fuck me up the arse. Why did I tell her my real name?

"Sorry?" she asked, her beautiful brows rising high.

Beautiful brows? What the fuck, man?

Rubbing a hand roughly through my hair, I said, "My name's Trey. You can call me that instead of Dodge."

She bit her bottom lip, but I could still see the corners of her mouth rising. She liked that I'd told her that.

"Ah, anyway, this place is safe even if I'm not here. That panel,"—I pointed to the wall beside the front door where it held the security system—"is a top-of-the-range system. Tomorrow, I'll give you the passcode, so when I'm not here, you can feel safe. It also has a panic button and will contact my phone. Not only mine, but Dive's, as well. He lives just next door, so if I can't get back, he'll be here. Not that you'll be alone often. Not until we get this fucker off your back."

"So, I can't go to work?" she asked with a cute worry line on her forehead. I wasn't sure she was more worried about missing work or when I said she could be alone in the house. Why was she so content to stay with me when we didn't know each other? Fuck, I could be a murdering wanker...uh, okay, I could kill for the fun of...shit, it wasn't exactly like that. I enjoyed killing those who fucked with us. Still, I could be a man with no soul, not caring who I killed, but I did. *She* didn't know for sure I only killed those who fucked with my family. So why was she so trusting with me?

"No work for now," I said.

"I'll have to call them. If I don't, Lucia will worry."

"The woman you work with?"

"Yes. She's a friend and if I don't talk to her, I'm sure she'd go to the police. She'd keep trying to find me. I would...I'd also like to see if they would keep my job open."

"Not sure how long all this will take, little bird."

"I can't do nothing, Trey."

Jolts of pleasure shot right to my dick hearing her say my name.

"For now, you have to. Then I suppose I could try and find somethin' for you to do." If I trusted all my brothers, she could work the desk in the garage. After her small nod, I added, "Tomorrow, you call your girl and your manager. Tell them somethin's come up."

"Lucia won't believe it. She knows how much I needed that job, how much I wanted to get out of my cousin's house. She'll get suspicious."

"You trust her?" I queried with a raised brow. I rested my arm along the back of the couch. If I reached a little more, my fingers would graze her shoulder, but I didn't.

"Yes." Her tone was definite.

Still, I pushed. "With your life?"

"Yes," she bit out with a nod.

"Tell her what's goin' on then. But I'll be there for the call. I want to listen in. I can catch a person's lie in seconds."

"Okay."

"For now,"—because it was getting to me—"I wanna know why you trust *me* so much."

She stiffened. I visibly saw it; her eyes went wide and heat touched her cheeks, which caused me to want to know even more. I tilted my head and waited for her answer, an answer she obviously didn't want to give, but I wasn't letting her get off...well, I could get her off, but she wasn't getting off from answering.

"Um." She licked her lips. Her gaze went to the floor and then, it was just like earlier. She straightened. Her chin jutted out and she glared at me as she said, "You told me you killed people. Why else wouldn't I think I'd be safe with you?"

I smirked from her attitude. "How'd you know I wouldn't just hurt you?"

"I-I, the way you were. You got those men out from the room. You called people you trusted to help me. The thought of not trusting you wasn't a question. You're big…" I winked and she rolled her eyes. I wanted to laugh. "You look like you could cut a brother down if they tried anything against you…or anyone you know. I-I just knew I would be safe with you." Her shoulders slumped. Fuck. "But then, I didn't know what Josie had gone through. My troubles don't seem that bad when someone has lived through something like that." She looked up to me. "If you just let me go with Lan, I could be out of all your lives and not bring—"

"No," I snapped and sat forward, my elbows resting on my knees, my hands clasped in front of me. Turning my head enough to share my own glare, I added, "And saying another word about it will just piss me off. You don't wanna see me pissed off. You stay here. Hawks will take care of it *while* taking care of our own problem."

"Trey—"

"No, Low. Not another word about goin' anywhere and, if you try to leave, sneak out, I'll fuckin' find you. And it won't be good when I do."

My cock pulsated under my jeans from the challenging spark in her eyes. "What would you do?"

Eat your pussy out until any thought of leaving would vanish. Then fuck you hard so it'll take at least a few days until you could get outta bed to walk. But then you'd be so in love with my cock, you wouldn't want to leave it...leave me.

Yeah, best not to say that. "You'd have to try it and see, but I highly suggest you don't, little bird," I said before standing. "I'm headin' to bed. I'll set the alarm, which also goes off if anyone tries to go out any door or window in this house." I went and did just that before turning back to her, and before I could drag her to my room. "You can do anythin' you want. Watch TV, a DVD, grab whatever you want to eat." *Come to my room and sit on my face.* "Night," I growled.

"Night, Trey," she whispered with her sweet voice.

Yep, I was fucked for sure.

CHAPTER ELEVEN

WILLOW

ONE WEEK LATER

Slowly drifting my hand down my stomach and into my panties, the first touch to my clit caused my lower body to lift off the bed. One week I'd been living with Mr Sin. One week of seeing him walk around the house in boxers when he first got out of bed. One ducking week of seeing him leaning against the kitchen counter in nothing but jeans that rode low on his hips. Hips I wanted to touch, to lick. And one stuffing week of smelling his delicious scent after he freshly showered, after he'd finished a workout in the spare room—even his sweat smelt divine.

My body wasn't my own. It wanted to reach out to Trey to demand he take us. My mind was mad with lust, and I couldn't hold off not touching myself any longer.

Biting my bottom lip to prevent my moan from being heard, I slid my fingers lower and straight into my tight, wet tunnel. I covered my mouth with my free hand. My legs spread wider, pumping my fingers in and out as my orgasm worked closer and closer to the edge.

Thoughts of Trey filled my mind. His face between my legs, him lifting his body over mine then slowly sliding his large—somehow I knew it would be large, if the bulge I saw behind his jeans was an indicator—penis inside of me. Him teasing me with how slow he wanted to take it when all I wanted was him to slam himself into me, claiming my snatch as his.

Which was why I didn't hear the door open. "Little bird, do you want… what the fuck are you doin'?" Trey yelled as he stood in my doorway. His phone and drink bottle clattered to the floor because his hands went to the doorframe to support himself.

You would think I'd be embarrassed, and I was. However, I was more frustrated that he'd interrupted what I knew would be a mind-blowing orgasm.

Flattening my legs, I got to my elbows and glared over

at him. "What did it look like I was doing?" I demanded and watched him gulp hard. It was quite funny, and I would have laughed if I wasn't wanting to get back to it.

Over the week, our relationship grew into friendship of the teasing kind. The sexual tension was there, only there was no way I was making the first move, and I wasn't sure if Trey actually wanted me. Yes, I saw his heated looks, but they, most of the time, were replaced with a scowl. As if I'd done something to upset him for being female and in his house. Three times I'd said I'd find another place if he wasn't comfortable with me being there and those three times, he'd quickly shut my suggestions down then threatened me if I tried to leave.

My days were spent with either Trey or Josie, while my nights were always with just Trey. We watched movies, ate dinner together and got to know one another...at least somewhat. I knew Trey moved from Sydney to get away from an arsehole—his word, not mine—stepdad who brought him up when his mum passed. Trey had been twenty-two when he'd moved to Ballarat, which was also where Talon had found him in a backyard fight, taking him straight into the biker fold. He'd said it was the best day of his life.

The more I got to know him, the more I wanted him. In my twenty-two years, I'd never wanted a man as much as I wanted Trey.

Never, which scared the bejesus out of me.

Trey cleared his throat, his wild and wide eyes looking from my face to my private area under the sheet and back to my face. "Y-you were touchin' yourself."

"Yes, Trey." I smirked.

He glared then and barked, "You just make this harder and harder."

"Do I?"

He jerked his head back in confusion. "Do you what?"

"Do I make you hard?"

His intake of breath was audible. "Jesus, woman. I'm talkin' about the situation, not my cock."

Sitting up, I folded my arms over my tee-covered chest. "Well, excuse me, but my brain is muddled, and I was *this* close"—I held up my finger and thumb an inch apart—"to coming, and you interrupted it. Now, I'm annoyed, and you just want to stand there and talk. So, I'm sorry if my foggy brain got mixed up and thought about your cock."

"Don't," he growled low.

"Don't what, Trey?" I snapped.

"Don't talk about my cock," he hissed through clenched teeth.

Snorting, I glowered and sang, "Your cock, your cock, your lovely humping cock."

Oh. My. God. What's wrong with me? Pissed-off, 'close to orgasm, but interrupted' Willow was a crazy wench. *Did I really just sing that?* I sang about a man's cock, while

116

he glared at me with burning eyes from the doorway. At least The Black Eyed Peas would be proud they'd inspired my song.

Note to self: never get angry if you get interrupted again while playing with yourself.

It was obvious in the past week I'd let my guard down, let my inner crazy out to see if Trey could take it. And he did. Every time I snapped, teased or talked, he did it right back, if not first to get a reaction from me. Admittedly, since living with Trey, I'd been having the most fun I'd had in my life.

"That's fuckin' it," Trey grunted.

"What?" I asked icily. But then, holy mother Mary, he ripped off his tee and somehow, so quickly it was hard to follow, his jeans were down at his ankles and he was kicking them off. "Trey," I breathed, because he went commando under his jeans and now my eyes were admiring his large—*yeah, baby, I knew it*—erection as it bobbed up and down.

"I told you not to talk about my cock. Now I have to deal with you."

Rubbing my thighs together, I breathed, "Deal with me?"

He stalked towards the bed and flung the sheet from my body. "Yes, little bird, deal with you. Or more important, my cock wants to deal with your pussy."

Licking my lips, I asked, "Um, what type of deal?"

"You'll fuckin' find out soon enough. Let's just say the deal will be pleasurable many times over." He smirked and climbed on the bed. "Take off your panties, Low."

Without thinking, I did as I was asked—no, ordered to. I peeled them off my body and threw them to the side, causing Trey to don a huge grin, showing all his wonderful teeth. I loved it.

He grabbed my ankles and dragged my body down to him. I squealed and then laughed.

"You want my humpin' cock, Low?" he growled.

"Yes."

"You want it, you take it."

Oh, there was no doubt I wanted his lovely humping cock. I reached between us, wound my hand around his thickness…just as there was pounding at the front door.

"Fuck," Trey hissed.

"Ignore it," I pleaded.

Another knock, that one louder.

"Christ," Trey barked. He leaned in, rested his forehead against mine, and then placed a gentle, quick kiss on my lips, too quickly for my liking.

"Yo, brother, where you at?" we heard yelled from the living room.

"Dive," I groaned, annoyed for the interruption.

"Motherfucker," Trey bit out and jumped up from the bed, placing the sheet over me. "You move, I'll hurt you."

Then he mumbled to himself. "Shoulda never traded keys with the bastard."

"You'll hurt me in a good way, right?" I teased.

"Just try it and see, woman." He tugged on his clothes. I saw him wince when he tucked away his still-hard dick and walked out of the room.

"Brother, where's Low?"

"Resting. What do you want?"

"Maybe I should just check on her—"

"You walk to that hall, brother, and I'll take you down."

"You dawg," Dive cheered. "Was she good? I bet she was. With the attitude she's been showin' us in the last week, I bet she—ah, fuck, fuck, fuck, brother. You grab my balls again, I'll gut you."

"You say one more word about her *I'll* gut you," Trey snarled.

"I'm guessin' you didn't get to finish—"

"Fuck, enough! What'd you want anyway?"

"Oh, yeah. There's a black chick out front demandin' to see Low. Said she used to work with her, was supposed to come tomorrow to see her, but didn't want to wait any longer. She said she needs to see with her own eyes that we haven't fucked with her girl in any way."

Lucia. I smiled. I'd rang her the morning after my first night under Trey's roof. First, I spoke to my manager, who said he couldn't hold my position which saddened me, but once Lucia was on the phone, I'd found myself smiling. She could always, no matter the mood I was in, make me smile.

"Girl, Larry said you wanted to talk to me, said you ain't comin' to work here anymore. What in the fuck, girl? You can't leave me alone. I'll get bored. B.O.R.E.D, and it'll all be your fault. Shit, I could get so bored I'd have sex with Larry just for the heck of it." She paused. *"No, Larry, I was just talkin' shit. I ain't lettin' you stick your white little pecker anywhere near my va-jay-jay."* She sighed. *"Tell me, what's gone down, girl? Prince Aladdin come to fly you away on his magic carpet?"*

Dodge, like he said, was listening in. Obviously, he recognised she was indeed a friend, even a crazy one. He rolled his eyes and hung up his line. I stayed on and told her all about my rotten cousin selling me for money, how I escaped and was hiding out in a house that belonged to a member of the Hawks motorcycle club. Before she could rant and rave, I told her the Hawks had nothing to do with the men selling women as slaves. They were trying to stop it and were willing to protect me from anything like that happening again.

"You playin' with me?" she whispered into the phone.

"If I was, you'd be crying my name out by now."

"Bitch." She giggled and then asked, *"That shit actually happened?"*

"One hundred percent truth, Luce."

"Knew it. Knew that cousin of yours was no good. Fuck me. Fuck me, Low. He sold you," she seethed. "Tell me where you're at. I need to see with my own eyes you're good and ain't bein' held at gunpoint sayin' this. If those new bikers fuck with you, I'll cut their balls off with a blunt fuckin' knife and while I do it, I'll be smilin' away."

"I promise you they're taking good care of me."

"Where are you?" she demanded.

"I'll talk to Dodge, see if I can tell you and you can come visit."

"I don't need some male to tell me whether I can come see my girl or not."

"Luce, we have to make sure it's safe for the both of us."

"Fuck me. Fuck me with a ten-inch dildo." Her voice cut off at the end.

"I'm okay, girl."

"You better be."

"I am and I'll talk to you tomorrow, but please, please don't say anything to Alex about this."

"I won't. Never. You and me, girlfriend. You and me together forever." She paused, waiting for my part.

I smiled and said, "Until dick do us part." It was something Lucia and I had made up one day at work while we were going loco with boredom.

Trey appearing in the doorway brought me from my thoughts. "Baby, get dressed. Your girl's here."

Mutely, I nodded. He'd never called me 'baby' and my stomach melted from it, warming my insides.

He disappeared from the room and I heard him tell Dive, "Let her in, brother." I quickly got up, dressed, and then ran to the bathroom to wash up before I went out to see my one and only friend.

CHAPTER TWELVE

DODGE

*J*esus, *fuck. Jesus, fuck.*

I'd almost had her. My cock was so goddamn close to touching her sweet spot and she was raring for it. She wanted me. Wanted my dick inside her and hell, I wanted to get her back in the room and make it goddamn motherfucking happen. My cock was so hard I swear it was growling out its frustration through the slit at the end. I was fucking surprised my balls didn't turn into hands and claw their way out of my jeans, demanding Low to see to my aching cock.

It was all her fault.

When I'd walked into her room, fuck me, I'd just

about choked on my own tongue. Her legs were spread under the thin sheet, in a way I just knew, *I knew,* what she'd been doing. And when she didn't deny it, instead got pissed that I interrupted her, I was a goner. I wanted to show her something better than her fingers.

Stupid fucking Dive.

Fuck him. Fuck her friend, too.

If they didn't show, I'd be balls-deep inside her perfect pussy.

I could almost weep.

Actually cry like a two-year-old having a tantrum.

Whether she liked it or not, she'd be accepting me in her body as soon as the fuckers were out of the house.

The front door opened. Dive walked in with a smirk on his face, after him was the other chick I'd seen at the grocery store. I didn't take her in at the time; all my attention had been on Willow. The woman looked around the same age as Low, twenty-two, which was something I'd found out in the week just gone. My woman was only twenty-two. I felt like I was cradle snatching, but she acted older than she was, which I knew was because of her upbringing. Defending herself in life on her own.

Lucia was also black, with a short bob, dark eyes and a slim figure. She was pretty; still, she had nothing on my little bird.

"You," Lucia gasped when her eyes landed on me. "You're the hot dude from the grocery store."

Hmm, seemed Willow didn't tell her who she was staying with.

"That lucky bitch," Lucia uttered, more to herself. Still, Dive and I heard it, causing Dive to laugh.

"Hey, girl." I turned in time to see a bright smile on Willow's face for her friend. She glanced my way and blushed. She'd better not get shy on me and back the hell out of me having a piece of her.

"Oh, you wanna 'hey, girl' me when you forgot the most important part about where you're stayin'. Girl-friend,"—she pointed to me—"Mr Yummo, seriously? I don't know whether to hit you or kiss you for good luck." She stepped in more then made her way to Willow, taking her in her arms and hugging her tight. Willow reciprocated the hug. She whispered something in Low's ear, causing my little bird to giggle.

After stepping back, Lucia looked at Low from head to toe then smiled big before saying, "You're glowin'. Is he givin' it up for you?"

"Lucia," Low snapped.

Dive burst out laughing then added his part. "Not yet, I think we actually interrupted somethin'."

Lucia looked from Dive, to me, to Willow. "Well damn, do you want me to come back? Or I could wait

here while you two go at it. Promise I won't listen…
much." She winked.

Low rolled her eyes and said, "No, we're fine."

We were?

Fuck, I wasn't.

I wanted my hands on her curves. I wanted her small
body under mine, and I goddamn wanted my cock buried
in her wet snatch.

What I needed was to get the fuck out of there before
I went all caveman and took her in front of people.

"Brother, kitchen," I growled.

"Whoa, hold up there, hunk." Lucia came at me, her
hand moving forward. "I'm Lucia, and you are?"

"Dodge," I barked.

"Okay," she drew out. "Now, Dodge. I gotta say this
and I hope you won't hurt me in the end. But, if you fuck
her over, after the shit she's been through, I will come at
you with guns blazin'."

"Can see why you and Low are friends. Both got attitude too big for your own good," I commented.

"Hey," Low snapped.

I leaned in to Lucia and her eyes widened. "She's safe
here. I won't fuck Low over in any way, except maybe to
actually fuck her—"

"Trey!" my little bird yelled.

"She's Hawks business now, which means, either way,
she will *always* be safe. You can be a part of her new life

126

or not, but her new life comes with all of us." I asked with a raised brow, "Good enough for you?"

The smart-arse put her hand up in my face and tapped her finger to her chin, pretending to fucking think about it. I would have laughed if I wasn't so goddamn frustrated.

"I suppose." She sighed. "At least you're all eye candy."

"Is your friend taken?" Looking to Dive, I saw he'd asked Low that question.

"Yes." She smiled at my brother.

"Dammit."

Lucia turned to Dive. "And who said I'd let you have a piece of my arse, white boy? You ain't man enough to handle me."

Jesus. She didn't know who she was talking to and Dive being Dive, he just saw that as a challenge.

"Oh, baby. I'd rock your world. It's obvious your man ain't doin' you right or you'd be less cranky. Let me show you what a *real* man can do." He smirked and grabbed his crotch like he was some Michael Jackson impersonator. Next, he'd try the fucking moonwalk.

Lucia rolled her eyes. "I notice you don't have much to grab there, little man, so how could you teach me what a real man can do when you haven't got the equipment?"

"Lucia," Low warned.

Too damn late, though.

Dive whipped down his jeans and stood there with his frank and beans showing.

"Jesus, Dive, put it away," I growled.

"Not much, hey?" Dive taunted Lucia while he swivelled his hips. Holy shit, the way his junk swayed could entrance anyone. Motherfuck, I was even looking.

Christ. Eyes burnt.

"Oh." Willow sighed. My head spun to her to see both women studying Dive's junk. I stalked over, covered her eyes with my hand and brought her back against my front.

"Don't fuckin' look," I barked in her ear and felt her body shiver.

"Take a photo, if you want," Dive offered Lucia.

She nodded and reached into her purse over her shoulder. "Don't mind if I do."

"Lucia, you have a man," Willow scolded.

"Oh, yeah." She giggled. "Good show, white man."

"Why you hidin' Low's eyes, brother? Scared she'd be after me instead?" Dive joked and palmed his dick. Bile rose in my throat.

"Fuck o—"

"Won't happen," Low interrupted, moving my hand from her face then turning to me. "You're way bigger than him." My chest puffed up with pride.

"Get the fuck outta here," Lucia cried out.

"Hey," Dive started with a growl. "Pine over my dick, not his, woman."

Shaking my head, I asked, "Is anyone findin' this whole situation fucked-up?" No one said anything. And there I thought Wildcat and her crew were strange. Looking down at Low to see her eyes bright with humour and heat, I bent, touched my lips quickly to hers and received a moan in response. Only, I wasn't having our first *real* kiss with people around. Because once I had my tongue in her mouth, I'd want more. Instead, I pulled back, my hand going to the side of her neck, where I applied pressure and said, "Thanks for defendin' my junk. I'm gonna take the dweeb to the kitchen, let you catch up with your girl."

"Okay," she breathed.

Touching my mouth to hers again, I pulled away and started for the hall. "You reckon you could put it the fuck away now? I never want to see it again. If I do, I swear on my goddamn ride, I'll snap the thing off."

"Damn, you're moody when you don't get some," Dive said as we walked down the hall, pulling up his jeans.

"One more word outta you and I'll call Julian up and tell him you need a massage," I warned.

"Cold, brother, cold."

IN THE KITCHEN, with a bottle of beer in my hand, I sat at the table with Dive and wondered for the hundredth time that week if I was doing the right thing. I'd been fighting myself all week to stay clear of her, not to try anything... but all that was wiped away as soon as I saw her in her room with her hand down her panties.

Was the risk going to be worth it?

Jesus, I didn't know, and I felt like a pussy-whipped dickhead for even thinking about it. But Willow could be different. She could be like Wildcat was with Talon, his one and only. Hell, my brothers in Ballarat were glad and proud to have their balls around their women's necks, and in a way, I could understand why. Those women were one of a kind. They were all special.

Was Willow?

Fuck, she was special. She was sweet, sexy as hell and very tempting.

Hell.

Shit.

Motherfucker.

I was going to do it. I was going to risk it once again and let her in. Let her all in.

If my heart ended up fucked, then that'd be the end of me, as well.

"Do you think I could entice Low's friend over to the white side of things?" Dive asked. Obviously, his thoughts were totally different than mine and honestly, I sometimes wondered about my brother, if his mind was 100 percent there.

"Brother, she has a fella."

He shrugged. "So?"

"Even I know you ain't one to steal a woman away from another man. You'd never sink that low."

"There's just somethin' about her."

"That's what you said about Simone, Josie's girl, as well."

"Yeah, well, that turned to shit, didn't it?" It did, but only because he'd fucked it up while he was trying to chase her. He got impatient as she was taking her time accepting him, so he went out and screwed some bird. Simone found out. She thought if he'd been totally serious about them, then he wouldn't have slept with anyone else, which was fair.

"Maybe if you keep your dick in your pants, things would be different."

He rolled his eyes, sat back in the chair, and smirked. "Where's the fun in that?"

Full of shit. Like me, he was over dipping into pussy that didn't matter.

My phone in the back pocket of my jeans started ringing. I pulled it free, saw it was Dallas and hit the button, saying, "Yeah?"

"We got him," he hissed.

"What?"

"The snitch. Got him on camera, brother."

At church, we'd all been surprised when no fucker showed their colours, guilt taking over after it was announced I was president. Every one of those little shits sat calmly at the table and congratulated me. Not that they'd had a choice in the first place, because Talon ruled it to be so. Still, I would have thought the snitch would get cold feet with the sudden changeover. No such luck, until Dallas rang.

"I'm comin' in," I growled, ended the call and slapped the phone to the table. "Dallas found the snitch."

Dive smiled. "We goin' to have some fun?"

"Oh, yeah." I chuckled.

"What about Willow and her girl?"

"We'll set the alarm and get Beast here to watch from out front." With that, I stood from the table, a smile playing at my lips. I was ready to get the information out of the fucker any way possible, and I knew I'd enjoy doing it if it meant getting us to the fucker who thought he owned Low sooner.

CHAPTER THIRTEEN

WILLOW

TEN MINUTES EARLIER

*L*ucia and I watched Trey and Dive walk towards the hallway. Once they were out of sight, Lucia turned to me and smiled. Her hand flew over her mouth and she squealed into it, jumping from one foot to the other. Laughing, I rolled my eyes, took her hand and dragged her over to the couch to sit down.

"How lucky are you, girl? When everythin' and I mean *everythin'* has turned to the worst shit in your life, you find help from hot bikers. And one who wants to follow you around and sniff your crotch every five seconds."

"Shut up." I laughed.

"Seriously. My God, I would have fanned my coota from the way his eyes fucked you on the spot every time he looked at you." She fanned her face instead, thank God, then took my hand and gave it a squeeze. "Babe, you know I love you, but you gotta know that man's on heat for you."

Shaking my head, I said, "I do know. We... um... nearly, before you arrived."

"*But*... I know you have a 'but' in there, woman."

"It was the heat of the moment, for him mainly. He caught me rubbing one out and things went straight to fast-forward. However..." I smirked. "I..." I started but couldn't finish.

"You have feelin's for him." She smiled sadly.

"Yes. How could I not? Living with him for the last week has turned the lust into something else, something I feel in my gut, in my head and heart, and it scares me. I want to know all of him. I'm wanting..." I sighed. "It's weird because it's only been one week, but I'm finding myself wanting to never leave his side again."

"Go with it," Lucia declared.

"What?" I dropped my voice low.

She placed both hands on the side of my head, met my eyes with her serious ones and said, "Go. With. It. You deserve this, and I just know…I can feel it in my bones, this is right. And when it turns out right, you hav'ta shout me to an expensive dinner. I want to be wined and dined, bitch." She squished my cheeks together then left a big smack-a-roony on my mouth.

"We walked in at the right time," Dive said.

Lucia let go and burst out laughing.

"Too bad we can't stay," Trey commented with a smirk.

I stood. "You have to go?"

He studied my face and whatever he saw, he liked. His eyes warmed and his smirk turned into a sweet smile. "Yeah, little bird, but I'll be back soon."

"Okay." I nodded. He winked and walked to the door with Dive following. Before he headed out, he said, "Arm it as soon as we step out." I nodded.

"Nice to meet you, Lucia," Trey said.

"You also, hunk." She smiled. "And you, ding dong." Dive winked at her, sent a chin lift to me, and they were gone. I went straight to the alarm and armed it.

He wasn't back soon. To start off with, I was annoyed, but Lucia stayed to keep me company and when we heard a Harley drive up the street, we ran to the window to see who it was. Only it wasn't Trey, but Beast. I'd met him a couple of times. He was the quiet type, like Dallas, only Dallas was broody as well as quiet.

"Should we invite him in?" I asked.

"Ah, no. Your man didn't say to invite anyone in." As we watched Beast, we saw a car pull into Trey's driveway. When Beast didn't react, I slowed my heart down. Then I saw Josie with another woman get out of the car, and my heart settled back to its steady pace.

I disabled the alarm and opened the front door. Waving to Beast and getting a chin lift in return, I moved out of the doorway as Josie made her way to me and walked in with her friend following. Over the last week, Josie had become my friend. She was something else. What she'd been through was heart-breaking, but how far she'd come was amazing. Josie and I had become firm friends and that friendship would never be broken. I'd fight for Josie, any battle, and I knew in my soul that Josie would do anything for me in return. She was a woman filled to the brim with heart and she was lucky to have two men who saw her as theirs, who saw the full heart Josie had and claimed it. Billy and Pick were the best thing Josie could have found, and I was glad for her, so happy for her because after everything, she deserved happiness. She deserved the world.

"Hey, honey." She smiled.

"Girlfriend," I said and kissed her cheek.

"This is Nary. She's a friend from back home and

just moved here to get settled in before she starts uni next year." Back home was Ballarat, a country town an hour away. The town where her mum, brother and sister still lived with their families. Looking to Nary, I noticed she was a stunner, even with a scar that ran from the side of her mouth up to her cheek bone. Nothing could take away her beauty. Her shoulder-length, light brown hair was silky, her body amazing. She was tall and slim, but with curves in the right places. But what made her truly beautiful were her green eyes, a similar colour to mine, which sparkled in excitement.

Josie had told me about Nary moving and how Nary was eager for the change, eager to get out from under her parents' roof and their rules. She was also eager to start afresh. You could see it all in her eyes. I hoped to God she would find what she was searching for in Caroline Springs.

"Hey, girl." I smiled and pointed to Lucia, who was back to sitting on the couch. "That's my girlfriend, Lucia. Babe, this is Josie and Nary."

"Hey," Lucia called with a wave.

"I brought supplies." Josie grinned and waved a bag I hadn't noticed out in front of her. With my puzzled look, she added, "The guys are out, so I thought for Nary's first night here, we could celebrate with a few drinks."

"Oooh, baby, you're my new best friend." Lucia

clapped then patted the spot next to her, causing both Nary and Josie to giggle.

Josie made her way over to the couch and Nary stepped in further. I turned to her and said with a wink, "Welcome to Melbourne, girl."

She grinned. "Thanks, it's great to be here." I closed the front door after waving to Beast and armed the alarm again.

"Sweetheart," Lucia called, her eyes on Nary. "Tell me you got the shithead who did that to you?" She gestured to Nary's face.

"I shot him," Josie said while pouring out the alcohol into plastic shot glasses, ones she pulled out of her plastic bag.

The room fell silent as we all looked to her. Then I turned my wide eyes to Nary who nodded.

"Say *what*, woman?" Lucia whispered.

"It's a long story," Josie admitted. I knew about her past with her sister's dead ex-husband, but she'd never mentioned her shooting someone.

"Um," I started, and then sucked back the shot she'd just handed me. "I think we have time."

"Plus." Lucia grinned. "What's better than a juicy story about shootouts while drinkin'? Nary, come sit, get your drink on with us."

After three shots were downed, Josie started talking about her stalker and how he showed at her father's wake to steal her away. When Nary screamed, trying to warn people, she'd been shot. Josie was taken until she'd had enough, until all her grief, of thinking Pick had been killed, came barrelling back in and she couldn't deal any longer. She told us she would never, for the rest of her life, regret aiming that gun and shooting that man.

After five more shots, Nary told us about her mum's issue back in Ballarat. How Stoke, a Hawks' brother I was yet to meet, came in and claimed her mum as his own. We also learned about Saxon.

"Fuck'im," Lucia slurred. "He ain't worth it if he treats you like that."

"But—"

"Fuck'im," she stated again.

I wasn't so sure. Saxon obviously cared for her. He seemed to always be in the right spot when Nary needed someone to save her. Like when she was nearly raped at school, and his reaction when she'd been shot made it pretty clear. He'd stayed in the hospital until she was awake. She wasn't supposed to know that, but her mum told her anyway. He was there at every operation. Again, she wasn't supposed to know, but she did. So I could understand why she would defend him. She had *big* feelings for him and everything he did for her showed he felt something back, only he wouldn't make a move. He steered clear of her when she was around. It broke my heart when she told us he'd said she was too immature for him, that he wanted a real woman. One who knew how to use their body, and *that* was after she'd tried, and failed, to kiss him. It was even *before* her accident.

It was all so confusing.

Pain etched her face talking about him, yet the depth of her feelings and hope she held for him played across her features with every word.

I was afraid, though, that one day, he would break her and she'd move on. If she did, he would be miserable. No one went to the length he did to protect someone if they didn't feel anything for that person.

Nary had her own shit to go through and I decided that, if she needed me, I was going to be there for her. I was happy, so ecstatic with the girls in the house, drinking, talking and sharing. They were *my* girls.

"Anyway!" I shouted, seeing Nary had enough of Lucia and her advice. "Let's drink to friendship because, girls, I can honestly say I love you all like you're my sisters from another mister."

"Cheers," they sang. We picked up our shot glasses and tossed them back.

HOURS LATER, we'd somehow talked Beast into the house. Well, Nary and Lucia convinced Beast into the house, while Josie and I stood at the door laughing our arses off.

Once he came in, he sat on the couch and watched as we laughed, talked, and danced when Lucia turned on some tunes—we had a merry old time. I'd just been in the kitchen and walked back into the living room to find my girls playing charades, and I couldn't help but think how lucky I'd become after my life had taken a turn for the worse.

Lucia, since I'd moved in with my cousin, had always been close to me. We'd always bonded, but now I found myself with two more girlfriends. I'd been blessed. Maybe my luck *was* changing and finally Luck *was* gracing me.

Trey…God, Trey was amazing. To take me into his home and help me out when I had no money and had pretty much nothing to my name showed me the person he was.

Loyal.

Strong.

Caring.

Sweet when he wanted to be.

Also scary, possessive and mean when he wanted to be.

All in all, he was perfect.

He'd even gone to Josie, gave her money, and told her to buy me clothes and all the girly shit—his words—I needed to start over.

Yes, perfect.

Just thinking of him brought a smile to my face. I was excited to see him when he got home. Desire reared its head because I wanted to start where we'd ended things in the bedroom earlier. If my snatch could sing, she would be.

To keep my mind occupied, until I saw that powerful man walk through that door, I headed into the living room, took another shot and grabbed Nary into my arms to get my wiggle on. She giggled as we spun. I dipped her and we swayed against each other.

What I didn't expect was to trip over Beast's foot behind me and land on my arse in his lap...which happened to be when Trey walked—no, barrelled—into the house.

CHAPTER FOURTEEN

DODGE

A FEW HOURS EARLIER

We reached the compound and walked straight in. Saxon stood outside Dallas's room. He gave us a chin lift before he opened the door and went in with us following. Billy, Pick, Memphis, Lan and Dallas were already in there, either standing around or sitting where they could.

"Someone could think we're havin' an orgy in here," Dive muttered. Before I could slap the back of his head, Memphis had already done it.

"The cameras are hooked up to Dallas's computer, dick," he barked.

Dive rolled his eyes. "Just playin'."

"Now's not the time," Pick said and gestured with his head to the computer Dallas sat in front of. He clicked on the mouse and the video turned to life. It was of Handle and Slit in the garage. It looked like it was just after closing time. They were the only ones left, but it was their words—not their actions, *their words*—that got my blood pumping for some violence.

"What the fuck you mean you're pullin' out?" Slit spat at Handle and shoved him back. "You can't pull out now, dickhead. Not only will he kill you, but he'd take your girl's life, as well."

"This shit's wrong. I said it all along," Handle snarled. "I only got in it to have your back, brother. You and your fucked-up, get-rich-quick schemes. Where'd it get ya? Got any money yet? No, because a prick like that don't pay in money."

"It ain't about the money now. You know that. Can't wait to see Dodge's face when we take his life apart. He thinks he's hot shit bein' president now. He don't scare me."

"He should. You just got no brains for it."

"You sayin' you're scared?"

"Fuck, yes."

"You gonna rat out your own flesh and blood?" Slit asked.

Holy Christ, they're blood brothers.

Handle sighed and looked to his boots, crossing his arms over his chest before he raised his head and looked to his brother with vengeance in his eyes. "Don't have to."

Slit glared. "What'd you mean by that?"

"They have cameras in here. You just told them everythin' they need to know."

"The fuck?" Slit spat just before the garage door burst open and Dallas rolled in, gun raised, with Saxon behind him, also carrying a piece.

"Move a muscle and we'll fuckin' shoot," Dallas barked.

Slit looked to his brother. "You've just killed me."

Handle's wince was small, only his hard eyes never turned to regret. No, they were still travelling the vengeance wild ride. "You killed my woman," he uttered. "*He* took her a week ago. *He* took her so I'd keep you doin' what you're doin' for him. He fuckin' took her from *my house!*" he bellowed. Pain and deep loss etched over his features. "He took her, broke her and then…fuck, *fuck,* I found out last night, *brother,*" he spat. "He killed her. Killed my woman 'cause of *you.* I wanted to kill you with my own hands, but I think the way Dodge will deal with you would be more enjoyable."

"You didn't fuckin' tell me. I would have got her back!" Slit yelled.

Handle snorted in disgust. *"Bullshit!"* he roared. "You knew. You fuckin' knew, you *sick cunt*. You knew he had her because you went to him worried I'd back the fuck out and wouldn't help with the delivery. I saw the tape, brother. I saw it and when he said he'd take *my woman,* you nodded. You fuckin' signed *her* death warrant right then."

A shot was fired. We saw Slit fall to the ground, his hand over his thigh. Before Dallas switched off the recording, we saw him turn to Saxon. As the room quieted, I looked to Saxon, who shrugged and said, "He moved."

Fuck me.

The kid was born to be a brother, like me.

Looking to Dallas, I asked, "Where are they?"

"Down in the basement. Muff is guardin' Handle. Knife has Slit's room."

"Right. Pick, Billy and Dive. I need you lot to find out all Handle knows."

"Any way?" Pick asked.

"Sucks his woman got killed, and he's in this shit for havin' his blood brother's back, but if you think he's leavin' anythin' out, get it outta him in any way you can," I said. "Dallas, me and Saxon are gonna go pay a visit to Slit."

"The kid?" Memphis asked.

Looking to Saxon, his jaw clenched, his eyes vicious, I also saw he wasn't a kid any longer. He may be nineteen nearing twenty, but he wasn't a kid.

"Yeah, Vicious is comin' in with us."

"Vicious?" Saxon asked.

"Your club name. You down with it?"

He smiled. "I'm cool with it."

Lan cleared his throat. "Time for me to leave."

"Yeah, brother. I'll get someone to call with an update later." He gave me a wave over his shoulder before walking out the door. He was a good cop—fuck, detective —and a clean one. Which was why I probably should've had him out of the room before I said the plays. Not that he seemed too fazed by them. He understood how it went down with a dirty brother, and he'd be the same once they found the dirty cockhead in the force. Though, for him to keep clean, he may need to call upon us to get rid of his problem.

And we'd do it. He had our backs and we had his. He'd proved himself many times. Even when he was in the law business, he saw Hawks was good, pure. We didn't deal in pussy, drugs, guns or other shit. We were on the straight and narrow. He liked the way we were and knew we'd do anything to bring justice to the fuckers who did us wrong. Even if that meant he'd have to turn a blind eye to something.

I spun back to Memphis after Lan had left. "I want you to spread the word. Have a sit-down if need be, but tell the brothers what's goin' down. We had a snitch. I'm dealin' with it, and when I'm done, have the brothers walk through the room to see what would happen to them if they fuck with Hawks. This brotherhood is not about snitchin'. It's not about fuckin' each other over or playin' games. It's about loyalty, about trust. It's about family, friends and fuckin' hard. Livin' strong and findin' our peace. Hawks *is* safety. Remind them of that after they've seen the room."

"Done," Memphis said.

"Let's get to it then, ladies." Dive smiled.

KNIFE SAW ME COMING, and he had the door open before I reached it. With a chin lift, I walked past him to see Slit sitting on a chair, his arms tied behind his back and his ankles tied to the chair. His head was down, but it came up with a smirk on his face when he heard someone walk in. I waited until Saxon and Dallas were in there with the door closed before I stepped in front of Slit. He tilted his head back more so our eyes clashed.

"Whatever you're gonna do will be nothin' compared to what *he'd* do to me."

I shrugged. "We'll see." Glancing at his leg, I saw a

white bandage wrapped around his thigh where Saxon had shot him. "You gonna tell us anythin' freely?"

"No." He glared.

"Be quick for you if you did. Less sufferin'," I offered.

"Get fucked."

My fist connected with his face, his stomach, the wound on his thigh. He puffed, panted and screamed, but it didn't make me stop slamming my fist into him over and over.

No one fucks with Hawks.

Suddenly, I stopped. His breath heavy, I could hear each intake he took. It was slow, pained. His eyes were black and blue already, but that wasn't the end for him yet. I drew my gun free from my jeans.

I needed answers, answers he'd give me. I'd make him tell me all he'd hidden while double-crossing his club. Hunching down in front of him, I offered again, "It can go easier."

Defeat shone through Slit's one squinted eye. Still, the fucker had will in there, also.

The bastard had to tell me, and he would with his life. He spat at me, blood coating my black tee and face. The gun in my hand caused my palm to sweat. I stood, wiped the blood splatter from my face and threw a sinister smile at him. "Last chance."

He looked down, not acknowledging me. I lifted the

gun slightly. His good eye tracked my movement to his left boot that was still tied down.

A smirk reached my face. I fired. Pain radiated through his features as he bellowed. Screams tore from his throat. My smile didn't leave my mouth.

No one. Fucks. With. Hawks.

"Next one?" I questioned. He violently shook his head back and forth. Now was the time to get the answers I wanted. Then I'd give him what he needed. A six-foot hole in the ground, with bugs crawling through him, making him the piece of shit he was.

"You don't understand. I do what I have to do, and I would do it again just to fuck up your life. You think you're too good, untouchable, but you're not. He's gonna come for you. He's gonna wreak havoc through your life until you have nothin', and I can't wait for it."

Shaking my head, I asked, "Who's he? Where does he take the women?"

An evil laugh burst from his busted lips. "Your worst nightmare." Without thinking, I aimed and shot. His other foot received a bullet. He screamed again. "Stop, fuck, stop. It's Baxter Davis, also known as Blade, and guess what, motherfucker? Bad shit will be comin' your way. He's gonna take that black bitch. He's gonna ruin you and Hawks, so there will be nothin' left for you before he takes your life." His voice was mixed with pain and satisfaction.

What. The. Fuck?

Baxter Davis.

I knew that fucker from years ago, during the time I was involved in backyard fighting.

Again. What. The. Fuck?

Through his good eye, Slit looked up at me. *He knows.* His time had come. I knew that was all he'd give, so that was all I'd get. The bastard was going six feet under. Tired, his head flopped down, his breath hardly recognizable. I pocketed my gun and walked behind him. Reaching into the back of my pants, I pulled my knife out. The blade came up over his neck. He didn't even move, the fight gone from him.

Yeah, he knows. "See you in Hell, snitch," I whispered just as the blade sliced his neck. Blood coated his clothes then dripped onto the floor.

"You left us with nothin' to do," Dallas complained.

Actually, I'd forgotten they'd even been in there.

"Do you know who he was talkin' about?" Saxon asked.

"Yeah," I started as I stood and wiped the blade on my jeans at my thigh. "He was from Ballarat. Before I met Talon, I was into backyard fightin'. He was one of my opponents. He never liked that I'd win. He'd been undefeated 'til I'd come along. Hated I took the glory away from him. I also stole his girl at the time. Guess the fucker never got over it." I shook my head and grabbed the towel Dallas threw my way. "Knew he was a sick fuck back then. Was glad to take his woman away. I saw the bruises he'd given her. But fuck, sellin' women into slavery and waitin' to cause shit with Hawks? He's not just a sick fuck, but a sick and twisted one seekin' revenge after losin' a fight I'd fuckin' forgotten about years ago."

"What's the plan?" Saxon asked.

Smiling, I said, "Find the fucker and eliminate him."

"I'll start a background check," Dallas answered.

"I want all the information you have on that dickhead, and I want it fast. This is the last time I hear that fucker's name and the last time he thinks he can play with Hawks."

As I WALKED out the door, my phone rang. Wiping my hands on the towel, I pulled it free of my jeans and answered with, "Yo?"

"Mr Monroe?" a woman's voice asked.

"Yeah?" I said and kept walking down the hall, up the stairs and into the compound common room.

"Mr Monroe, I'm sorry to inform you, but your sister was in a car accident and she passed away."

"Who's this?" I barked.

"This is Jennifer Lucas. I work with Child Protective

Services. I'm sorry about your loss, but I also rang to discuss her children."

Fuck. Fucking Christ. I hadn't seen my sister in nearly sixteen years. Before I moved out of my stepdad's house, she was already gone. She was nine years older than me and hitched to some loser. She managed to stay with that loser for too many years before she left him. She'd had two kids in that time and, as far as I knew from the minimal phone calls we'd shared, she had no one else in her life.

"Mr Monroe, are you still there?"

Shit. My sister was gone.

Hell. She'd hated me because I was a biker, so we weren't close, but that loss was tight in my gut. Was that what Slit meant? Bad shit was going to happen. Had they killed my sister?

No. Fuck no, couldn't be. He meant something else because no one knew I had a sister. No one knew of my life before I moved to Ballarat and Talon found me. My name wasn't common knowledge. Everyone knew me as Dodge and that was it.

So shit. Fuck. Christ.

My sister was dead.

"Mr Monroe, *are* you still there?" the Jennifer woman asked with an impatient tone.

"Excuse me for takin' my time while I *fuckin'* process the death of my sister," I hissed down the line.

"Yes, well, sorry." She sighed. "But I need to tell you about tomorrow."

"Is it her funeral?"

"Mr Monroe, I don't think you heard my earlier comment. I'm calling about her children. You were put down as their guardian. You need to come to Sydney and collect the children, sign some papers and help them see to the funeral."

My mind was blank.

Nothing.

Absolutely fucking nothing.

"Mr Monroe?"

"She left her kids with me?" I uttered.

"Yes. She *was* your sister, am I right?"

"Yes."

"Dodge." I looked up to see Pick had called my name. I waved my hand at him for 'not now', but he still walked my way.

Jennifer started talking again. "As far as I know, there is no one else. Your stepfather passed away a year ago and you're the only living family member left. But most importantly, you are in her will as sole guardian to Texas and Romania."

Texas and Romania.

What in the fuck was she thinkin' naming her kids that?

I knew she'd had them. I'd sent presents each time one was born, but they got sent back.

Why would she leave the kids to me when she fucking hated me?

"Mr Monroe, can I expect you tomorrow?"

"Yes. Text me the address and I'll let you know when I can get in." Closing my eyes, I asked, "Why didn't the police call?"

I opened my eyes to see Pick standing there before his hand went to my shoulder. I shrugged it off as Jennifer answered me, "As far as I know, they did. They'd had trouble getting a hold of you, but I was under the impression they'd left a message."

They'd left a message.

They'd left a message to in-fucking-form me my sister was dead and now I had two kids to take care of.

Fuck!

I didn't even know how old they were. "How old are they?"

"Who?"

My upper lip rose at the stupid question. "The kids," I snarled.

"Oh. Um…" I could hear some papers being shuffled around. "Texas, the boy, he's fourteen, and Romania, the girl, she's just turned seven."

Shit. Christ. Fucking hell, what am I gonna do with kids at fourteen and seven? I don't do kids. I can barely take care of myself. What do they eat? Can they fuckin' bathe themselves? Go to the toilet on their own?

"Okay, Mr Monroe. I shall text you. Please let me know when you land. The children will be happy to see you."

I highly fucking doubted it.

She hung up. I slowly pulled the phone away from my ear and looked at it in my hand.

My sister was dead.

She'd given me her kids.

I was now taking care of kids.

Crap.

"Dodge?" Pick said in a quiet tone. "Everythin' cool downstairs?"

"Huh?" I asked and blinked up at him.

"Brother, what in the fuck is happenin'?"

Rubbing a hand over my face, I cleared my head and said, "Tell Memphis to send in the brothers. Dallas will give you the info you need to know. I have to go."

"Go where?" Billy asked, stepping up.

"My sister was in a car accident. She's dead. I have to go to her kids, organise a funeral, and bring the kids back here."

"To live with you?" Pick asked, shock in his voice.

"Yeah... fuck!" I looked to both of them. "I'm their legal guardian now. A boy fourteen, a girl seven. What in the fuck am I gonna do?"

Pick straightened. "Give me a sec, I'll talk to Memphis, then we'll get you outta here and organised.

The women will know what to do with the kids. First, you need to go shower and clean the fuckin' blood off."

Shit. Yeah, a shower was good.

Kids.

I was going to Sydney to collect my dead sister's kids.

Fuck, my chest hurt.

As soon as I stepped in the house, anger took hold. Seeing Low sitting on Beast's lap pissed me right the fuck off. I had enough shit going on without having to deal with a slut sharing herself around. She didn't get my cock today, so it seemed she was seeking it elsewhere.

Fine. Fuckin'. Fine.

Bitches were all the fucking same.

Using, motherfucking cunts.

Knew no good could come from her.

"Trey." She smiled and stood.

"Get the fuck out!" I bellowed from the front door.

"Dodge," Pick warned.

"Brother," Dive snapped.

"Fuck!" Billy swore.

They knew what had been said in the room with Slit. They knew Baxter was still after her, so being Hawks men, they were still protecting her.

"Trey," she uttered.

"You listen here, dickhead—" Lucia started in.

"No. I don't have to listen to any of the shit you bitches say. Whatever it is will be fucked-up anyway. Get the fuck outta my house, now," I demanded. "Dive, *she* can go to your place. I want her outta here, and now."

"Trey." Not a whisper that time. No, she snapped it at me, her backbone kicking in. Any other time, my dick would have got hard, but not then. I was too pissed for anything.

"Low, it's not what—" Dive tried to say.

"Dive," I growled before he could finish. "Get the bitch the fuck out. Now," I ordered and stalked off to my room at the end of the hall, slamming the door behind me.

I had to pack a bag. My flight was in two hours at five a.m. The flight was only an hour and a half, then I'd be off the plane and heading to my sister's house to organise the funeral. If I kept myself going, kept moving and thinking about what I was going to do with two kids, I'd be okay. I'd forget about seeing Willow in a brother's fucking arms.

Thank fuck I didn't dip my cock into the bitch's snatch.

If I had, I would have been weaved into her web more and been led by my cock into another dangerous situation that I didn't need right then.

Christ.

My tee slipped from my hands when I heard sobbing

coming from in the room on the other side of my en suite. Closing my eyes, my head dipped. My chin touched my chest as I listened to the next words.

"They're all the same," Low growled through her crying. "He didn't even let me explain. He didn't care. Fuck him. Fuck this shit. I don't need anyone's help."

"Girl," Lucia groaned.

"No! I did nothing, Lucia. Nothing but trip and fall and land in some guy's lap, and that's how Dodge reacts. It gutted me. My stomach is hollow. My heart hurts. I just want it all to end. I want to be left alone." A wail of pain, pain that pierced my soul, followed by her voice filled with utter devastation. "I didn't ask for this life and right now, I don't want to be in it."

"Girlfriend, don't—"

She sniffed up. "I'm sorry, babe. I shouldn't have said that."

"You ready?" I heard Dive ask.

She must have nodded because I heard no more except retreating footsteps.

Moments later, my door burst open and Josie stepped in with Pick and Billy behind her. She looked hurt more than anything.

Before she could say anything, I held up my hand. "Don't." Fuck. I couldn't take a lashing after hearing what I just heard. So I said, "I was wrong. I let my emotions fuck me up and took it out on a person who didn't deserve it. I'll fix it when I get back."

"Her face, Dodge," Josie uttered. "It was like you took a knife and stabbed her in the chest then twisted it for fun." *Jesus fuck. That killed.* Josie shook her head sadly. "I know you have things going on yourself and I hope when I tell her what they are, *which* I will be, that it will ease some of her pain. But I can tell you now, you will have to make it up to her when you get back. Prepare to have a fight on your hands."

I was a cunt.

A motherfucking, low and dirty cunt.

To take my shit, my fears, out on her like that.

I knew I was going to have to fight for her forgiveness and I was more than ready to do it. How-fucking-ever, I had a flight to catch, two kids to take care of, and that shit scared me more than being shot.

That was until I called Talon to update him.

"Talk," he answered in his signature response.

"Baxter Davis," I growled into the phone.

"You're fuckin' kiddin' me?"

"No. He's the one sellin' women into slavery. Found the snitch tonight and got it out of him."

"Fuck me. That cunt came to me after I got you into Hawks and wanted to join, as well. I turned him away. He's a dirty prick."

"Guess he never got over you shuttin' him down. Not

only that, but me winnin' the fight when he had the undefeated title and also stealin' his woman he used to beat."

"Jesus motherfuckin' Christ. Knew that guy was fucked in the head. What's the play?"

"Got Dallas lookin' for him. Gotta head outta town for a while, though."

"Yeah, heard. Fuckin' sucks, brother."

"S'all good. Talk soon."

"You need anythin', and I mean fuckin' anythin', you call, hear?"

"Yeah, brother, 'preciate it. Keep your ear to the ground, not sure if the fucker will wanna start shit in your area."

"Will do."

Throwing my phone to the bed, I quickly packed some shit into a carry-on bag.

I was off to collect some kids.

Shit.

CHAPTER FIFTEEN

WILLOW

TWO WEEKS LATER

$\mathcal{M}$y emotions had been like a wild roller coaster. Deep-seeded hurt, where I would curl up in a ball and cry, happened often. However, my emotions would then quickly switch to anger and I'd find myself cursing while cooking, watching TV or reading. Those hot, smoking heroes in the books pissed me the hell off because I had one, only he turned out to be a bastard. The way Trey's eyes sizzled with hate on that night taunted me even in my dreams.

The way he spoke played on repeat over and over in my mind.

Usually, I wasn't one to hold a grudge. The speed in which I forgave my parents was testimony to that. My cousin, however, I didn't have to forgive. What he did was unforgivable. When I'd been told he was no longer an issue, I half expected the guilt to kick in.

That never happened.

Instead, relief had brushed over me knowing he had received exactly what he'd deserved.

Still, I found myself holding a big, fat, ugly grudge when it came to Dodge.

It was as if he'd hurt me more than any one of *them*. I couldn't explain it, nor could I understand it. All I was able to do was guess, and my guess had to do with the fact I trusted and relied on Trey too much. So when his actions tore me apart, I had no one else to blame but myself for letting my emotions for him take control.

No more.

I understood what he went through before he arrived at the house. How he found the snitch and... took care of it. How some of the trouble with Hawks was because someone had a vendetta against him over stupid, petty stuff. And especially how he lost his sister and was since responsible for two children.

He would have been a ball of confusion and hate.

Still, if he had let me, I would have been there for him.

I would have helped him through it all. However, he'd pushed me away by being a stubborn prick who wouldn't listen to me, and I found that his words speared my heart, fracturing my already-frail emotions.

None of his treatment I deserved.

Three days. It took me three days to stop the tears springing to my eyes when that scene would pop into my head. Poor Dive thought I was going crazy; he also thought I had my period. Men didn't understand that woman were emotional a lot of the times, especially when the hope for a happy life was ripped right out from under them.

On the fourth day, he'd had enough of me moping around. With the help of Josie, Nary and Lucia, they all snapped me out of my funk with kindness. We watched movies, we went shopping—with five bikers tagging along. I'd borrowed money off Lucia to buy some clothes. With no questions asked, she'd lent it to me. It was only Josie who questioned why I'd gone to her and asked for her help to sell the clothes Dodge had given me online. I wanted the money so I could pay him back. And as soon as I had a job, I would give him some more money for the short time I was under his roof. After all, bringing two children back with him would be expensive when he'd have to feed, clothe and arrange schooling for them.

I could say I cared about the children more than Dodge, but I'd be lying and that irritated me so much.

It peeved me that Dodge was on my mind, which was another reason my anger felt fuelled.

At the start of the second week, Dive—who was becoming another fast friend, though sometimes an annoying older brother—came to me and asked if I wanted a job. I jumped off the couch and wrapped my arms around him, screaming, "Yes, yes, yes!"

His reply was, "You aren't outta the crap yet. We'll still keep you close, but we need someone at the garage to man the phones. You willin' to do it, babe? There'll be a lot of horny bikers around wantin' to tap your arse."

Rolling my eyes, I said, "If I can put up with your horndawg ways, I'm sure I can put up with them." I'd lost count of the times I'd heard Dive get a visitor at night. What I could *count* was the times I'd heard the women cry out their orgasm, causing me to feel a little jealous. Not that I would ever go there with Dive. He was a Player with a capital P.

I started work the next day. Dive drove me in. He wouldn't have me on the back of his Harley. One, it wasn't safe and two, that spot was for his old lady. I wondered if that meant his mum. Weird.

To start with, after Dive had led me into the front office, I was scared and overwhelmed when I spotted the overflowing paperwork all over the desk. I knew it wasn't my job to organise and file, instead just to answer the phone and jot down appointments for all the employees—and there were a lot of workers. Still, I couldn't even find the phone under all the paperwork. After Dive left me to it, with a kiss to my temple, I started tidying. I didn't like to work in a cluttered environment. I was sure the men knew most women were like that, because when Memphis came in at the end of the day, his whistle was long, his brows were high, and he smiled big. "Never thought I'd see the place like this. You rockin' this work shit, sweetheart."

Laughing, I told him, "It only took me all day, but I finally found the phone."

"And cleaned, filed all the shit… fuck, you even put a fresh pot of coffee in the machine. The men won't want you to leave now." He walked to the door that led into the garage and yelled, "Low's got the coffee machine workin'!" He turned back, moved out of the doorway and folded his arms over his chest as he leaned back, as if he was waiting on something. That *something* came barrelling through the door. At least five big men came striding in to stare at the coffee machine.

"Thank fuck," one said.

"Miracle," another added.

"I think I'm in love." That one was looking at me.

"Hated going to the diner down the road, woman. You've made a fan outta me if it tastes as good as it looks," said the only one I actually knew, Saxon.

"I'm tryin' it first, you fuckers," replied the last guy, who ran at the coffee pot.

With wide eyes, I looked to Memphis as the other men crowded around the coffee pot. He shrugged and said, "The kettle in the lunch room stopped workin' 'bout a month ago. That thing was outta action before that. We're all lazy fucks and couldn't be bothered fixin' it when the diner opened down the road about the same time they broke."

Men were strange.

The days that followed were something special. I got to know most of the guys as they came in and got their coffee when they wanted one. Some stayed around to chat and others said a quick hello.

On Friday, at closing time, I was shocked to come back from a toilet break to find the front office filled with most of the guys. Upon opening the door, they all started clapping and cheering. Then they parted, and Josie, with Pick and Billy behind her, stepped forward with a big bunch of flowers.

"They all wanted to do something special to show you how much they appreciate you being around to deal with the paperwork, phone calls, *and* for fixing their coffee machine." She rolled her eyes and I giggled. Tears brimmed in my eyes. I quickly wiped them away.

"Glad to have you here, Low!" Bulldog shouted.

"Yeah, be lost without ya, beautiful!" Sunny yelled from the back of the group.

"Babe, if Dodge doesn't get his finger outta his arse when he gets back, I'll claim you," Muff teased with a wink.

Though that comment confused me.

My head jerked back and I said, "But Dodge and I aren't—"

"Anyway," Dive interrupted. "It's time to party!" he shouted. Cheering, hollering and whistling echoed around my small office.

Things calmed down and almost everyone left the office, either walking out the side door to the garage or out the front. That was when I saw women arriving and the men claiming them with an arm around their shoulders.

Looking to Josie, who stood beside me while I shut down the computer, I saw her wince.

"Babe, it's party time," Dive said. "Means the club girls are here to get the party started."

"Club girls?" I asked.

Josie nodded with a look of disgust on her face. "They're a bunch of women who freely offer themselves up for…"

"They like the attention and to get fucked by us bikers," Dive finished for her.

Suddenly, I felt sick. Women did that? They came here

to get it on with bikers and let the men use them in any way? Why?

"Women get hot for biker cock," Billy said plainly. He sent an apologetic look to his woman. "They're up for anythin', and they don't care who they get it from. They share themselves around. Some even have a few men goin' at them at the same time."

"That's..."

"Shameful," Josie said. "I'd never seen it before until the first time I joined in at a club party with Billy and Pick. Though, I wasn't really welcomed by the women. They hated me because I had two of the new, fresh meat."

"Screw them then," I snapped. Josie laughed and Pick came forward to pull her back against his chest, wrapping his arm around her waist. I watched her melt. I quickly glanced at Billy to see the small smile playing on his lips as he watched Josie and Pick, before I asked, "Wouldn't you have seen this in Ballarat, though?" I asked.

"No." She smiled.

"Talon got rid of all free pussy before he took claim to Zara. Knew she'd hate it, didn't want anythin' to wreck his chance with her. Pussy still showed, just never when Talon was there. But now, a lot of the brothers are hooked to an old lady, so club pussy stopped altogether in Ballarat."

Oh, now I got it. 'Old lady' meant they had a woman.

"But they still do it here," I stated.

"Yeah, Memphis didn't care. He had a woman at home, and all the girls knew not to approach him after he shoved one bitch outta his face for even tryin'. Still, he was fine with the brothers havin' their fun."

"But Dodge is now president."

"Dodge loves gettin' it on… fuck," Dive groaned. "That was back when we just got here, before he knew you."

Shaking my head, I offered, "I don't know why you keep defending him like I'd be hurt with what he's done. He and I weren't *and* never will be a thing."

"But—"

"Dive," Billy barked and shook his head.

"Anyway," Josie said. "It's up to you if you want to party at the compound, or we're heading to our place for drinks and then a nightclub. We wanted to know if you wanted to come to celebrate your first week finished working here."

Taking her hand in mine, I gave it a squeeze. "I appreciate the thought, I really do, but I think I'll just head back to Dive's."

Dive groaned. "That means I'll have to go with you and miss out on free pussy."

"Pig," I coughed into my hand. "But no, you can stay. I doubt—"

"Never doubt," Pick said in a low tone. "You never know what can happen. Look, we'll take you back. Dive can get his fill and meet us back there. We'll stay with her until you're done, brother."

"Lifesaver," Dive cried, slapped Pick on the back and walked out the door.

I wasn't really in the mood for company. After finding out about the club women, it kind of put a dampener on my happy mood from my heart being filled to the top with the appreciation the men had shown me with having me work there.

Still, because I didn't want Dive to regret taking me into his house…after Dodge ordered him to, I was glad Pick had offered.

On the drive home, Josie said to Billy in the back of the car, "I put the final touches on the rooms today."

"Good, sweetheart. He's all set then."

"Yes. It's kinda scary that we'll see Dodge with children."

"He'll have our help, precious," Pick reassured her. I thought it was nice that Pick, Billy and Josie had gone to Dodge's place to clear out the spare rooms and install new bedding and such to go with the children and their ages. Josie was excited to have kids around again; she'd told me how much she missed seeing her nieces and nephews.

What was also nice was that they didn't hide those things from me. They still included me in things, even after what happened between Dodge and me. Instead, for the children's sake and because I loved spending time with Josie, I went shopping with her and her men in my spare time and helped pick out items for the kids' rooms. *I* was even excited to see how they'd like their new rooms.

Though, because they'd just lost their mother, I wasn't sure they'd be too happy about anything.

When we pulled into Dive's driveway, my heart took off in a wild gallop. There was an SUV parked in Dodge's drive. He was home.

CHAPTER SIXTEEN

WILLOW

"I'll take Willow inside and lock the place up if you two want to go see Dodge," Josie offered. I was glad she did. There was no way I was going over there.

"We'll get you both inside first," Pick said as he climbed out of the car. We all followed and made our way inside. Billy asked us to stand by the front door as he walked through Dive's house. He came back out stating all was clear. Josie gave them both a quick kiss before they walked out the front door and Josie locked it, which was then checked by one of the guys from out the front.

I slumped down on the chair in the living room and

sighed. I wanted to go over there, I needed to know he was okay.

But how could I want to after the way he treated me?

Looking to Josie, I asked, "Did you leave it?"

She sat in the chair opposite me and nodded. "On his nightstand. He shouldn't miss it. But...honey, are you sure you should have done it?"

No, I wasn't sure.

However, I did.

I'd asked Josie to leave money and a note in Dodge's house. It took me multiple times to write what I wanted to say and still, I remembered every word.

Dodge,

I wanted to thank you for taking me in when you did. For wanting to protect me, even when I pushed it on you. I'm sorry for giving you no choice and having me stay in your house. Thank you for the clothes you bought for me, but I can no longer accept them. I would have given them back to you, but somehow I doubt they would fit. So in return, I sold them. Here is most of the money back. Once I've worked some more, I'll give Dive some more money to give to you for the rest of the clothes and for other expenses while I was under your roof.

I hope you find happiness, and I hope you're okay after facing the loss of your sister.

I promise not to be a burden on your doorstep again.

Low

Regret for doing it filled me. Regret for saying I was a burden when I'd tried not to be in the first place and asked to stay with Lan ate at me. Was I being petty by leaving it? Probably. But at the time, I wanted to hurt him, even just a little, like the way he'd hurt my feelings.

Still, right then, I felt stupid.

We'd had a week together, yet somehow my emotions, my feelings were coiled tight around Trey Monroe. A week and I was a goner for that man.

Stupid, stupid me.

"Do you want anything to eat, drink?" Josie asked.

"Not really, girl."

"You have to have something. What about I order a pizza? The guys will want something soon."

There was a knock on the door. "Sweetheart, open up," came Billy's voice from the other side. Josie smiled and skipped over to the door. On opening it, she threw her arms around his neck like she hadn't seen him for months. He curled her into him and gave back the love she'd greeted him with.

That was what I wanted.

Groaning to myself, I slapped my hand to my forehead. God, how could I be thinking about my love life when I was still in hiding from the biker who owned me? I was still stuck in a situation that kept me where I was.

If it was over, I could move on.

If it was over, I could start again.

…And then be kicked up the arse once again when someone new chewed me up and spat me out like most people in my life did.

Pity party for one. Please take a seat and enjoy my morbid train ride.

"Low." I looked up to see Billy standing in front of me with a sad smile upon his face.

"He wants me gone?" was the first thing that popped into my mind, which I accidently voiced.

"No, babe. He asked me to give this back to you." He held out the money. "And then there's this." A slip of paper was in his other hand.

My hand shook as I slowly reached for it, worried it was going to bite me on the fingers. I pulled it free and he laid a gentle hand on my shoulder before he turned to Josie, tagged her with an arm around her waist and led her off towards the kitchen.

I didn't think he would find it that fast and then have time to reply. He had kids to take care of, get them settled in. But maybe, after he threw his bags in his room, he spotted it and got so angry he didn't want to wait to rip me a new one.

Licking my suddenly dry lips, I opened the note.

Little bird,

What the fuck were you thinking? You need a phone so I can ring you or text you instead of this old-school shit with passing notes. You can buy the fucking phone with the money that belongs to YOU!

I was an arse. A big, giant, hairy fucking arse. We need to talk face to face. I know now isn't the time. But soon. I'll come calling, and you will talk to me.

Trey (not and never will fucking be Dodge to you!)

My eyes teared. Then they widened and *then* they squinted into a glare. Who did he think he was? *He will come calling and I* will *talk to him.* No way and no how.

He was the one who called me a bitch and kicked me out of the house because he thought I was all over Beast like a dog on heat. *He* kicked me out. *He* spoke to me like a piece of dirt stuck to his shoe, yet he thought *he* could order me around in a goddamn note.

The whole letter pissed me right the heck off.

Sighing, I slumped back in the chair.

I was annoyed because my stupid, pathetic heart fluttered, and I smiled a small smile.

God. What was I going to do?

One thing I did know was I was never letting him treat me like that again, and if it meant keeping my distance, I had to do it.

After everything.

After my family screwed me over time and again, I did not need some alpha male dictating to me what he wanted from *me*.

What about what *I* wanted?

God. What do *I want?*

It seemed I got out of one mess and straight back into another.

I knew for certain, though, I was not going to buy a phone with *his* money. Somehow, I would get it back to him. Even if it meant spending it on his niece and nephew.

Josie walked back into the room with Billy following. "How was it?" she asked, and then her footing stalled when she saw my glare. "That good?"

"Oh, no, it was fine," I said sarcastically. "*He* thinks *he* can come back and expect me to get over it because he called himself an arse and then boss me around. Then things are all peaches."

"I'm thinkin' it's actually not," Billy mumbled.

"Damn tooting it's not all good," I growled and stood

from the chair.

I watched Billy's lips twitch. He turned to Josie and asked, "Did she just say 'damn tootin'?"

"Um, yes," Josie said, her lips also twitching.

"Not funny." I glared and stamped my foot.

"All right, take a breather and calm your tits, woman."

Josie turned on him. "Did you just say 'calm your tits' to Willow?"

He groaned and stepped back, arms folded across his chest. "If I say yes, does that mean I'm not gettin' lucky tonight?"

"Yes." She glared.

"Then no." He smiled and winked.

Josie rolled her eyes and turned back to me. "Dodge probably didn't think when he wrote the note. Billy said he's had a hard time with the kids."

My venom eased a fraction. "Are they okay?"

Billy shrugged. "Dodge said the girl, Romania, is cool about movin', but the boy is bein' a shit."

I threw my arms up in the air. "Of course he's acting out. He just lost his mum and now he's moved away from his friends who could have helped him out, and in with a man he hardly knows. And let's face it, Dodge can come across as a scary guy. All tall, big shoulders, sexy... anyway, I was saying the boy will need time to settle in."

Josie giggled then sobered when I lasered her with a

look. "Yes, you're right. I totally agree. Sexy Dodge can be scary."

Groaning, I slapped my forehead.

"Though, you're also right. If he gives... Texas, right?" She looked to Billy who nodded. "Some time to settle in, start at the new school, things should settle down. Dodge isn't the most maternal man." Billy snorted at that, and Josie glared at him. "But with help, he should be fine."

I hoped so, for the kids' sake, at least. *What must they be thinking after going through losing their mum and now living with a big, scary biker dude?* It would be hard.

There was a knock at the door. "That'll be the pizza," Josie said and started for the door until Billy grabbed her arm and shook his head. Instead, he went to the door.

Once he'd paid and gave the... heck, *five* boxes to Josie, he said, "I'll be back soon." He spun, walked out the door and closed it behind him.

"Where's he going?" I asked as I helped Josie place the boxes on the big coffee table.

"Going to get the others for dinner."

I was bent over, looking in the boxes to see what toppings they'd got, when I paused and looked up at Josie. "And by others, you mean Pick, right?"

She wouldn't meet my gaze. She shrugged then mumbled, "And Dodge and the kids."

Standing quickly, I faked a yawn and said, "Wow, I'm so tired. I think I might just go to bed."

180

Why would Dodge write me a note when he knew he was coming over in the first place? Was it to piss me off before he got there? What was his game? I didn't understand it, and I didn't have to stick around to find out.

I moved. Josie got in front of me. I sidestepped. She was there.

"What are you doing?" I hissed. "I thought you were my girl?" I snapped with my hands on my hips.

"I am. But I'd love for you to meet the kids with me."

I raised a brow at her. "And?"

She sighed. "It's got to happen sooner or later, you two in a room together, so why not let it happen when other people are around? At least you'll have a buffer then and be able to dodge Dodge." She giggled. It *was* actually funny and I would have laughed with her or smiled at least, but my stomach was all of a sudden wrapped up tight in a ball of nerves, annoyance sliding around, as well.

My eyes widened when I heard the rattle of the doorknob.

CHAPTER SEVENTEEN

DODGE

They hated me. Maybe I was exaggerating. Romania seemed to warm to me straight away, but the boy, he couldn't stand me and I couldn't blame him. We didn't know each other and even in the two weeks we'd spent together, he'd said hardly a word to me. So we still knew nothing about each other. I'd tried. I asked him questions, but he'd ignore me. I'd left him alone, thinking he'd soon come around. However, he hadn't.

The kids were still dealing with losing their mother. Not that it was much of a loss, which I found out the first night with them. Still, it'd be something to deal with, thrust out of one situation and into another. Knowing it was hard for them, I didn't push anything on them.

Romania was a cute, seemed a little slow on some things. But she was one who went with the flow on things. Her, I could deal with. The boy and his attitude, not so much. Still, I had to give him time to adjust.

As soon as I'd walked into my sister's house, I knew I was going to have trouble with Texas. Jennifer introduced me to them as they sat together on the couch. Romania jumped up with a smile and flung her tiny arms around my waist to hug me. Texas took one look, turned up his nose at me and walked out of the room. Romania, who told me I could call her Rommy, skipped out of the room after her brother. I learned then that they also had no father; he'd died five years earlier, and it wasn't like he was even in their life before that, either.

Fuck. The kids had no one.

Except me.

It was then I decided I'd try my best to be there for them.

Having no one sucked, and I knew how they felt because I'd felt it after my shit, until I was welcomed into Hawks. Now, I had a huge-arse family and I couldn't be happier.

A vision of Willow smiling at me as we sat on the couch slipped through my mind.

Yeah, I needed to make things right when I got back.

God, I was such an arse.

The two weeks with the kids had been the hardest in my life. Kids and me? I had no fucking clue what I was doing. So after Jennifer left that first night, I sat on the couch and stared at nothing. My mind couldn't think of what to do next.

Did I have to feed them?

Was I supposed to make sure they washed?

Fuck. Was I supposed to tuck them into bed and read them a story? That thought actually scared the crap out of me.

Rommy came out hours later and sat next to me. I blinked down at her as she placed her tiny fucking hand on my arm and said, "It'll be okay."

I nodded, not knowing what else I was supposed to do. *Shouldn't I be the one reassuring her?*

"Ah, you hungry, kid?" I asked.

"Yes." She smiled.

"Got the number to a pizza joint?"

"On the fridge." She beamed and skipped off to get it.

"You a biker?" was asked from behind me. I turned to find Texas standing just in the mouth of the hall where the bedrooms lay.

"Yep."

"You movin' us with you?"

"Yeah, you'll like Melbourne."

"I won't. I'll hate it."

"Don't know that for sure, kid."

"My mother hated you, but she hated us more, which is why she left us to you in her will, so we'd suffer more."

My body tensed. *What in the fuck?*

"You don't know *that*, kid."

"I do. She told me. She hated us because our father didn't like us, and he left because she kept us around. If she had gotten rid of us, then she'd still have had him."

Jesus fuck. Jesus. Fuck.

I'd thought she'd got rid of him.

My sister. Always the bitch.

Those were the first and last words he'd spoken to me while we were in Sydney. His replies took to grunts and head shakes, or he'd confide in his sister and she'd mention something to me instead of him coming to me.

The pain and loss I'd felt for my sister was wiped away that night from her son's words.

Instead, I wished she were alive. Then I'd harm her myself for letting her kids believe she'd hated them, and for *making* them believe they weren't worth being born.

Rommy came back in with the pizza list. After ordering, we sat in front of the TV she'd turned on. Out the corner of my eyes, I'd looked down at her. She'd chosen to sit next to me, as close as she could get while she sang along with some theme song for some kid show.

The pizza arrived, and I opted to sit at the kitchen table. While I set out the pizza on the bench and found some plates, I asked Rommy to go get her brother. He walked in with his head hanging low, loaded up the pizza for him and his sister and then sat at the opposite end from where I did. Rommy sat next to me.

"Uncle Trey?"

Fuck. Hearing her say it in her sweet little girly voice was something special.

"Yeah, darlin'?"

She giggled. "Do you work?"

"Sure do, I'm a mechanic."

"What's that?"

"I work on cars and bikes in a garage with a heap of other guys."

"Cool." She smiled and took a big bite of her slice.

"Uncle Trey?"

Smirking, I said, "Yeah, darlin'?"

She giggled. "What's the school like?"

Shit. I had no clue. I wasn't even sure there was one near me. I'd have to ring Josie to look into the best one around our area. I guessed Texas would be going to a high school. Kind of wished they were closer in age; I knew I'd prefer Texas with his sister to protect her.

Christ. What if she got bullied? What if he did? I couldn't beat the shit out of some kids. How the hell was I supposed to deal with stuff like that?

I'd have to call Talon and ask him.

"Ah, not sure just yet. We'll both take a look when we get to Melbourne."

"Yay." She grinned. "Uncle Trey?"

"Babe, I'm right here. You don't need to say my name every time you wanna ask a question. Just ask it, 'kay?"

She bit her bottom lip. "But." She stopped and looked to her brother, who was silently eating his pizza and watching the table. Rommy shrugged and then blew me the fuck away. "I like saying your name. I haven't been able to say it, and now that you're here, I like to say it because... because it... it means you came here to help us and, and you're like family and, well, because you came, it must mean you care about us." She looked up to me with hope shining in her light blue eyes. "Am I right?"

Fuck me.

Even though they both looked like their mum, with blond hair and blue eyes, they acted nothing like her. Rommy was pure heart. Texas, even when he sat at the end of the table all tense and shit, I could see he was holding his breath, waiting on my answer. The kids cared. Nothing like my cold-hearted sister at all.

"Yeah, darlin', I'm here because I care."

Texas scooted back his chair quickly and left the room. When I felt a small hand over mine, I looked down at Rommy. "He gets cranky, but I'm sure he likes that you care."

I wasn't sure she was only seven.

THE FUNERAL SUCKED. No one turned up. It was me and the kids and that was fucking all. It was obvious she'd made no friends and from the way she treated her kids, I understood why.

I sat on the end of the bench as the reverend talked up front about a sister I didn't really know. About how loving and great she was. It was all full of fucking shit, and I would have stormed out of the place if it wasn't for the kids. When Rommy started crying, I curled my arm around her and brought her in close to my side. I looked down at Texas sitting next to Rommy. He watched his sister in my arms with tears in his eyes, but they never fell. I stayed sitting there listening to the crap for those kids. It was their chance to say goodbye to the woman who birthed them and, from the way Texas fought with his emotions and won by not crying, I swear it was his way to stick it up to my cunt of a sister. It was his way to show he didn't care she'd left the world.

I was fucking proud of him because I would have done the same.

The rest of the week was spent packing up shit and getting stuff sent to Melbourne, so it'd be there when we arrived. Pick had rang me. They'd offered to set up the kids' rooms. It meant I'd have to get rid of my home gym so the kids didn't have to share a room, but at that stage, I didn't care.

All I wanted was to give them the best chance they could, something that became obvious they'd never had. They'd had a shit life with my sister. Hell, they'd cringed when I'd shouted at the TV over some game and would cower if I moved suddenly.

She must've yelled at them a lot, and I was worried she'd hit them, as well. All the signs were pointing in that direction. After just a few days, I'd wished she were alive so I could fuck her up for it.

They were good kids. At least Rommy was. Texas, with time, I'd know more about, but he was still getting around like a robot. Least he did what I asked. Rommy was a ray of sunshine. She actually made me laugh when she asked stupid shit. I'd see her brother roll his eyes at his sister, but every time, I didn't miss the small smile playing at the corners of his mouth.

I was nervous about getting them back to Melbourne and into my house. It meant it was final. It meant I was permanently in charge of two young kids. They'd be under my roof until I saw fit they could move out on their own. Would be a long fucking time coming. They'd have to find the safest place to live and the right people to be around.

Holy motherfuckin' shit.

My chest got tight.

They'd eventually want to date.

I'd kill anyone who fucked with them.

Kill them slowly and painfully.

Jesus. That was if all of it didn't kill me first.

It was the last night in their house when Rommy came into the spare room where I slept. I was sitting up in bed talking to Pick on the phone, finding out they'd still had crap-all on Baxter when Rommy walked in like a bloody zombie, rubbing her eyes, hair all crazy. I quickly told Pick I had to go and asked Rommy what was wrong.

She shook her head, climbed onto the bed and shocked me when she proceeded to sit on my lap, her head resting against my tee-covered chest.

"Rommy, darlin', what's up?"

Tiredly, she asked, "Do you think Mummy's happy now?"

I turned to stone. Shit like that I was no good at. I didn't know what to say, and I knew I'd fuck it up in some way.

Still, I had to give it a go. She was feeling the loss. Even if her mum was a shit mum, I still knew Rommy loved her. Pure heart of gold, that kid.

"Yeah, babe. I reckon your mum's happy, even though she'll miss you. I mean, who wouldn't? You're a great kid to be around. Same with your brother. Even when he's bein' a moody shit... hell, I mean..." *Ah, crap! Don't swear in front of kids.* I felt Rommy's body shake. She was laughing. "Rom, the answer is, yeah, your mum would be happy."

She sighed a content little sigh. "Are you, Uncle Trey?"

"'Course, darlin'. Only a fool would not be happy if they got to have you and your brother in their life."

"'Kay." She shifted on my lap to wrap her arms around my neck. "Love you, Uncle Trey. So, so, so, so, so happy you came to get us."

My eyes closed. It felt like I was punched in the gut at the same time my heart grew double its size.

I'd kill any fucker who fucked with them.

THE FLIGHT HOME WAS UNEVENTFUL. Both kids behaved themselves, both on the plane and off. Rommy was a ball of excitement, loved everything she saw, and regularly pointed shit out that I'd seen a million times over. Texas sat in the front of the car looking out the window, saying nothing except for when his sister said something to him. At least he wasn't freezing her out of his life like he was me.

Give him time.

How much time did a kid need when it was a sure thing to say he didn't like his mother?

As soon as they were settled in, I'd be having a word

with Texas, and he'd better listen if we're to live under the same roof.

We weren't long home before the kids were in their rooms checking out their new things. Rommy loved her girly room, no doubt thanks to Josie. She squealed and pounded on her new junk. All *I* saw was pink crap everywhere. Texas was even surprised about his room. It held posters of skateboarding people, motocross guys, a desk, a new bed and some other stuff scattered around. What I liked the best was the smile I saw. Only, he quickly wiped it away with the back of his hand. When I asked if he liked it, his answer was a shrug.

Walking out, I picked up my bag and went to my room to dump it. That was when I saw the fucking note. Goddamn Low tried to give the money back from the shit I bought her. It was not happening.

I was home. Things had to get back to what they were before I fucked it all up, and I was going to see to it.

I'd already written my own note when there was a knock on the front door. I stalked down the hallway and swung it open to see Pick and Billy.

"Fuckin' good to have you back." Pick smiled and slapped me on the back before moving around me to get into the house. "You had dinner yet? We're thinkin' about pizza. Wanna join us at Dive's?"

"Who's 'us'?" I asked after greeting Billy with the same slap to the back.

Pick shrugged. "Josie, me, Billy and Low."

"Sure, I'll give it ten, though," I said.

"Why?" Billy asked.

"Need you to run next door, give Low this, and the note."

"Fuck. You sure you want to get her fire goin' before seein' her?"

"Always loved a good fire brewin' before I got to it." I smiled. Billy shook his head, but walked back out the house with the money and note.

"Hey," I heard Pick say. I turned to find Texas standing in the living room.

"Don't be rude, man," I warned.

"Hi," Texas said with a glare. "You a biker, too?"

"Sure am. Name's Pick."

"Tex."

So, he didn't like Texas, either.

"Good to meet'cha." Pick smiled.

"Uncle Trey!" was screamed from Rommy as she ran down the hall. "Uncle Trey." I ignored Pick's laughter beside me as Rommy ran into the room and headed straight for me. I braced. She attacked and clung to me with her arms around my waist. She looked up at me and smiled. "I love my room. Love it. L.O.V.E it so, so, so, so much. Already I love living with you because you haven't yelled at us once. You yell at the TV, but not us and you don't get cross when we do things wrong, like when I spilt my drink. You don't smack us." Her head turned to its side. "Is it wrong to like it here when Mummy's not here?"

Fuck, fuck, *fuck me.*

"No, kiddo. I don't think it is."

Shit. I should of realised it. I should of felt the change in the room, but Rommy had all my attention.

Looking to Pick, I warned on a growl, "Brother." His eyes snapped to me. Christ, he didn't like the fact my fucked-up sister treated the kids badly. "Cool it."

"She smacked 'em for spillin' drinks? She yelled at 'em?" he snarled.

"Tex, take your sister to get cleaned up. We're gonna have dinner next door."

"But," Rommy started, "I wanna meet him. Hi." She waved at Pick. With his clenched jaw, he gave her a chin lift.

"Tex. Now, kid."

"Rommy, come on."

I caught her eyes and said, "Darlin', you can meet a lot of my friends soon, yeah?"

"Okay, Uncle Trey." She smiled and walked to her brother, who took her hand. He gave one last, strange look to me and Pick then walked her out of the room.

"She smacked 'em about. Yelled at 'em. What else did she do, brother?" Pick asked low.

Running a hand through my hair, I said, "It's as much

as I know. Tex hasn't really opened up to me, and Rommy isn't one to talk bad 'bout her mum. But Tex said the first night I got there that she often told them she hated them. If they weren't around, she'd still have her low-life husband. She didn't treat them good, brother."

"Fuck," he hissed. "*Fuck!*" he roared.

Grabbing his neck, I pulled him close. "Look at me." His rage-filled eyes hit mine. "They're good now. They have a good place to stay and we'll all make sure of it. Won't we, brother?" He said nothing, his eyes closed, his breath heavy. "They'll never feel fear again. They'll never be treated like shit again. They'll know they're worth something and we'll all make it so. You get me, Pick? They'll be happy from now on, brother."

He nodded.

I let go of him and said, "I'll go get the kids and we'll head over. You calm down, yeah?"

"I'm good, brother."

"Good. Besides, I need to get the fuck over there to see to my woman." I smirked.

He snorted. "May take a while until she agrees she's your woman."

"I'm lookin' forward to the fun and games then." I left Pick chuckling in the living room and walked down the hall.

"Uncle Trey," I heard called as I passed Tex's room. I looked in and found him sitting on his bed.

"Yeah, mate?" I asked, hands to the doorframe. Excitement ran through me from hearing my nephew call out to me for the first fucking time. Progress was a beautiful thing.

"Is… your friend, he okay?"

I nodded. "He just hates to hear about kids bein' treated the way you and your sister were. But he'll be cool now."

"Okay," Tex uttered and glanced to the floor.

"You all right, kid?"

His eyes met mine and he said, "I-I think I will be."

"Good, I'm glad." Bloody ecstatic, I couldn't comprehend the relief I was feeling. "Now, where's your sister?"

He actually smiled then, and fuck was I glad to see it. "She's in her room tryin' on clothes."

Fuck. There'd be a huge mess of girly shit everywhere, one I didn't want to see.

"Ah, you wanna go get her and we'll head next door for some pizza."

"Cool."

Knocking on the doorframe twice, I moved off towards the living room smiling. Hell, things could actually work out. I just needed my little bird back in my life.

CHAPTER EIGHTEEN

WILLOW

*T*he front door opened and first in was Pick, then came a boy around thirteen or fourteen. He had blond hair and blue eyes. I saw his uncle's features in him immediately. The cute lips, the bottom one bigger than the top. The messy hair, the pronounced cheekbones. But then, when a blonde little girl bounded her way into the room, she took my attention. She must have been around six or seven and she was the cutest Skipper, as in Barbie's little sister, I'd ever seen. Her smile was bright, her eyes alight with excitement, and she wore the clothes I'd picked out. She'd chosen a sweet flowery pair of shorts, which could probably cause her legs to become cold since there was a breeze outside, and a purple tee, which didn't match her shorts at all. Still, nothing she wore would make her any less cute.

"Hi," she said to the room. "I'm Romania, but I like to be called Rommy. And that's my Uncle Trey." She beamed and thumbed behind her to Dodge, who placed his hands on her shoulders. She looked up to her uncle with devotion in her eyes. "Oh, and that's my grumpy brother, Texas, but he likes Tex better. Uncle Trey said we were having pizza with his friends. It's really nice to meet you all."

Swoon. Totally adorable.

"Rommy," Dodge began. "You met Pick next door. But that's Billy. The women are Josie and Low."

"Low." She giggled.

Stepping forward, I held out my hand to Rommy. She took it attentively. "It's actually Willow." I smiled and added, "But I like Low better."

"Cool." She grinned.

"Little bird." His voice was deep and growly. I tensed.

Standing tall, my eyes roamed up and glared at the sinful man, looking sexy as ever, as he stood behind Rommy. "*Dodge,*" I said blandly.

"Why do you call her 'little bird', Uncle Trey?" Rommy asked, looking from her uncle to me and then back again.

Not giving him a chance to answer, I turned to Tex and walked over to the coffee table, gesturing to the pizza boxes. "Hey, Tex. We've got all kinds of pizza. What do you like the best?"

He shrugged and said quietly, "Anythin', really."

"Awesome, I'm the same. I'd eat just about anything, except snails."

Rommy giggled and walked over to us. "No one eats snails, silly. That's yuck."

Nodding, I said, "People in France love them."

"Really?" she whispered.

"Really," I uttered back.

From then on, everything exploded into action. People talked to the kids, made them laugh—though, I could see Tex was holding back a bit more than his sister —so Billy and Pick took up picking on their uncle, which seemed to relax him more and enjoy a laugh without feeling as if he was being watched or judged.

We ate pizza while we discussed what they didn't like to eat. For Rommy, it was vegetables. Josie managed to talk her around, saying that eating a few most nights was good because it helped people grow and become smarter. Since she wanted to be a monster truck driver, she knew she needed to be strong, because if that fell through, she wanted to be a stunt-girl—her words. I noticed Dodge blanched at those ideas of possible future positions. Tex, after some encouragement, told us he hated broccoli. I managed to get a smile and chuckle out of him when I told him that if his uncle tried to feed him that stuff, I would come to the rescue because I hated it, also.

The night went smoothly until I stupidly went into the kitchen on my own to get rid of the rubbish. I'd just placed the boxes on the counter when I felt heat at my back. I stiffened and went to shift to the side, but hands caged me in on both sides when they landed on the kitchen counter.

"Dodge," I hissed. "Move away."

"Call me 'Dodge' one more time, little bird, and I'll have you over my knee in seconds."

He was so full of it.

"Sure, Dodge, with the kids in the house and all."

"You think I'm lyin'?" His tone told me he wasn't messing around, but still I pushed.

"Yes."

Why did I say that? I shouldn't have, because he picked me up and a moment later, I was laid out over his knee after he'd sat on a kitchen chair.

"Dodge," I warned while pushing up to get away from him. I couldn't move, though. He had his arm over my upper back and the prick was strong.

"Last chance, little bird. Call me 'Dodge' one more time and see what happens."

Stilling my struggles when his hand roamed over my jean-clad bottom in a circular motion, I said, "Don't be silly, let me up. The kids could come in here."

He chuckled. "Noticed your game tonight. Talked to everyone but me. The kids were a good distraction for you, Low. But no more. Josie, with my brothers, took them home while I have the chance to have a talk with you." While he spoke, his hand never stopped running over my arse.

Snap. Snap. Snap! Why did I like it? Why did I like that he wanted the chance to talk to me? Why did I like that he made it happen?

Still... "Dodge, you're being a—"

Crack.

His hand slapped down on my butt. My back arched and I cried out in surprise and...dang it, desire.

"Don't you dare—"

"You gonna stop callin' me 'Dodge'?"

"You can't do this. We have to talk properly. You can't just do what you did and expect me to be—"

"I'm not and I didn't. But the ignorin' game ends now. You willin' to talk about what happened like adults now?"

That just pissed me off.

Turning my head, I glared up at him. "Act like adults? Like you did before you left? Like you gave *me* a chance to explain how I ended up in Beast's lap? Don't be an arse, *Dodge*, and think—"

Crack.

A stupid moan slipped from my mouth.

Oh, God, I was panting. "Don't," I uttered.

"Don't call me 'Dodge' and I won't. Though, I think you like—"

"Let me up!" I yelled and pushed against his leg again.

"No," he growled. His hand rubbed around where he'd slapped it. "Two weeks, Low. Two weeks while I was dealin' with my fucked-up sister's funeral, takin' care of her kids and feelin' like a loser, all the time you were on my mind."

Oh, man, oh, man. Why did he have to be sweet when I was still annoyed and hurt? My heart, already erratic, sped up.

"Dodge, you seriously can't."

Crack.

God. Damn. It.

Licking my lips, I panted through them until I stopped breathing altogether when his fingers ran down over my pussy. Thankfully, I think, I had jeans on. Still, I felt that heated touch. I felt it and liked it too much.

"Low," he growled. "I'm sorry for bein' a dick." His fingers pressed in more, causing me to moan. The prick chuckled. "I'm sorry for leavin' you after what we nearly shared that day." His fingers slipped down further, and I jolted when he pressed them down hard on my clit and rubbed them up and down on it. "Most of all, I'm sorry I hurt you."

"You're," I panted. "Two weeks," I moaned. "Too," I groaned. "Late," I snapped and swiftly rolled and fell off his knees, my butt hitting the ground hard. However, I was on my feet and straddling his lap next. I took note of his surprised look with satisfaction before I got close and hissed, "I don't forgive you yet, but I'm willing to *use* you." With that, I kissed him. It was a hot, heavy and dark kiss, one I enjoyed very much, especially when his fingers slid into my hair and gripped to tilt my head to the side to deepen it. Our tongues slipped and slid over one another, as though they were memorising the way they moved and felt against each other.

I rocked back and forth on his hardness, causing him to growl low down my throat.

"What do we have here?" a highly amused voice asked. We broke apart and I quickly stood, taking a few steps away from my desire.

"Dive," I breathed. "You're, um, home."

"Sure am." He beamed. "Good to have you back, Prez. I'd come and welcome you back, but it looks like I could get my eye poked out." His eyes dipped down to Dodge's crotch, and I slapped my hand over my mouth to hide my laugh. Even though Dodge had jeans on, somehow, his pecker was so hard, it just about tented in the denim.

"You reckon you could come back later?" Dodge snarled at his brother.

"Nope." Dive smirked.

"He, um…" I licked my dry lips. Had Dodge sucked all my saliva out of my mouth? Too bad I wanted him to do it again. "Dive and I. Uh, we have something to tell you. We're together," I said my lie and crossed my arms over my chest.

"What the fuck?" Dive cried. "We're not. No way would I touch her, brother." Dive's tone was high-pitched as Dodge stood slowly. Dive backed up, and his glare to me meant I would pay. "You tryin' to kill me, woman? After I take you in, you want my own brother to kill me for *thinkin'* I touched you?"

"S'all good, brother," Dodge announced, and Dive visibly sagged in relief.

"Well, I guess if Beast had told you nothing was happening between me and him that night, you'd have believed him over me? Oh, wait, you didn't even give me a chance to tell you, *Dodge*. Nooo, instead, you kicked me out and spat nasty words at me." I glared.

He smirked. "You think you're safe now my brother's here? You're not. Call me 'Dodge' again, woman, and see the show we'll put on for him." He shrugged. "Dive won't care. He likes to watch. It'll be like porn for him."

"You wouldn't." I scowled.

"Wouldn't I?" He quirked a brow at me, testing me.

Snap. He really would.

"So, I see you have a new game now, to piss me off so I don't wanna get close to you." He stepped towards me, taking my chin between his finger and thumb before he pulled my gaze up to meet his. "Won't work, little bird. I know I was a dick, and I apologised. Now it's you bein' a bitch for not accepting it and gettin' over it. Still, I reckon I'll enjoy the games you'll give me." His gaze heated. "You seemed to like the last one real good." He chuckled at my hooded eyes, which then turned hard as I scowled up at him. "Talk soon, Low," he uttered, pressed his lips to mine and walked out of the room. Moments later, I heard the front door close.

I jumped when Dive said, "He's bloody good." I'd forgotten he was even in the room.

"He's a pain."

He laughed. "Yeah, okay then, woman. How about you take your lust-filled self into your room and knock one out." He paused. "Even better, how about you let me watch while you do it."

"Dive," I scolded. "Didn't you get any tonight?"

"Sure did. Which is why I'll only watch and save it for my wank bank later."

Snorting, I rolled my eyes and said, "No, Dive. I will not let you watch me rub one out."

"Noticed you didn't say you weren't goin' to do it."

Glaring, I asked, "Do you want me to tell Trey you asked to watch me?"

He blanched. "No."

Walking towards him, I patted his arm as I passed. He called my name just as I reached the door. Looking back, I asked on a sigh, "Yes, Dive?"

He smirked. "You called him Trey. Looks like you're learnin'."

Shaking my head, I gave him a smile and wave before leaving. Did I want to learn, though? Because the outcome *had* been enjoyable.

Trey 'Dodge' Monroe was the most annoying, sexy, possessive man I knew. He got under my skin, pissed me off, and hurt me. Yet, his words when asking for forgiveness were sweet and tender, caring even.

Could I forgive him?

I realised I already had. Still, I'd let him stew on it for a while longer.

It was too much fun otherwise.

CHAPTER NINETEEN

DODGE

*M*y little bird was playing with fire. It'd been two long-arse weeks since that fucking scorching kiss, and I wanted more. How-fuck-ing-ever, life got in the way, so I was stuck with flirty looks, light touches and her teasing me with small smiles as she worked at the front desk.

My cock was hard all the goddamn time and my hand had seen more action in the last few weeks than it had in my whole bloody life. I couldn't get a moment alone with her, and it was driving me insane. Every time I caught her alone in the office, someone would walk right in after me. It made me think she had my brothers' ears and told them to come in if they saw me entering. If that was the case, then she'd better look out because my hand was itching to get on her arse again. Her arse, her tits, her body, her pussy. Fuck, anywhere on her body would do.

The kids were also putting a dampener on my sex life. Not that they planned it or knew about it, of course. But they kept me busy with setting up their school, cleaning shit at the house and cooking. It seemed my life now played out the same every day. I'd wake up hard, wank in the shower, get the kids ready for school then take them, which they seemed to be enjoying; the teachers loved them. Then I'd head to work, finish early to pick them up from school, head home, and help them with their home-work. After that, I'd do other stuff with them, like play ball with Tex or draw with Rommy. Both I didn't mind doing. Then I'd cook dinner, wind them down before bed, and get them into bed, which was always a feat with Rommy. She wanted to stay awake all the time. By doing that, she'd get up several times until she'd eventually crash. Then I'd be too fucking tired to do anything else, so I'd go to bed and wank while thinking of Low, waiting for it to happen all over again the next day.

What was also frustrating was that we'd gotten nowhere with Baxter. It was like he'd cooled off and wanted nothing to do with Willow anymore. While this was good in one way, it wasn't in another because knowing the fool, he was just waiting on the sidelines for us to slip up in some way. So I made sure Low always had protection around her.

Venom MC seemed to be still wanting to fuck with us, which was why I'd made the play to have a sit down with their prez to see what the fuck his problem was. It couldn't be just because he wanted our turf. There had to be something else. My guess was Baxter had something over him, and the Venom prez was doing shit to us for Baxter's benefit in some way.

It was all fucked, petty shit, boys playing in the real man world, and they needed to stop, to be taught a lesson. Time had come for me to do it.

I'd felt shit for not doing it sooner, but I had the kids to handle first. If that shit hadn't gone down, I would have already had a sit-down with Switch, the Venom prez.

Better late than never, I guessed.

I could have left it to my second, Pick, or even to Dive, my third. Hell, even Dallas or Billy, but I wanted to do it. I needed to show them that since I was prez, I wasn't some pussy. I didn't hide behind my brothers.

As the last brother walked through the door in the room we held church in, I cleared my throat. They knew to shut the fuck up when I did that. "First order of business. Beast, Knife and Muff, you guys pick a strip club to go to tonight. You know the drill. If anyone sees anythin' outta place, call it in. Don't try and be a fuckin' hero like Bottle did." Bottle was at a club last weekend when I got the call he'd been taken down. Thank fuck it was only a flesh wound and Nurse had stitched him up. Nurse was a medic from the Army who'd joined Hawks a year ago. Fucking glad he joined. Saved us going to the hospital with little shit and having docs or cops asking questions. "He'll be back in business next week, but until then, I need another out at the last strip club tonight. Any volunteers?"

"Me," Saxon said. He'd never done security detail as of yet. I guessed it was time to tell if he'd be good for it. I sent him a chin lift and Billy wrote his name down against the club he'd be on that night.

"Right, movin' on. Anyone got anythin' to tell me about business here?" I asked.

"Prez, gotta get some time off," Elvis announced. He was an older member, but a good one.

"What's happenin'?"

"Family shit. Some dick thinks he can fuck with my sister. I need to take time out to get to Geelong, spend time there lettin' him know it ain't fine to mess with my family."

"Done. Take off tomorrow and take Eden with you."

"I can handle—"

"We have each other's backs," I interrupted. "You don't

do this shit on your own. Havin' a brother with you will also help get the message across."

He sent me a nod. A small smile played on his lips. He agreed and approved.

"Right. Handle comes back next week." A few grumbles started around the table. I slammed my fist down. "He learned his lesson. He has the injuries to prove he learned them. He was lookin' out for his blood brother, but in the end, he had our back—"

"Only after they killed his woman!" someone yelled. Every brother knew of the situation, the one where we had a snitch in the club, and what went down with Baxter and Low. They'd already admired my woman, but had since cherished her for how bloody strong-willed she was. They were prepared to do anything to fuck Baxter up.

"Don't matter how it all went down. When he gets back, I don't want shit to start for him. Brothers' through and through. We all fuck up in some way or another. What counts is if we can see the errors and fix that shit. He did. He's paid, a lot. Now it's time we have his back again." I looked around the room. "Does everyone get me?" A chorus of *yeahs* and *okays* were sent my way.

"Good. Anyone got anythin' else to say?"

"We need to get new club pussy in," Gamer voiced.

"What's wrong with what you got?"

He smiled big. "Been there, done that. Want somethin' new to play with."

"If you want to recruit more pussy, do it or have a club girl you trust to pick clean girls out. I don't give a fuck."

"You used to like the girls, Prez. They're missin' you," Gamer said.

"*Used to* bein' the word there, Gamer."

"Somethin' else, somethin' chocolatey taken your eyes now, Prez?" He chuckled.

I sat forward, my eyes hard. "Learn now, brother. No one says shit about Low. No fuckin' one."

"You claimin' her, then?" Dive, the smart arse, asked.

"You know it," I growled and saw smiles around me. Some even cheered. *Fuck me.* "Enough pussy talk. Get the fuck outta here."

The room cleared except for Pick, Billy and Dive. Dallas hadn't even been there. He was out already at the most popular strip club Talon owned doing security.

Knew my brothers were in for a chat, but I stood. "You guys still right to watch the kids for a little longer?"

"Our woman's already there, s'all good," Pick said.

"'Preciate you lendin' her for the kids." If it wasn't Josie, it was Willow, always stepping in to spend time with the kids when I couldn't be around. Made me wonder if my woman liked the kids more than me.

"Josie wouldn't have it any other way." Billy smiled.

"Where you goin' in such a rush?" Dive smirked.

"Gotta get *my* woman off Lan's hands," I said, walking to the door already.

"So, you gonna claim it true tonight? For Low to be yours?" he questioned.

Turning, I said, "Should'a already happened. But yeah, she'll be mine, enough games. Which means don't come home for a while."

He chuckled and gave me a chin lift before I walked out the door. My dick was already hard because it knew it was going to get some action, and soon.

THE RIDE HOME was long and awkward. Never in my years had I been embarrassed. The ride became awkward when I sat on my Harley thinking of the ways I was going to take my woman, thinking of her sweet pussy and how I was eager to be inside her. I didn't realise I was rubbing my hard-on through my jeans until I heard the gasp. I looked sideways to see an old lady sitting in her car in the lane next to me with a disgusted look upon her face.

"You,"—she pointed to my dick area—"you leave that for behind closed doors," she'd scolded.

I actually felt my face heat. Thank fuck the lights changed and I took off before she told me off again.

Could not fucking believe I'd been reduced to a teen

again where I couldn't control my erection and the urge to touch it.

Pulling into Dive's drive, I looked next door to my house, seeing the lights on, knowing Josie would be in there with the kids. Bloody grateful I had such a kick-arse family.

Slipping off my ride, I stored my helmet on the seat and made my way to the front door. Dive and I had a key to each other's place, so I unlocked it and flung it open to find Low sitting on the couch beside Lan. His hand was to her back, and she was crying in her hands.

"What did you do?" I growled, stalked in, slammed the door and made my way to them, ready to beat the fuck out of him even though I respected the guy.

My hand just gripped the front of his tee, ready to pull the dick off the couch when Low looked up. Tears streamed down her face and she yelled, "No, don't! Lan didn't do anything. I-I was watching *My Sister's Keeper* and…oh, Trey, it was so sad. S-she, the sister…" She stopped to cry again.

Letting go of Lan, I looked down at him and his amused expression. His lips were twitching, his eyes alight with humour.

"I'll leave this in your hands," he said before kissing Low's temple, standing, slapping my back and saying, "Good luck." Then he was gone.

Crying women and me did not get along.

I was lost.

Didn't have a fucking clue what to do.

I'd expected to come here and get the sex on. Dammit, I wanted to pound my woman and claim not only her, but her pussy.

Jesus. Now *I* felt like sobbing.

"Ah, little bird. Can I, ah, get anythin' for you?"

She sniffed up. Not a pretty sight. "It was heart-break-ing, Trey," she mumbled. At least she was calling me Trey. The monster had taunted me with Dodge for the last two weeks, and my hand had been itching to give her punishment.

"Fuck," I hissed. She glared at me. "Look, ah, do you wanna shot or somethin'?"

"No, I don't want a shot." She stood and wiped her face so it was free of tears. "I want you to help me forget that sad, sad movie," she snapped as her hands went to her hips.

Attitude, I could handle.

Smirking, I asked, "How you want me to do that?"

"Play Monopoly with me."

What. The. Fuck?

She wanted to play a board game? I had something else I'd rather her play with. Fuck me, sobbing was defi-nitely up on the top of the ladder for me. My poor cock wanted to pack a bag and go on vacation, because I was about to be a pussy.

"Okay." I sighed.

Her expression changed. Her eyes heated. She smiled wide, showing her perfect white teeth, and then she jumped me. My hand went to her arse as she climbed me like a pole. *My* pole perked up again.

"I was kidding. I have something better in mind to make me forget that movie." She ran her nose up my neck to whisper in my ear, "Though, I'm happy you wanted to help me in some way."

"Low," I growled when she bit my earlobe.

"Dive rang," she said, and I stiffened. "Told me you were on your way and apparently you wanted to claim me as your woman." She laughed at my fierce glare then said, "I was told in my younger years at school that I was good at acting."

She'd played me.

Fucking played me.

"I fully accept the making me yours, as long as that means you become mine and no one else's. However, you treat me like you did that night ever again, I will gut you myself and serve your innards up for dessert." She smiled.

"Fuck, baby. How could words like those turn me on?"

"Because you, Mr Sinful, are a weirdo."

Gripping her hair in my fist, I pulled her head back so I had her eyes. "You're my woman? My old lady? Your body is fuckin' mine for the takin'. Your body, mind and soul are mine to consume in the wickedest ways I want."

"Yes," she uttered before she crashed her mouth to mine, only to pull back again. I groaned in frustration. "But you're mine for all that, as well. Yes?"

"Fuck, yes, little bird."

She giggled. "Good. Now, take me to bed."

CHAPTER TWENTY

WILLOW

*W*hen Dive rang, my heart pounded hard behind my ribs. My body quivered and my hands shook with shock and eagerness. Trey *wanted* me. He wanted me, as Dive put it, to be his old lady, to be the one and only to ride on the back of his bike.

It was weird, Dive ringing me and telling me, but it was his way of showing he cared about the both of us. For me, it was so I could make up my mind on what I wanted. For Trey, it was Dive's way to warn me to get out of his friend's way before he could make his intentions clear and I was to break his heart.

Dive was protective, like all members of Hawks.

Still, I knew my answer straight away. I wanted Trey in a big way. The last two weeks had been exhausting. Watching him around work, or with the kids in the back-yard playing, or even when we'd all shared a meal together—it had been a test of my willpower. Every day, every hour, my feelings grew for the man.

However, it didn't mean I couldn't play with him a bit and make him pay for what he did to me once and for all. I'd told Lan my evil plan. He knew, like himself and many males, that Trey wouldn't know what to do with himself if he saw me crying. The fact that when he came in he was about to beat up Lan said a lot.

A smile lit my face as Trey dragged me by my hand down the hall. He'd looked devastated when I'd asked him to play a board game. I, however, found it highly amusing, as well as sweet. He put *me* before himself, before what he wanted, so I could calm down and be satisfied.

He made me happy.

That was all I needed.

Once in my room, he tugged on my arm and I ended up on my back on the bed with a girly squeal. I took to my elbows and eyed my man. *Oh. My. God. The beautiful specimen* is *my man. He's mine. M.I.N.E. No ho-bag can touch him. If they do, I have the right to take them down, and believe me, I will go all* Bride of Chucky *on them.* My eyes glided over his body as he pulled his tee over his head. I loved,

loved his arm tattoos. I enjoyed and wanted to lick his six-pack and...oh, snap it, I just wanted the sinful man in every way.

"Trey," I breathed. He raised a brow as he undid the top button of his jeans. I cleared my throat and asked, "Who's with the kids? And will Dive be coming home soon?"

"Josie and her men. If anyone comes through that front door and interrupts us, I'll kill them. You're mine tonight, to take, to claim, to fuck—hard, fast and sweet-like."

Dang. He was a wonder with words.

Licking my lips as he slid his jeans down his legs to reveal tight cotton boxers, I asked, "Does everyone know you're claiming me tonight?"

He shrugged and smirked. "Just about. At least then they'll know no one is to fuck with you." He waved his hand over me. "You have too many clothes on. Get naked."

I saluted, sat up, and pulled my tee over my head. "Yes, boss."

"Damn, little bird, I like that."

"Me half-naked?" I asked.

"That, but also you callin' me 'boss'."

A laugh escaped. "Don't get used to it, mister."

"Pants," he said with a growl. His hand flicked towards my waist.

"Boxers." I smirked.

He eyed me with a heated stare before he placed his thumbs in the sideband of his boxers and slowly slid them down.

There he was. I sighed.

Little Sinful was glorious. I only had a chance for a quick look last time when I was singing about him, but now I got an eye-full. He was proud and sitting high. From the twitch, he liked my gaze on him. He was long and on the thick side of cocks. I was happy to see Trey was circumcised; I wanted to suck on the tip to see if I could get him to dribble with pre-cum.

"Woman," Trey groaned. "Your eyes fuckin' my cock are makin' me hungry. Pants, little bird. Now."

Laughter erupted from me. Still, I did what I was asked—or rather, what I was told. Arching my hips up, I wiggled my jeans down, along with my panties.

"Fuck." Trey eyed me with a smile. "Beautiful."

I flung them to the side and lay flat, totally bare before my man while his eyes graced over every inch of my body as he palmed his rigid cock.

"You my woman?" His voice was thick and low with emotions.

"Yes," I whispered. "You my man?"

"Hell yes. After I take you, claim you, we gotta talk about gettin' your arse back to my house."

"Trey," I warned.

"No. I want you with me. I want to wake up to you, smell you, finger you and take you when I can. I need you in *our* bed in *our* house. For now, my woman needs her man's cock. I can see how slick you are with need, baby, and it's fuckin' glorious."

"Then take me, Trey. Make me yours. But we'll be talking later."

He smirked. "We will, and you'll submit to what I want."

"Cocky."

"Yeah, little bird. Cocky enough to say once you get a taste of my cock, you'll want more of it every fuckin' day."

Rolling my eyes, I laughed. "What have I gotten myself into?"

"Nothing, Low, but I'll be in you soon."

"Less talking, handsome. More showing."

"Up on all fours, little bird," he growled. Excitement fluttered in my belly as I rolled over and got to my hands and knees, my bottom facing him. "Move up the bed a bit." I did. I felt his weight hit the bed, but when I felt his hands on my lower thighs, I looked down because I expected them on my hips or arse.

No, Trey wasn't kneeling behind me. He was lying on his back and shifting up so his head was between my legs.

"Fuck my face, Low," he ordered. "I wanna taste how much you want me."

Oh, snap.

My body shuddered. I didn't have to move, though, because my man was impatient. He gripped my arse and pulled my pussy down on his mouth. I had no time to fuck his face because his mouth was fucking me. He groaned on the first taste as he glided his tongue from bottom to top. I gasped and cried out. He brought me down closer again and slipped his tongue inside of me while he ran his nose over my hardened nub.

It was driving me wild, and I was loving every moment of it.

"Trey," I whimpered and rotated my hips forward and back on his mouth. He grunted his approval. "Yes, babe. God, yes!" I moaned. I wanted his cock in my mouth while I was getting pleasured. I wanted to do the same to him. "Let me move around," I said. I felt him shake his head side to side, saying no. "Trey," I snapped. "I want to suck you." He shook his head no again.

He kissed his way up to my clit and paid special attention to it, driving me to the edge. My hand ran over my stomach, over my chest and I gripped my breast, pinching my nipple as Trey sucked, gently bit and tongued my nub.

"I-I'm going to—" I didn't get to finish, I cried out through my orgasm, running my pussy up and down his mouth as he drank my juices down with a groan.

I fell forward, my body still trembling from coming hard. "Give me a second, babe," I muttered into the sheet.

The bed tilted as he moved. He chuckled against my lower back. He licked my no-doubt salty skin up along my spine then gently bit down on my shoulder. "Never seen a woman come that powerfully, little bird. Good to see I got my woman off good and proper."

"I'll let your smugness pass, Trey. For now." He swatted my bottom and I giggled. Rolling over, I wrapped my arms around his neck and brought his mouth down to mine.

Passion fuelled our kiss and filled it with promise of more. He pulled back, pressed his erect cock into my side and said in a delicious, grumbly voice, "Fuckin' love that you don't mind a taste of yourself on my lips and tongue. Makes me crazy, woman."

Before I could say anything, he kissed me again, not that I objected. My hands ran over his back, down to his perfect arse to give it a squeeze. He growled into my mouth and without breaking the kiss, he climbed on top of me. My legs spread to fit his large form between them.

"Love your mouth," he said against my lips. "Love your body, your smooth-as-fuckin'-silk skin. Christ," he bit out, slanting his mouth along mine again before his tongue dove inside.

His hand shifted between us and ran over his length. Up and down, again and again. I lifted my hips to show him I wanted him inside me. He chuckled against my mouth while I growled against his. Having enough of the teasing, I wrapped my legs around his thighs. Ripping his hand away, I pushed my arse up while my legs pulled him down, impaling myself on his cock. Our mouths tore apart and we groaned.

He was big, long, and delicious inside me.

"Trey," I moaned when he shifted slowly out of me.

"You're greedy, little bird, and I fuckin' love it. You wanted my cock, now you're gonna get it." He pushed back into me hard and fast. My head jerked up, my neck stretched and I cried out in pleasure. He wasn't done, though. His hands slid under my arse. He then pulled my lower half up and he fucked me. His thick cock in my tight pussy filled me to the top and touched that sweet part inside of me. My belly dipped and swirled. I gripped his shoulders and forced his upper body down more so my teeth could latch onto the skin between his shoulder and neck.

He grunted and moaned against my ear when I bit down. "Fuck, yes! Harder," he snarled, so I did. "Christ, stop. Fuck, I'm gonna come."

Licking his neck, I ordered, "Not yet." Because I was so close, in fact. My hands fisted his hair and I held on as the warmth of the orgasm washed over me.

He pushed into me three more times and then my arms dropped away from him as he slid his dick out. He got to his knees and I watched in awe when he gripped his cock in hand and pulled. His cum shot out all over my stomach and chest. He groaned through his release.

He smiled down at me after, his hand going to my pussy and cupping my mound, and then he slid two fingers inside my sensitive hole. "Best pussy I've had. Only pussy I want. My pussy. My woman and old lady."

"Yes," I whispered. He pumped his fingers inside of me a couple of times, withdrew them then sucked on them while looking down at me. "Fuckin' beautiful. Wanna come in you next time, little bird. You covered?"

"Yes."

"I'm clean," he offered.

Mood dampener, still, I answered, "So am I." He grunted his approval.

He didn't stay that night, had to get back to the house for the kids. But he took care of me, his woman. He cleaned me up and ran me a bath before he carried and deposited me in the warm water. With a tender kiss, he left me to soak with a promise I'd be seeing him in the morning.

I didn't know what the next day or so would bring, but with a man—my old man—like Trey, I was looking forward to finding out.

CHAPTER TWENTY-ONE

WILLOW

*T*he next day, I woke with a smile. I stretched, enjoying the aches in all the right places. Those places couldn't wait to be played with again. Already, as I lay there in bed thinking of Trey, I was wet. I would have dealt with myself, knowing I couldn't get Trey inside me until maybe that night, only Dive suddenly burst through my door.

I franticly pulled the sheet all the way up to my nose. "Ever heard of knocking, you douche canoe?"

"I thought you'd be in a better mood after gettin' some last night." He smirked, leaning against the doorframe.

Rolling my eyes, I said, "I would be if someone didn't barge right in. You need something, Dive?"

"Nope." He winked.

"Dive," I whined.

"Oh, wait. There was somethin'. Just got off the phone to your man. He wants his woman over there for breakfast with him and the kids."

Up on my elbows, I smiled big. "Really?"

Dive chuckled. "Yeah, woman. Get up and ready. We're headin' out in ten."

"We're?"

"Low, if you think I'll miss a chance for food, you'd be wrong."

"But there's food in the cupboards here," I told him as he began shutting my door.

"True, but then I won't get to see the two lovebirds together. That's entertainment *and* a meal." He laughed and shut the door completely.

I was up out of bed with a giddy feeling of joy. Then I paused. What would the kids think with the change between their uncle and me? I hoped they'd be okay with it. I wouldn't want anything to come between them, especially considering Tex had finally warmed to everyone and was more his true self around us all.

There was only one way to find out. I needed to know how Trey and I were going to approach it, so I got myself dressed and headed over there.

It seemed I didn't need to worry. As soon as Dive and I were through the back door and into the kitchen, I was knocked back a step by a little girl. Rommy's arms were tight around my waist. When I looked down to see if she was okay, I saw she was already looking up at me with a bright smile.

"It's so cool you and Uncle Trey are boyfriend and girlfriend. We'll get to do more girly stuff together. I always knew he had a crush on you. It was weird how his eyes always followed you around. Anyway, it's so cool." She squealed, let go, and hugged a laughing Dive. "Hey, Uncle Dive. Uncle Trey cooked bacon and eggs. They're on the stove warming."

"Awesome, kiddo. Let's eat."

Tex sat at the table, and I walked to him and placed my hand on his shoulder. Leaning in, I asked, "You okay with it?"

"Totally, Low."

"Cool, little dude." I smiled and kissed his cheek, which he quickly wiped off. Before I went in search for Trey, I made myself a coffee.

He'd told them already. Trey really wasn't stuffing around any longer. I was tagged, bagged and claimed in the whole sense.

Walking into his room, I heard the shower in the en suite going. My clit pulsed and my heart skipped a beat at the thought of my man naked. Butterflies circled in my lower belly with a *swoosh* feeling. Slowly and quietly, I opened the door and spotted him through the glass straight away. His head was down, eyes closed. One hand and elbow rested against the tiled wall, his other hand wrapped around his erection as water beaded down his back.

It was obvious he hadn't heard me enter, because he kept sliding his hand up and down his cock. What helped drown out my approach was the sound of the fan drawing out the condensation—*yippee*—swirled above his head. I decided to take a seat on the closed toilet seat and enjoy the show. I licked my dry lips before bringing my mug to them and took a slip of my coffee.

Live porn. Exactly what a woman liked to see.

A grunted moan fell from his mouth. I zig-zagged my legs together. I wanted what was in his hand inside of me. I was wet and needy.

"Fuck," he murmured before opening his lids. He must have seen me out the corner of his eyes because his head whipped around so fast he stumbled back. "Willow," he said softly, his gaze heating and taking on a possessive look.

Smiling, I said, "Just enjoying the morning show." I shrugged, like it was every day I went into a bathroom and found a man wanking. "You should really lock your door. You never know what pervert could walk in." He seemed surprised by the laugh that came from him. I gestured with my hand to his junk and said, "Continue, please." Then I took a sip of coffee.

"Woman, are you serious?"

"Heck yes. I'm so wet and hot right now I could come just from watching you."

"Don't."

"What?" I asked confused.

"Don't come. That's my fuckin' job."

I raised my brows. "I could say the same to you."

"Fine." He squinted at me. "I'll finish for your pleasure, of course."

I giggled. "Of course."

"But tonight, it'll be my pleasure while I watch you make yourself come."

My breath caught in my throat. My ears rang as all the blood rushed to my face. "Um, okay?"

He chuckled, but soon sobered as he stepped closer in the spacious shower and took his cock in hand again, stroking up, down, up and down, again and again. God, it was mesmerising, hypnotising. He groaned through clenched teeth, "Love your fuckin' hungry eyes on me."

"Love seeing you handle yourself. Biggest turn-on so far."

"I'm sure I can change that when we play again." He smirked.

No words came to me as I watched his hand, his hooded eyes, the straining in his neck and arms as he pleasured himself. My breath became laboured. I wanted to rip my clothes off and join him, drop to my knees and finish him off. I licked my lips just thinking of the taste of him.

"Jesus, little bird." He sighed right before his cum shot out of the tip and onto the tiled floor. Still, I kept watching until the last drop, mixed with water, landed. His chest heaved up and down and still I kept watching, frozen in place as he cleaned himself up, turned off the shower and stepped out. He grabbed a towel and wrapped it around his waist. In his next move, his hand was tugging me by my wrist and I was up in front of him.

"Watch my coffee," I complained. Precious coffee could not be spilt.

He chuckled and took my mug from my hand. I glared up at him when he placed it on the basin. He ignored it and as soon as his mouth hit mine, I forgot I even had a coffee.

From the moment I'd stepped in on Trey wet in the shower, manhandling his cock, I'd forgotten pretty much anything of consequence.

I gasped and pushed him back. I didn't get far, though, as his arms were tight around my waist. "The kids."

"What about them?"

"How could I forget? I've been in here for a long time, and they're probably wondering what we're doing. Oh, snap. Tex is at the age he would *know* what we were doing." My flushed face hit his damp chest. "I'm terrible."

"Low, it ain't like we fucked."

Smacking his chest, I looked up at him scowling. "That's not the point. We can't do this when the kids are in the house." I nodded to myself. "It's decided. We can't be alone with each other when the kids are around."

"Like fuck." He actually shook me by his hands on my shoulders. His face took on a look as if I'd just told him I was a man. "Woman, they know we're datin', and they're old enough to understand what comes with datin'. I won't fuckin' be keepin' our PDA in private, and we'll be doin' stuff, *lotsa* stuff, behind closed doors. That shit won't slide by me. I want every fucker to know you're my woman."

"But—"

"No, buts, no ifs, no nothin'." He turned me, slapped my arse and added, "Now get outta here before I *do* fuck you."

"Trey," I snapped, but then I was gone because I knew he was serious.

THE MORNING TURNED HECTIC. After I walked back into the kitchen, I waited for the sly or disappointed looks from the kids. I got nothing. It was as though they didn't take notice I'd disappeared. Thank God. The only sly look and wink I got was from Dive, which was understandable because he was a horndog.

Dive went off to work on his Harley, while Trey and I drove the kids to school. It was the sweetest moment of my life. Especially when we dropped Rommy off first and she leaned over to kiss her uncle on the cheek, but then she turned to me and kissed me, as well. I melted and, in fact, got teary. Still shocked after she jumped out of the car, I was half-turned to the back, so I didn't miss the soft look on Tex's face. He saw what that meant to me, and he liked that it meant something to me.

"Right," I said and flipped back around to the front. "Off to high school now to fill your brain with important stuff." Trey shook his head, but moved the car off.

The trip wasn't far from Rommy's school. On the way, though, I listened to Trey and his nephew bond over mundane things—sports, bikes, work and school. When we stopped, Tex gave a chin lift and fist touch to his uncle, while I got a hand on the shoulder and a tight squeeze.

Again, I found myself teary.

Before we took off again, Trey chuckled and said, "You're a nut."

I didn't say anything. He could have called me anything he wanted at the moment, because nothing could have burst my bubble of the high, loveable emotions I was feeling for those two kids.

When we pulled up out the front of the compound, the garage that joined next to it was already bustling with customers and brothers working. However, I turned to Trey and said, "I think, while we're still new, that I should keep staying at Dive's. Christmas is coming up soon, and I'm sure the kids would love their first Christmas with *just* their uncle. And besides, what happens if things don't go as planned and we end up breaking up? It won't be good for the kids. Not that I would ever forget them. I do hope if anything did happen that you would still let me see them. They're great, amazing kids. Still, um—" Snap. He was glaring at me. "I think it would be best to, ah, stay at Dive's and just date for a while. We could go to the pub or movies. I mean—"

"Shut it," Trey snapped in a low voice through clenched teeth. Yes, he was pissed. "You move in tonight. You don't talk about breakin' up because we ain't fuckin' datin'. You're my old lady. I'm your old man, and that's it. I don't do movies, but if I have to, I won't see any romance shit. We can go to a pub, but it won't be a date. It'll be me with my old lady goin' out and enjoyin' each other."

Sounds a lot like dating to me.

"But when it's fuckin' over, we'll go home, to our fuckin' house, where the kids will be, and after I pay the sitter, I'll be takin' my old lady to our fuckin' bed and fuckin' her hard. And then, come fuckin' Christmas, we'll wake up together and enjoy fuckin' Christmas mornin' together with the kids." There were a lot of fucks in there, which told me he was more than pissed—he was furious. He went on, "Then you'll cook for us while I put shit I hate together for the kids." He stopped, glared and snarled, "We clear?"

Even though my heart warmed when he stated he wanted to share that with me, because it was a big something, annoyance sat in my chest. He expected me to agree with everything he said, as if I had no say.

Instead, with a shrug, I said, "We'll see."

"Willow," he warned, his tone hard and scary. But the fact was he didn't scare me. He never once frightened me, even when he told me he'd killed people. I knew I was safe with him. I knew he had my heart in his hand, and I knew, gruffness and all, that I loved him with everything I had.

Because of this, I felt content to be myself. And when I *was* myself, I'd become annoyed when he bossed me around and stated how *he* wanted things without taking anything I said into account.

So, I smiled, gave him a quick kiss and opened the passenger door, saying, "Got to get to work. Have a good day, babe."

"Little bird," he bit out low, dipped in displeasure. Only, I closed the door and skipped off into the office.

Thankfully, I knew he had a busy morning scheduled, so I didn't need to worry about him coming in to continue our conversation. I wasn't in the mood for it.

Despite my irritation, my smile played easily on my lips.

Because I loved that man, *my* old man, so much.

CHAPTER TWENTY-TWO

DODGE

Her arse is mine. I swear to fuckin' Christ, my hand is burning to take her arse in my hand and teach her a lesson.

All day, I knew she was up to something. All goddamn day, she was as sweet as pie. She didn't shy away when I wanted to kiss her or claim her with my arm around any part of her body in front of the brothers. Next step would be to get her a club vest, stating she was my property, so every outsider knew I'd claimed the woman. My brothers knew. They'd spread the word immediately and knocked the flirty attitude off towards Willow, cementing their respect for me. Instead, they treated her like the old lady she was.

They talked to her with high regard instead of with playfulness. Hell, even when some still attempted to flirt, my woman sliced it down real quick, which turned me the fuck on.

When my day came to an end and I had to collect the kids, I went into the office to see Low buried in paperwork. I didn't give a fuck, though. I said, "Gotta get the kids. Get your purse and let's go."

She looked up with a glare. "I can't. I have so much to finish."

"Low, when I go, you go."

"Trey, when I say I'm staying, I'm staying."

"Little bird." I sighed.

"No, babe, please don't order me around again." She pouted. "This is my work. I love my work. I enjoy doing it because not only does it help the club out, but it helps the family you have going on. I will not have you come in here and tell me—"

"Okay," I said with a smile.

Her head jerked back. "Okay?" she whispered.

"Yeah, baby. You wanna stay and finish, stay. I'll see you at *home* later. I'll cook. What time do you think you'll finish?"

"Um, I can't have dinner." She looked away quickly. That was when I knew she was up to something.

"Willow?"

"I promised Josie I'd have dinner and a few drinks at her place tonight. She'll be here later to pick me up."

Wanting to see what her play was, because I knew I'd bloody enjoy her punishment, I sighed and ran a hand over my face. "Okay, little bird. One of the boys will give you a lift back home to me. I'll see you when you get there."

"Um, okay, babe."

Fuck me.

She said she was a great actress and I believed her when she turned on the waterworks, but right then, she was losing her role.

Smirking, I bent, gave her a kiss she'd remember and walked out to the car to go get the kids.

After I'd collected them and we were home, and before they ran off to do their homework, I sat them down to have a chat.

"Wanna ask you two somethin'," I started as we all sat at the kitchen table.

"What's up, Uncle Trey?" Tex asked. Fucking proud the kid was now out of his shell and showing me the awesome person he was. He took care of his sister, was smart and skilful in sports, and with a wrench. Loved having him and his sister in the house. Loved hanging with them and talking with them. Life without them would be dull as fuck.

"I need to know your thoughts of havin' Low livin' under our roof."

"She can sleep in my room," Rommy piped up.

Jesus. I walked right into that one.

"Rom." Tex laughed. "She'd be sleepin' in Uncle Trey's room 'cause she's his woman."

"Oh." She frowned, then smiled. "No matter where she sleeps, Low is awesome and it'd be so cool to have another girl in the house. We can paint each other's nails, and oh, oh, oh, she can do my hair in the morning because"—she sighed—"I'm sorry, Uncle Trey, but you don't do a good job."

That was when I burst out laughing. I ruffled Rommy's hair and said, "That's fine by me, darlin'." Turning to Tex, I asked, "You okay with it?"

"Yeah." He smiled. "Like Rommy said, she's cool."

"All right then." I grinned. "Homework time." They both groaned but went to get their books. They knew they had to get that shit out of the way before they could relax. At least they got to do it while listening to music and eating a snack.

It was while they were doing their homework that I went into my room and called Pick. "Yo," he answered.

"Brother, my woman at your place?"

"No, why?" His voice held an edge.

"Don't stress, she's just fuckin' with me. I bet she'll be hidin' at Dive's."

He started laughing. "Let me guess, you told her how you wanted it."

"Uh, fuck yeah."

"Brother." He sighed. "Did you think of askin' her?"

"What for? She's *my* woman now."

"Shit. How long has it been since you last had a woman? And I ain't talkin' about some random chick you screwed."

"Dunno, 'bout twelve years."

"Brother, advice. She'll have her back up. Even though she probably liked you wanting her in your house, she'll hate that you *ordered* her to do it. Especially with the 'tude your woman has."

"Fuck."

"Yeah. Now you got me."

"She said she'd come here tonight. If she doesn't, then I know how her game was played."

"Prepare. But I reckon the game's already playin' if she told you she was comin' here tonight."

"Figured as much. She was sweet all day."

Pick burst out laughing before he hung up.

I'd give her time, see if she came to me. If she didn't, her arse was mine. Even though I knew I fucked up the situation, goddamn, she was my woman. I wanted her under my roof, not a brother's roof where he'd get to see her all the time. I knew it hadn't been long between us, but hell, I *knew* she was the one, and I'd fight with everything I had to prove it to her.

First, though, before I got the kids' dinner, I had to make another call.

The phone rang twice before Talon answered, "Talk."

"You alone?" I asked.

"No, got Blue, Griz, Killer and Stoke in the room."

Christ. It just had to be all those taken fuckers.

Sighing, I said, "Put me on speaker."

"You're on," Talon said.

"I'm a pussy," I stated, and laughter rang out over the phone. *Fuck me.* "Proud to be a brother whose balls are around the neck of his woman."

I swore, *bloody swore,* I'd never get hooked, and one night while I was drunk and swearing it, I happened to make a bet with my brothers that if such a thing happened, I had to call them with those words exactly.

"Welcome to the crew, brother." Talon snorted.

"Good luck, brother," Killer added.

"Yeah, you're gonna need it." Griz chuckled.

"Especially from what we hear about Low. By the way, thanks for the money. Pick had us in on the bet. I was the closest to guessin' when you'd claim your woman," Blue commented. My brothers laughed.

Jesus Christ. I'd fucking forgotten about that damned bet.

"Lookin' forward to meetin' her, Dodge," Stoke said.

"My woman and I are gonna be your way soon to check in with Nary."

"Sounds good, brother." I grinned like a fucking fool. "And the lot of ya can get fucked," I added. Just before I hung up, the room up-roared in laughter again.

It was after we ate, after the kids had long gone to bed, that I stood in my living room with only the lamp in the corner shining. She hadn't come, and she wasn't answering her phone. It was time to play.

Putting my phone to my ear, I waited. "Prez," Dive answered with a smile in his voice. "Took you long enough to call me. What do you want me to do?"

"Bring her to me," I barked.

He chuckled. "This is gonna be fun to see."

WILLOW

I was lying in bed when my door was thrown open. I screamed, threw the covers back, and was on my feet in the next moment on the bed. I expected it to be an angry Trey, but it wasn't. However, in the doorway, stood a grinning Dive.

"Dive?" I questioned.

"Nope, nothin' you say can charm me into listenin' to

you." How was his smile bigger as he stalked his way towards the bed?

"Dive, what are you doing?" I asked, backing up so I stood near my pillows.

"When you told me about your game, I knew the prez wouldn't go for it, and I was right."

"Dive," I whined as he stopped beside the bed near me.

"Still, I didn't want to get involved, even when I thought you were bein' stupid."

"Dive," I snapped, my hands going to my hips as I glared down at him.

"Low." He sighed. "You're bein' stupid." He held up his hand when I went to talk. "And so's he. He shouldn't have told you, he should have asked you. But what you don't get with us, honey, we bikers? We get what we want. We bikers make it happen. He's claimed you. My brother has never fuckin' done anythin' like that in the whole time I've known him. He sees somethin' in you he hasn't with anyone else. Now, stop bein' a shithead and get your arse over there."

"But—"

"Nope, don't wanna hear it." And he didn't; his actions when he hurled me over his shoulder and out of the room said it all. Thank God, I'd gone to bed with clothes on. In fact, I wore Trey's boxers and tee. Dive walked right out of his house, while I struggled and cursed at him from over his shoulder. He jumped over the fence, my stomach hitting his shoulder, which caused me to lose my breath for a moment as he made his way to Trey's front door. Like he knew it would be unlocked, he opened it and stepped inside. Dive planted me on my feet then spun me around to face a scowling Trey. I silently rubbed my stomach and glowered at my man.

"Thanks, brother." Trey sent Dive a stiff chin lift.

Dive chuckled. "Anytime." And then he left, closing the door behind him.

"Little bird," was growled low. I turned my head back around from where it had followed Dive out and glared down at Trey. I liked that I was taller as I stood up on the ledge before it stepped down into the living room.

Crossing my arms over my chest, I waited for him to continue. I wasn't going to apologise...or maybe I should, maybe Dive was right. I *was* being a shithead. But I hated to be ordered around by someone I cared about the most.

Placing my arms down at my side, I started with, "I'm—"

But he interrupted with, "I'm sorry. I suck at this shit. Never have I liked change or been scared. For fuck's sake, I terrify and fuck people up for *my* club. But what's changed has freaked the fuck outta *me* for once. Low, I don't get scared, but I am now when I have two kids to take care of and a woman who could be taken from me at any second. Even though I won't let it happen, I've still seen it enough to know shit can go down that I can't stop.

I've claimed you as my old lady. It puts a message out that no one touches you or I fuck 'em up. So havin' you still want to sleep next door…fuck, it didn't feel good, because I put myself out there for you and it felt like you threw it back in my face."

"Trey, I never—"

"I know." He sighed. "It ain't on you. You're just bein' you, and I went about it all the wrong fuckin' way. I should have asked instead of orderin'. I was bein' a prick like your fuckin'—"

"Don't," I ordered. "Please, don't compare yourself to anyone. I know this is all new and scary to you, but it is for me, as well. I've never been in a relationship. I don't know how to do things, and I got my back up over something silly when I should have told you how I was feeling and how the way you went about ordering me…well, I didn't like it. But I know you meant to do right by me and you have, Trey. You really have. I've never felt anything like I do with you with anyone else."

"Does this mean you're gonna move in?"

"The kids—"

"I've talked to the kids. They're down with it. They think you're cool."

My eyes went to the floor. I couldn't help but smile. "Okay." I sighed teasingly. "I'll move in with you."

I looked up with a grin on my face to see his smile was light, happy and carefree. Amazing. His eyes were warm and held a hint of something else. His next words told me what that something was, "You're still gettin' punished for playin' your game today."

"What game?"

"Little bird," he said with a tone of warning.

Rolling my eyes, I said, "Okay, bring it on."

He chuckled. "With pleasure."

"I hope so," I added and then gasped when I found myself up and over his shoulder. He stalked down the hall to his room, went in and threw me to the bed.

"Play with yourself," he ordered. That didn't seem like punishment to me, so I happily obliged. Shredding myself of his boxers, I spread my legs wide, so my man standing at the end of the bed could see my already swollen, wet pussy. "Run your fingers through your juices, Low," he said and then hissed through his teeth when I did just that. His eyes stayed glued to my privates as I slipped in two fingers and pumped them in and out.

"Trey," I whispered.

"Feel good, little bird?"

"Yes," I moaned and ran my thumb over my clit. "Oh, God, I'm already close."

"Stop!" he demanded.

"What?" I snapped.

"Stop!" he barked. Leaning forward, he held my hand down to the bed.

Okay, he did intend to punish me. He ordered, "You touch yourself again, I won't let you come all night."

"Trey," I whined.

"No, little bird." He smiled, stood tall again and hooked his thumbs in the sides of his jeans to shove them down. My man had gone commando, no boxers in sight. "I saw how hungry you got when I touched myself," he said and ran his hand over his cock. I glared while he chuckled. He looked down and I followed his line of sight. Running his forefinger over the tip of his cock, he then took it to his mouth to suck off his pre-cum.

Snap. It.

That was hot.

"Doesn't taste too bad, Low. Bet you'd like a taste."

Yes. Yes, I would. I nodded as I slid my hand between my legs.

"No touchin'," he warned on a growl.

"Trey," I cried, but removed my hand.

He smirked and started tugging himself. "Look at you. Can't take your eyes away. You fuckin' love it."

I really did.

"Feels good, Low. So fuckin' good."

"Taste it again," I whispered.

"No."

"Please." I moaned and rubbed my legs together. God, the pressure to come was still building and I wasn't even touching myself. Instead, my incredible man touching himself may be enough to do me in.

He was so dang hot.

"Come 'ere," he demanded. Sitting up, I wiggled to the end of the bed. He stepped closer, fisted my hair and ordered, "Suck me."

Yes, please.

He moved his hand and my mouth wrapped around his hardness. I licked and tasted his pre-cum like a starved woman. Then I glided my slick lips down along his cock. He grunted his approval. "Suck me harder," he ordered. Applying pressure with my lips, I sucked harder up and down his dick, feeling it swell. I knew he was close to coming, and I was eager to have it fill my mouth.

"Stop!" he bit out.

Snap it. I groaned and sat back.

"Good girl." He smiled down at me. "Stand up and turn around." I was ready to explode. I didn't like him holding me off from pleasure, yet it was such a turn-on, as well.

Once my arse was to him, his hand went to the middle of my back and he forced it down so my hands went to the bed.

"You want my cock?"

"Yes."

"Tell me how much."

"A lot. Please, Trey." Instead of his dick, I felt his fingers slip into me, and I moaned.

"Fuckin' hell, so fuckin' wet." I lost his fingers and mewed in complaint, until I looked behind to see him on his knees. I gasped when he spread me wide with his fingers while his tongue lapped up my wetness.

"Yes, babe." I sighed and pushed my pussy onto his mouth. My belly dipped. My core quivered, ready to release on his face—until I lost him again. "Trey," I grumbled, desperate for more.

"You come on my cock tonight, little bird."

"Yes," I whispered. His hands went to my hips and the tip of him nudged at my entrance. And then, with one quick push, he was inside of me, causing us both to cry out.

"Love your pussy. Fuck, the taste, the smell, the feel of it. All fuckin' mine," he said as he pounded into me fast and hard.

"I, yes, oh…I…" It all crashed over me. He'd worked me up so much I was coming within seconds of having his cock in me.

"Jesus. Fuck," he grunted before his release spilled into me.

CHAPTER TWENTY-THREE

DODGE

*C*ouldn't for the life of me stop smiling. Even though I knew there was a cunt out there gunning for my woman, I was smiling. But I knew something was going to go down. I could feel it. It made me nervous, as if there were a pit bull in my stomach gnawing away, but I had to put it all aside and enjoy the time with my woman and the kids.

It'd been a month since Low had moved in, and it was as though she was made to be there, made for me and for the kids. They loved her and the company she kept. Lucia called in a couple of times and they thought she was a crack-up. We shared all the responsibilities, helped each other with the house shit, and with the kids. One afternoon, Tex had come home in a crap mood. I'd picked him up and told him he'd better snap out of it before we got home. He wouldn't tell me what his problem was, so I couldn't help fix it. When he walked in the door and Low greeted him, he told her to leave him alone. She looked at me worried, but then, I watched her back snap straight and she scolded, "Hang on there, little dude."

Tex paused in the mouth of the hallway. He didn't turn, though. Rommy stood by me, concern showing in her eyes and stiff posture. I hoped to Christ she didn't think Low would hit Tex for his attitude. I knew it wouldn't happen, but they may not have if it was what their mum had done.

"Turn around, Tex," Low said, and when he did, she asked. "Who peed in your Cheetos this morning?"

A snort escaped me. I looked down at Rommy to see her cover her mouth and giggle. I glanced over at Tex to see the anger had died down a little.

"No one," he said.

Low rolled her eyes. "Texas, tell me what has your boxers in a twist. I need to know if I have to go beat a kid up or yell and rant at a teacher. No one upsets anyone in this household."

Fuck, she was beautiful.

My chest expanded in pride. She wanted to protect

the kids, and I knew she'd do it, even if it meant she beat a kid up.

My eyes moved from my woman to nephew, where I saw Tex wipe at his eyes with the back of his hand. "Nothin' I can't handle."

"Tex," she uttered and took a step towards him. "Mate, you don't get it. You have to learn that you don't have to handle anything on your own. We're all in it together. We fight any battle *together*. That's what friends and family do."

He wiped his nose and nodded to the ground. "Some guy at school. Just givin' me shit about... damn, about you bein' black and bein' with our uncle and—"

"Enough," I growled.

Low sighed. "I'm sorry he's being a di..."—she looked at Rommy and changed her word from 'dick' to —"dinosaur."

He shook his head. "I don't care what he says to me. I don't. I just care that he's sayin' shit about you."

Low's eyes warmed.

"We'll deal with it, Tex," I said, before my woman started crying. "Tomorrow, Dive can take Rommy and Low to school and work, and I'll take you. We'll sort it."

He nodded again. "Okay."

That night, I called my brothers. The next morning, Tex was on the back of my bike and with Pick, Billy, Memphis, Saxon, Beast, and Muff following, we rode into the school car park. Tex pointed out the punk who was saying shit about my woman. With the kid at my side, Pick and Billy at my back, I walked up to the prick who was hanging with his friends. The bastard looked like a senior.

"You the little dick who said shit about my woman?" I asked, folding my arms across my chest. The kid looked to Tex. "Eyes to me," I growled. "And answer my goddamn question."

"Yeah, I did," he said with a glare.

"You man enough to say it to *my* face instead of my nephew?"

"Look, I was only mucking around. I didn't think he'd tattle to his uncle."

Stepping closer, I looked down at him and that was when I saw it, the uncertainty in his eyes. "He didn't wanna. We forced it outta him because he belongs to Hawks and we take care of our own. So when we find out a brother is gettin' some pissy little kid annoying him, we come to back him up. You better leave him alone," I warned, getting real close so no one else would hear. "If you don't, I'll pay a visit to your house. Your daddy won't stand a chance against me, and it won't be just him I fuck him up." Leaning back, I asked, "You get me?"

His face paled and he nodded.

"Words, kid, I need them."

"I get you."

"Glad you understand." Turning my back on him, I asked Tex, "You good?"

He smiled wide. "Yeah, Uncle Trey. Perfect."

"Cool. Let's roll, brothers."

Tex got home that night to inform me the kid didn't give him any shit. If anything, he and his friends left a wide space whenever Tex walked around the school. Shyly, he also informed me that not only did he have new friends, but some girls were paying him attention.

Fucking Christ.

He was fourteen; I had my first fuck at thirteen. I asked him if he knew about protection. He blushed and told me he was all okay in that area.

Thank fuck.

THE VENOM PREZ, who was supposed to meet me three weeks earlier, had rang just before that to see if I could do him a favour and asked to set back our meeting. It seemed he had a family situation he had to deal with. I told him that'd be fine, as long as none of his brothers fucked with what belonged to Hawks. He agreed and did it quickly, so it made me wonder what had gone down.

The meeting was planned for the next evening, which meant we could enjoy party time the night before. I was at the compound with my woman. She was setting up chips and shit on tables. Said there couldn't be a party without nibbles. I told her I'd give her something to nibble on. She glared while Lucia, who was helping her, giggled, before they walked back into the kitchen.

The door opened and next was shouted, "The party has arrived!"

Goddamn. "Shoot me now," I begged the brothers at the table, Pick, Billy, Dallas and Vicious.

"You'd have to take us out, as well," Dallas said. He stood and quickly disappeared just as Julian, Mattie, Josie, Nary, Wildcat, Talon, Hell Mouth, Griz—Christ, the whole goddamn tribe from Ballarat—walked in.

I stood, moved around the table and greeted all my brothers with a big smile, chin lift and handshake.

"Where's this Low bird?" Hell Mouth asked. "I wanna meet the woman who took you to your knees. I'm even thinkin' of making her a plaque." She smiled.

"Fuck off, woman."

"Princess," Griz warned.

Behind me, I heard a gasp and then, "Oh, snap. Zara and her muffkateers are here. Lucia, come meet them. You'll love these bitches."

"I like her already," Hell Mouth said.

"Hey, sugar, come give me some lovin' first." Julian grinned with his arms wide open. She swiftly walked up and into his arms as Lucia came out of the kitchen.

"Hoo-wee, so many good-lookin' fuckers in one room. I'm gonna have a mini orgasm," Lucia sang.

Jesus motherfucking Christ.

"Now her, I *really* like." Hell Mouth laughed.

"Julian, take your fuckin' hand off my woman's arse," I snarled. Julian's hands dropped and he stepped back.

"Relax, buttercup, I'm gay. It's like a rule I can feel up the women."

"Not in my place."

He pouted. "You party-pooper."

While the brothers disengaged to greet other brothers, I stayed by my woman's side with my arm around her neck as she dribbled shit to the women. She drank, laughed and told me many times she loved my family. What I didn't like was how Lucia and Hell Mouth seemed to get on really well.

"Yo, Josie," Dive called from the other side of the room. "Where's Simone?"

Josie glared at my brother and said, "She's busy."

He gave her a chin lift and turned back to the others he was talking to. What was going down with my brother and Simone? I knew they wanted each other, only he'd fucked that up, but I still reckoned there was something else.

My eyes glided over the area. I saw Vicious and Nary having words—harsh words, by the look of it—in the corner. I wasn't the only one to notice, though. Stoke watched them like a hawk, and I knew he'd intervene if needed. But he didn't have to, because Vicious left Nary standing there and walked off just as the doors opened again and...

Fuck no.

Club whores walked in.

"What. The. Heck?" I heard Zara gasp.

"Kitten," Talon warned. "Not our business."

"Are you, or are you not, the president?"

"Yeah, woman, but what goes on here's up to Dodge."

Throw me under the goddamn bus.

All eyes turned to me.

What shocked the shit out of me was when my woman—my gorgeous, fucking strong, confident woman —said, "It's okay. I've had a word with them. They know if they fuck with a committed guy, their twats won't be in working order for a very long time. So long they'd never walk again. The bitches can stay for the single brothers. They need to have a good time, like I know my man will be with me."

If we'd been outside, crickets would be chirping. My hand slid into her hair. I tugged my woman's head back and when she looked up at me, I claimed her mouth. Hoots and woof calls echoed around the place.

"Kitten." Talon sighed. I lifted my head to see him take his woman in his arms.

"I'm fine. It's just baby emotions."

"Zara," Low uttered.

"Never seen it before, but you're right. The single brothers should get their fun, as well." She looked to her man. "Lift the ban on the whores."

"Kitten." He smiled. "No fuckin' way. I get where Low is comin' from, and it's great for her. But I don't want whores at the compound when our kids come in."

"I agree," Low offered, and she turned to me. "No hookers when you know the kids will be here."

"Same," Zara piped up, and the girls shared a look and giggle.

"Isn't this grand, bonding over sluts." Julian clapped. They all laughed again.

Later that night, I made sure my woman felt how much I appreciated her.

I was the president of the club, but I had the best fucking old lady at my side to run it with me.

CHAPTER TWENTY-FOUR

DODGE

*S*itting in the back office in the compound, I waited for the call to say the Venom prez, Switch, had arrived. The night before was crazy, but fuck, it was fun. Having my brothers over from the Ballarat charter made it even better. If felt like I hadn't seen them in years instead of a couple of months. It also made me want to get my woman down to Ballarat with the kids to show them around, knowing they'd never been.

My phone rang on the desk. Without looking, I picked up and placed it to my ear." Yo?"

"Dodge," a male voice replied.

"Who's this?" I asked.

"Blackie."

Strange. Why in the fuck was he ringing me? "What can I do for you, man?"

"Actually, it's what I can do for you. I have some information."

"You gonna say it or play with my cock like a tease for a while longer?"

He chuckled. "I'm not a cock man, so I reckon I'll tell you. You got Switch comin' to you soon. He's gonna talk shit about the turf he wants off you, found out it's all because of Baxter... Yeah, I know you now know. He's been in Switch's ear to cause shit with you Hawks. Switch, not havin' many brains, did what he's told. He's scared of Baxter, as well."

Jesus. Fucking Baxter.

"Somethin' else."

"Yeah?"

"There's been an in-house vote. Switch is no longer prez. He doesn't know it yet. It's just gone down and, when he gets back, *he'll* go down."

Holy shit. "Hold off on that for now. We got somethin' in play for Switch."

"Will do. Least I can do for the shit he's done to Hawks."

"So, who's in charge now?"

"You're talkin' to him. Good news for you, we don't want your turf. Bad news, we ain't helpin' you with

Baxter. He won't come near us now because he knows I won't let him talk me into anythin', but I'm stayin' right the fuck outta everythin' because I need to keep my family and the club safe." He paused. "You get me?"

"Loud and clear," I said before hanging up. At least it was fucking good to know Hawks just lost all trouble from Venom. Still, I knew it wouldn't cool some brothers' jets. They'd always remember the shit Venom put us through.

Crap, I actually felt giddy with the information I just got. No matter what, Switch was fucked, and Venom was no longer dicking with Hawks.

My phone buzzed on the desk. I looked to it. It was time. It didn't take Billy and Pick long to get them into the room. I didn't bother standing from behind my desk. Instead, when my eyes landed on the big motherfucker with a shaved head, beady eyes and a fat gut, I sent him a chin lift. He offered one back then sat in the chair opposite me. Two others of his people, a young-looking guy and a dude in his late thirties, came in and stood behind him. We waited until the door was closed, then Pick and Billy were standing behind me.

"Dodge, good to finally meet you. Heard many things 'bout you." Switch smirked.

Playing dumb, I said, "I have to say, Switch, I've heard nothin' about you. What I do know is that you've been fuckin' with Hawks for too long. What's your plan?"

"Straight to the point, I like it." He sat forward, his arms resting on his knees. "I want the north and south side."

"Why?"

"Our business would benefit from it."

I raised a brow at him. "Your business of pussy and drugs?"

"Yes."

"Then no." I smiled. "Actually, it was always goin' to be a no. It's our turf. We would never give it up, and we'd never let you fuckers deal your shit on our turf."

Switch rolled his eyes. "Yes, yes. Good old Hawks takin' the clean road in life."

"We get dirty when we need to, but that's often only in blood. We keep our territory clean of pussy, guns and drugs. Take a leaf outta our book, Switch. Get on the clean side of life and make your money the right way."

He scoffed and leaned back before saying, "Where's the fun in that?"

"It's safer," I offered.

"Safer?" He snorted. "We keep goin' the way we are, we'll soon have you pussies backin' down."

Smiling, I shook my head and shared a glance with Pick and Billy. Leaning my elbows on the desk, I said, "You do understand that I've taken over as president now, don't you?" I waited for his nod. The men at his back looked on warily. "My brothers at my back are Pick and

Billy the Kid. I've formed a new crew. Pick's my second, Billy's sergeant in arms, and Dallas is the enforcer. Do you know of our background?"

"I—"

"No, I don't think you do. You should have done your research when things changed over, Switch." I stood, my gun drawn. Pick and Billy followed with theirs. "We don't like games. We don't like anyone to fuck with Hawks. We deal with the cunts if they choose to play games and, by dealin', it means we ain't fuckin' afraid to shoot you in the goddamn head right now. My brothers at my back, and me, have so much blood on our hands. We've killed more than any of your pansy-arse Venom men have, and it's all to protect our goddamn clean, safe club from people like you."

"You want war?" Switch yelled, standing himself.

I chuckled, enjoying myself way too much. "There'll be no war, Switch. Right now, I have Dallas sittin' outside your house, watchin' and waitin' for my call before he goes in and tells your old lady exactly what you've been up to. If I know a scorned woman, she'd have your arse in jail before you've said anythin'. Sleepin' with teenagers, Switch. I should shoot you for even thinkin' it. You sick fuck," I snarled. "There'll be no war. You and your brothers will back the fuck off or I will not only invade your house, but your compound and business, and I'll shoot any fucker I see."

"Fuck!" he yelled. "Fuck!"

"Back the fuck away when you know you can't win."

"Fine," he barked. "Fuckin' fine." That was when I saw the kid behind him smile, just before the door was swung open and Nary stood there. Her eyes widened. Thank fuck, we'd just lowered our guns.

"Nary?" I asked.

"Oh, um…" She gasped when her eyes landed on the Venom kid behind Switch. "You, you're…no," she mumbled before running from the room.

The kid went to go after her, but I stepped in his way. "She's Hawks. Keep your fuckin' hands and eyes off."

"You don't understand—"

"Jerimiah," Switch growled, and the kid stiffened. The vicious glare he sent Switch was filled with so much hatred. "We leave," Switch ordered. With a flick of his wrist, he walked towards the door. I moved out of the way to let them pass.

Shutting the door, I turned to Pick and Billy. "What's up with that Jerimiah kid and Nary?"

"Don't know, but I'll get our woman onto it," Pick said.

"We need to find Nary, see why she walked in here in the first place."

"I'll do it," Billy offered. No woman interrupted a brothers' sit-down, and it was strange as fuck Nary did it. She'd know the rule from Stoke. Christ, she'd have to be punished for it, depending on her answer for why she'd barged in.

"That went well," Pick said as he sat in the seat Switch had been in.

I told him about the call from Blackie then added, "It was just a bit of fun. I wanted to see the fucker squirm. He'd been a pain in the arse too long for me to not do anythin' to him."

"Dallas in with his wife now?"

I smirked. "Sure is. The fucker will no doubt be goin' to jail with all the evidence we got from followin' him."

"Now we just got Baxter to deal with."

"He's a slippery fuck. But we'll find him and take him outta play."

"Got a call just before Switch turned up," Pick started. "Parker's outta Venom now. Seemed Blackie also informed him of the changes."

"Right. Do you trust Parker as much as Lan?" I asked.

Pick shrugged. "Not sure, brother."

The door opened and Billy came back in with hard eyes and a clenched jaw. "Vicious, the little shit, for some reason told Nary to come into the office. That you wanted to ask her somethin'."

"What the fuck? Where's he?" I growled.

"Comin'. I texted him to meet us in here." No sooner had he said it, the door opened and a scowling Vicious walked in, shutting the door behind him.

"She had to know," he stated, leaning against the door and folding his arms over his chest.

"Know what, brother? And it'd better be fuckin' brilliant for sendin' a woman into a sit-down. We had our fuckin' guns drawn, you dickhead. What would that have done to Nary if she'd seen it after all the shit she's gone through with that goddamn scar?"

"Fuck," he snarled.

"Yeah, *fuck*. What in the hell were you thinkin'?" Pick demanded.

"The prick that came in with Switch."

"The younger one?" Billy asked.

"Yeah. He's Switch's son." His upper lip rose, his body tense. "He and Nary have been gettin' to know one another. Don't know how they met. Don't know if it was set up. But I've been keepin' an eye on them, and I knew she didn't know he was *Venom* scum," he bit out.

Jesus. The jealous fuck could have done more damage than what had happened.

Running a hand over my face, I asked him, "Did you, at any fuckin' time, think of just tellin' Nary who that guy belonged to?" He said nothing, which told me everything. "No, because you and your weird-arse crush want nothin' to do with her, yet here you are wantin' to warn her she was in bed with a member of an opposin' club." I ground my teeth together. "Goddamn it, Vicious. Get your head outta your arse and either fuckin' claim her or leave her the fuck alone!" I stood. "Nothin' you do is helpin' her in any way. Christ, sendin' her into a room when you knew dangerous shit could have gone down was fucked-up. Are you tryin' to hurt her more than what you already are?"

"I'm not—"

"Don't," Billy growled.

"Man the fuck up, brother. You're hurtin' her," Pick said. "Get your shit together and go after the one woman who obviously consumes your mind."

"I can't!" he yelled.

"Why the fuck not?" I bellowed back.

His eyes dropped to the floor, but he didn't say anything.

Sighing, I said, "No club whores for a month. No pussy. You're on bar duty for that month, also. And you'll clean the bloody toilets in the garage."

His clenched jaw told me how pissed he was. Still, he said nothing. Vicious nodded and walked out the room.

"Fuck me drunk," I groaned and sat back down. "What's up with that guy?"

"I reckon it stems from his dad or some shit. What Vicious did was fucked-up. He deserved more than what you gave him, Prez," Billy said.

Nodding, I told them, "Agreed, but I think he's puttin' himself through his own hell enough by denyin' what he wants more than his next breath." Taking a deep breath, I said, "Change of subject here, but you guys notice the difference with Handle?"

Handle, before he backed his brother wrongly against us, had been one who'd smile and laugh. Now he was... dead, on the inside and out.

"The brothers are steerin' clear of him. They haven't welcomed him back as yet, which is understandable," Pick said, knowing exactly how it was since he'd done the shittiest thing to our prez in Ballarat and his woman. Still, we all got over it once he proved himself he was Hawks through and through.

"Yeah, it is, but still. Fuck, that guy is like a robot these days."

"He lost his woman to Baxter because of his blood brother. That'd fuck any guy up. He's lookin' for revenge, though, and if he's anythin' like us, he'd be huntin' it down in his own time."

"Have Beast and Muff watch him," I ordered.

"Done," Pick said with a chin lift.

My phone buzzed. Looking down at it, a message from a private number popped up. I opened the message then froze from the words I read: ***Do you know where your woman and kids are?***

The door was flung open and in it stood a heavy-breathing Muff. When I noticed his wild eyes, I stood, as did my brothers. "What?" I barked.

"Low, the shop, robbery," he said between pants.

"Fuck, what?" I roared.

"Dive… rang. He took Low to the supermarket to see Lucia after gettin' the kids." He breathed. "He waited in the car. She walked into a robbery takin' place."

"Where're they now?" Panic seized my heart. It ran cold like the blood drumming hard in my veins. There was no way some cockhead motherfucker was going to ruin what I had. No goddamn way.

"Fuck, brother. They're *still* in there."

Fuck. No.

Fuck!

I rounded the desk and barked at Pick, "Call Lan. We need a cover 'cause I'm goin' in there to get my woman and kids, and no one's gonna fuckin' stop me." I showed them my phone.

"Motherfucker," Billy snarled.

His guess was like mine. Baxter had finally made a move.

CHAPTER TWENTY-FIVE

WILLOW

*I*t had been a blissful month with Trey and the kids. We'd had our hiccups, but nothing that couldn't be smoothed over.

Last night had been amazing. I loved—like a huge girl crush—the muffkateers from Ballart. It was awesome to have spent time with them. Ivy—a giggle escaped me— definitely made her club name proud with the name Chatter. Damn, that woman loved to talk. Anything could come from her, both appropriate and inappropriate things. Still, her man Killer was hooked into her 100 percent.

Clary was a sweet, sassy and gorgeous woman. I couldn't believe she'd been blind. Blue, her man, found it hard, like mine, to leave her side. He was very protective. Heck, they all were. All Hawks men showed their love openly—which was amazing to see. They cherished their women and would do anything for them. I pinched myself knowing I was a part of that crew. I was a muffka-teer, and I couldn't be prouder.

Hell Mouth had declared Lucia was also an honouree muffkateer, even if she didn't have a bad-arse biker at her side. Lucia was a bad-arse woman enough to be a part of the crew. Griz looked on at his woman, Deanna, also known as Hell Mouth, with amusement and annoyance at times through the night. I could tell he found her taxing. Still, every time she got close, he would tag her in some way and show he'd claimed her just as she was.

Malinda was Nary's mum. She was the coolest mum I had ever met, and I ended up asking her if I could ring her for advice as Tex and Rommy grew. I wanted to do my best with those children. She'd said yes, on one condition. She asked me, *me*, to watch out for Nary while she lived and went to uni in Melbourne. Stoke, who stood beside her, grunted and mentioned he'd prefer to move them all to Melbourne so he could keep an eye on his girl, which Malinda squashed quickly. She told me later that the reason was because, like all Hawks men, they were possessive. So much so she knew Nary wouldn't be able to experience life without Stoke breathing down her neck.

Yes, the men of Hawks were very possessive. I knew it already from my own Hawks man. As Zara had explained, it could drive us crazy, but we knew they only had our heart in hand when it came to their women.

The best part of the night had been after the party, when Trey took me home and showed me how much he appreciated me. I didn't think threatening some hookers would turn him on, but it had, and I'd enjoyed the reward I got for it.

Trey had organised, with Dive, for me to pick up the kids from their schools the next day. I knew he had a lot on, especially the meeting with the Venom prez, plus I enjoyed picking up the kids anyway. Usually, we'd go get some ice cream or go shopping, even when Dive and Tex hated it. Rommy, however, loved it. I also took them, with whoever was our guard for the day, to the basketball court because I knew Tex loved to play. That day, though, I decided I wanted to cook something special, so I asked Dive to drive us to the supermarket. I couldn't go to any other market than the one where Lucia worked. It also gave me the chance to have a gab with her.

Dive stopped right out the front sliding doors. The area wasn't busy, as usual. I hopped out of the car with the kids following. They knew if they helped me shop, they'd get a treat at the end.

However, if I had known what lay ahead, I would have left them in the car.

But I didn't.

I walked, with the kids, straight into a trap.

As we stepped in and saw Lucia's tear-stained face, I knew something was wrong. The doors swished closed behind us and then I heard them being locked. Grabbing a hand of each child, I turned and pulled them behind me.

Two men, with ski masks covering their faces, stood at the doors with guns raised and pointed right at me.

"Girl," Lucia cried softly, her anguish showing on her face.

"Kids, go stand with Lucia," I ordered and started shoving them over to my girl, who I knew would keep them safe if anything happened to me.

"No!" one barked, the one with blue eyes. The other, I noticed, had brown. "They stay with you."

"Okay," I said, holding up my hands in front of me. Rommy gripped my side tightly, while Tex stood behind me but to my side, his fingers hooked in the back of my jeans. "You want the money? I'm sure Lucia will give it up."

"It ain't 'bout the money," the blue-eyed one said.

"Then what is it?"

"Girl." Lucia sighed. Looking over my shoulder, I locked eyes with her. She was as pissed off as she was terrified. "Jerry's knocked out in the back," she said. "They made me come up here and pretend like nothin' was happenin'. They—"

"Enough. Erik, go check on the guy in the back." So that was the blue-eyed one's name.

"You go, *Garry*." Erik obviously didn't like to be bossed around.

They were both obvious idiots for sharing their names…unless they knew we wouldn't be coming out of it alive.

Fear gripped my throat. I fought to swallow it down. It wasn't the time to freak the hell out like I wanted to. I had to be strong for the children.

"Fuck, you're dumb. Don't do shit 'til I get back. I'll check on the others, as well."

Others? They had more men around.

God.

"All this for money?" I whispered, more to myself than anyone.

Erik laughed. "Stupid bitch. It ain't got anythin' to do with the money. We were ordered to come here 'cause we were told you'd be comin'."

"There's a bug in your car. They heard you tell Dive to come here. They're goin' to kill us when Dodge gets here," Lucia said quickly, and Erik fired off a warning shot at the counter. She jumped away, screaming. We all did.

My eyes widened, and I wrapped my arms around the kids. They looked up at me with fright in their eyes. I couldn't let that happen, couldn't let the children lose their uncle. Was I fighting a losing battle, though? Because I knew Dodge would turn up as soon as he found out what was happening to us. Whatever it was, I had to fight. I had to do something.

"You, shut the fuck up!" Erik yelled.

Garry came running back into the room. "What the fuck?" he asked, looking at the counter in front of Lucia, which now had a hole in it.

Erik flicked his gun towards Lucia and said, "She told her the plan."

"Fuck," Garry snapped and ran a frustrated hand over his head. "If you hadn't told *her* in the goddamn first place—"

"If you'd have just let me shoot her in the fuckin' first place."

"Shut the hell up. God, go sit with your bitch and keep you trap shut," Garry snarled at me and the kids. We quickly ran around the counter and huddled together while Garry and Erik fought back and forth, over and over. All we could do was stand there, watch on, and wait.

I knew what we were waiting for. My man.

Once he was there, all hell would break out.

"Beside the fridge," I heard Lucia whisper.

"What?" I asked, my eyes still on the men.

I felt her eyes bore into me. "Beside. The. Back. Fridge."

Of course. Oh, God. My heart raced in my chest as the plan formed in my head. At least, if anything happened, the children would be safe.

I pretended to rest on the counter, my elbows on top and my head in my hands. Garry and Erik watched me, but kept talking.

Slowly, I slid a hand down to the pens and paper we always kept handy under the counter to throw notes at each other. I hoped to God they would understand my quick writing, but I had to be fast so the men, who looked across at us every now and then, wouldn't notice I was doing something. Tex, the smart boy, leaned over my shoulder, his arms curling around my arm under the counter, so it looked like he was just hugging me while hiding my arm.

Finally done, I lifted it then turned my back to the men for a second, long enough to pass the note to Tex. He nodded. I spun back around and we huddled close again.

I called out, "Can the kids at least sit on the floor?"

Erik's glare hit me before he nodded.

Thank you, Jesus.

Tex was first to sit, pulling a reluctant Rommy down beside him. I glanced down to see Tex opening the note and reading it. When I glanced down again, he was looking up at me and shaking his head.

"Get your sister to safety," I said through clenched teeth.

"Uncle Trey will come," he whispered.

That was what those guys were counting on. They wanted to crush my man by taking us out right in front of him. Even if they…killed me, I knew the children would help Trey live on eventually.

"I'm not—"

"Texas," I hissed low. "Do it. Now."

He bit his bottom lip. Tears fell from his eyes as he got to his knees and nodded up at me. I sighed in relief.

"No," Rommy breathed.

"Go with your brother."

Tex sighed. "Come on, Rom. You can do this."

She looked from me to her brother and then finally, *finally*, I saw her small nod. Tex quickly and quietly ushered his scared sister along the floor on all fours towards the aisles.

The shop owner, Jeff, being the cheap person he was, had found a hole in the wall that led outside. It was right beside the fridges, at the back of the bottom shelf with canned soup in front of it. Outside, the only thing covering the hole was a piece of corflute, thin material that Tex could easily kick out, and then hopefully they could get out without anyone noticing.

Please, please, please let them get out safely.

Lucia quickly gripped my arm. My body froze. We both heard it, the familiar sound of Harleys coming down the quiet street.

No. God, no.

Trey was walking right into the trap set for him.

I wasn't worried that my life was in jeopardy. What made me feel ill, what caused my stomach to drop, my hands to sweat and my body to shake, was the possibility I could lose my man, my family, my friends.

My life would be nothing without them in it.

The noise came to a stop right out front.

Holy…it sounded like there were at least about twenty Harleys parking out the front of the shop. I wondered if the neighbouring shops took notice. If they did, would they call for some more help…but if they did, Trey could get into trouble.

There wasn't going to be a good outcome in the situation we were in.

No matter what, lives would be lost, one way or another.

My hand went over my mouth. I shook my head back and forth when my eyes landed on the man who stood just outside the sliding glass door.

Behind and beside him were about twenty brothers.

Trey slowly slid down his mirrored sunglasses. The scowl on his gorgeous face was fearsome. He wanted to hurt people, and he knew he was going to have his way.

But I was afraid I'd lose my life before he could do anything.

CHAPTER TWENTY-SIX

DODGE

*M*y insides were in fucking turmoil during my ride towards death. It was death because I'd be killing, and taking goddamn pleasure in murdering those fuckers who thought they could mess with my family.

The thought of me going to jail didn't bother me. I'd happily go there. Hell, I'd even skip my way there if it meant my family were safe. I knew my brothers would take care of Low and the kids if that shit did go down.

I just hoped Lan had the chance to show before I did and had a fucking plan in place. If not, there'd be a bloodbath on my hands and he'd have to be the one to take me in.

Looking in my mirror on route had my chest filling with pride. My brothers had my back. As soon as they heard what was going down, they dropped everything and jumped on their rides with me. Fuck, even Handle.

She'd better be fine.

The kids had better be good.

If they weren't...

If I saw one drop of their blood on them, I would lose it.

And it'd probably take all my brothers to hold me back.

Or they'd join in with me.

Stopping right out the front, I climbed off my ride and stepped in front of Lan and Parker, who were already there waiting.

"They have four men at the back, two men are inside with the women and the kids. Not sure what their play is. The lines have been cut, so we can't call them inside."

"I'm goin' in," I growled.

"Fuck, Dodge, you can't." He looked around. "Too many witnesses."

Crossing my arms over my chest, I snarled, "You're wastin' my fuckin' time to save my family, and I don't appreciate it, Lan. I'm goin' the fuck in." Moving around him and Parker, who wore a fucking smile on his face, I kept walking.

"Shit," Lan swore. "I'm goin' 'round the back."

"Do that. Muff, Beast, Handle, go with him," I ordered.

As I moved close to the doors, Dive stepped out of nowhere, wearing a look of self-loathing on his face.

"Don't," I said. "It's not on you."

"But—"

"Don't." I reached out and gripped the back of his neck, bringing his forehead to mine. "Not on you, brother."

He nodded and stepped in beside me.

At the doors, I saw my woman. Scanning her body, I saw no damage. I let myself feel that relief for only a second. Lucia stood beside her with her arm around my woman's waist.

Where in the fuck were the kids?

Slowly, I lowered my shades, scanning the shop.

Two men appeared on the other side of the front doors.

"Open them," I snarled.

One smiled. "I don't think so. Baxter sent us. He sends his regards and for you to know this won't be the end. He'll take everythin' off you, even your club."

"He won't get the chance!" I roared.

"He will. He has eyes everywhere."

"Trey, go!" I heard Low yell.

Shaking my head, I looked to my woman. Did she honestly think I'd leave her there? I watched as she mouthed the words I'd been wanting to hear for some time: *Love you.*

Rolling my eyes, I said loud enough for her to hear, "Woman, I'm not tellin' you 'I love you' right now while there's fuckin' danger about, like we're in some romance novel. I'll do it later."

My brothers chuckled.

"You won't get a chance, dickhead," Fuckface said with a laugh.

My eyes sliced back to them and I prayed to Christ I'd given them enough time out back. "Ready?" I asked the brothers beside and behind me.

"Fuck yeah," Billy snarled.

The men's eyes widened as they saw all of us move at once. We crashed through the glass doors. Rolling, I was up on my feet in seconds. I heard the women screaming, but I wasn't taking my eyes off the target. The men had backed up, their guns high, pointed at me.

"Do it," I taunted.

"Trey," Low cried out.

"Do it now. You won't get the chance again because you'll be dead."

"Doesn't matter what you do to me. At least I know

Baxter will fuck you up. That's all I need to think about when I die," one said with a smirk just before I shot him right in the heart and he dropped to the ground. My eyes glanced off the dead guy to the other cockhead still standing.

"What Baxter didn't tell you fuckers is that I don't like anyone messin' with my family and club. He put you all up to this and knew you'd be dead for it. You dumb fucks. You die knowin' you failed and know you did it for nothin' 'cause Baxter won't get to me. He won't get to my family, and he sure as fuck won't get to my club, 'cause I'll make him bleed before that."

"Dodge, you can't shoot him," Lan said, coming in from the back.

I chuckled. "I won't have to with this one." I looked up and out the skyline to the roof. With a nod, the glass shattered and Dallas's bullet hit the fucker right between the eyes.

"Shit. Fuck!" Lan barked.

"Don't stress, Detective." Dive smiled and gestured with his head to Dallas. "His gun and bullet belong to Violet."

Talon's sister and private investigator gave us all back-up guns of hers when we got in shit situations, for when we needed cover. However, I didn't think I'd be getting off for what went down that day. I'd killed a man with my own gun. There was no way I'd get out of that.

At least seeing the threat to my family was dead, my heart finally calmed the fuck down.

Never had I been scared shitless in my life.

The thought of losing my family in one day…fuck, I couldn't go there. I still felt sick to my stomach.

"Trey," was sobbed beside me. She was in my arms in seconds. I wrapped her up tight, my nose going into the hair at her temple to take in her scent.

Peace.

Fucking beautiful peace.

"The kids?" I asked into her neck where I kissed.

"They got out." She nuzzled into me more.

Christ.

Jesus.

"They're with Vicious," Parker called out. His sudden movement caught my attention. He walked slowly over to the guy I shot and leaned over for the dead dude's gun. Holding it with his tee, he turned it on himself and shot himself in the shoulder. Shocked shouts erupted, but his eyes looked up and landed on me. "Self-defence."

Fuck, *fuck*, fuck me. He just shot himself to take the fall.

No one would question a detective.

Parker gestured to my gun with his hand. I held back. "Don't be a fuckin' fool," he snarled. "You got people to take care of."

Low took the gun from my hand and walked over to

Parker. She handed it to him, looked into his eyes. I knew he'd be seeing the gratitude within them, like I was fucking feeling for the guy. She hugged him quick and kissed his cheek before coming back to me and winding her arm around my waist.

Lan sighed. Glancing over to him, I saw his smirk. "He got to it before I did." *Shit, brothers to the fuckin' bone, even if they didn't wear the patch.* Lan continued, "Get the fuck outta here before the cops show."

"What about everyone out there? They've seen them," Low asked. I gave her shoulder a squeeze.

"They don't know what happened *in* here. We'll just say we flagged you down for some help. It'll work out." Lan winked at Low.

"Grateful," I said. "To you both."

"Just be ready when we need your help," Parker said.

"Will do. *Anythin',*" I offered with a chin lift before walking my woman out of the shop. I glanced just behind us to see Beast helping a still-shocked Lucia walk out, as well.

As we stepped outside, we heard bellowed, "Uncle Trey!" I turned around in time to catch Rommy, who ran and jumped into my arms. "Low helped us get out and Tex got us out by kicking in a wall. Then Mr Parker told us to wait outside with Saxon, but then Saxon got a call to say we could come see you. I'm so, so, so happy everyone is okay."

"So am I, darlin'." I looked down at her brother beside Low, holding her hand, and said, "You did well, kid."

I smiled when he gave me a chin lift.

EPILOGUE

DODGE

SIX WEEKS LATER: CHRISTMAS MORNING

I knew it wasn't over with Baxter. If his last message was anything to go by, not only did I need to protect my family, but my brothers, as well. He wanted to end it all. He wanted there to no longer be a Hawks in Caroline Springs, and he was crazy enough to get his way if we didn't stop him.

Security was a high priority. Not only at each and everyone's house, but the garage and compound, as well. Cameras weren't going to be enough; we needed state-of-the-art security systems, and there was only one man I trusted with the job. I'd previously called Warden and told him what was going down. His shit would soon be passing, he hoped; though he'd said even if it hadn't, he'd be there to help us out. He was another honorary brother, and it eased some stress knowing he was coming a couple of days after Christmas to get started.

I'd been worried about Low and the kids after the shit had gone down at the shop. However, I didn't need to. No one lost sleep. Even Rommy had a will of steel, and I found out why when she came to me a couple of nights after it.

I was sitting on the couch with Tex beside me. He was playing the Xbox, some car game, when Rommy walked into the room and sat right down on my lap, resting her head against my chest. If I didn't already love the kid, I would have then.

"Need to know somethin'," I said.

Tex paused the game and asked, "What, Uncle Trey?"

"You guys got any worries after what happened?"

Tex shrugged then shook his head. "I'm cool."

"Yeah, Uncle Trey, we're cool." Rommy smiled up at me. "Tex and I talked. We weren't too worried because we knew our tough uncle would come for us. We knew you'd stop those bad men and you did. You keep us safe."

Jesus.

I got fucking goose bumps. My eyes closed for a second and when I opened them, I asked, "You guys, you know I love havin' you both here, yeah?" They nodded.

Fuck, was I really going to put it out there?

Yeah, I was, because every kid deserved to know. "Best day of my life when I got you two here to live with me." Rommy's bottom lips wobbled and I felt Tex stiffen beside me. "There'll be many more kick-arse days while we live together. But, I wanted you both to know... you two are great kids, and it's a damn pleasure to have you with me. You know I love you two, right?"

"Loveyoutoooo," Rommy cried and threw her arms around me.

Tears formed in Tex's eyes. His lips quirked up and he nodded. "Same here, Uncle Trey. Same here." I reached out and tagged him with a hand to the back of his neck before I pulled him in to me.

It was time to share those strong-as-shit feelings with my woman.

A month. It only took me a month or so after the situation to get the tampon out of my arse and share the words with my woman.

Low started to shift beside me in bed. She was waking, and I wanted her to wake with need. Sliding my hand down her stomach and straight into her panties, I didn't waste time. I circled her clit. She moaned and slowly opened her eyes.

"Mornin'." I grinned.

"Good morning." She smiled and arched. Fuck, she

was beautiful. I never wanted a day to go by that I didn't wake up with her beside me, and I'd make sure that it happened. With quick movements, she removed her panties, which I hated her sleeping in, and straddled my waist. She kissed down my chest and mumbled against my skin, "It's a good morning now." Then she took my cock into her hot, slippery mouth.

"Fuck, woman," I groaned. I'd already been hard as anything before she woke from having her beside me, so I knew I wouldn't take long. I didn't want to blow my load in her mouth.

Grabbing her under her arms, I shifted her and her mouth slid off my cock. She mewed in complaint as I pulled her up to sit back on my waist.

"I want *in* you while I come," I growled.

"Yes." She smiled, pleased as she lifted to her knees and took hold of my dick in her hand. She then guided me to her tight hole and slowly shifted back so my dick glided into her body.

"God," she moaned.

"Never get enough of you," I said and ran my hands over her fucking perfect skin. I watched as she rode me— her hands to my chest, her head thrown back, her eyes closed. So damn beautiful.

I tugged her forward, her front meeting mine, and kissed her deeply. Pulling back, I said, "Love you, little bird."

"Finally." She smiled just as she climaxed around my cock. As she slid up and down on me still, she opened her eyes and kissed me before saying against my lips, "Love you, Trey Monroe. Dodge. So much." That was when I groaned and shot my load into her soaking pussy. Afterward, she lay down, with me still inside her, on my chest.

"Merry Christmas," I added.

She gasped and jumped up quickly, only to smile down at me. "It's Christmas. Christmas," she sang. "Get up, get up. Quick shower before we wake the kids. Oh, my God, I'm so excited." She danced on the spot, throwing her hands up in the air. "It's Christmas." Then she ran straight into the bathroom.

My woman was crazy. The night before, we waited up until an excited Rommy finally fucking fell asleep at the crack-arse of early hours, just so we could put out the presents from Santa. Rommy still believed. Texas was old enough to know, but still Low graced him with presents from the big fat guy. She'd said he couldn't miss out if his sister was getting some. They'd even placed a glass of milk, some cookies for the bearded dude and some carrots for the reindeers. Which I had to fucking nibble on in the early hours while Low got to eat the cookies. She tipped the milk out a little—not all the way, she told me, or else it looked too fake. Fuck me, the whole thing was fake, but I let her go for it without too much complaining.

In a way, I regretted giving her my bankcard to shop for Christmas, but there was no way in hell I would step foot in a crowded shopping centre. Instead, I'd sent Beast and Dive with her. Never seen them so pissed before when they got back. Of course, I laughed my arse off.

Still, I was glad my woman went all out. It was the first Christmas the kids had with us, and we both wanted to make it something special.

After Low had her shower, I quickly jumped in. Just as I got back into the bedroom wearing tracksuit pants, our bedroom door burst open. My head swung that way and Low's did as well from making the bed.

"He's been! Santa's been. Come on, come on, come on!" Rommy squealed and peeled out of the room on a run. We heard Tex's door crash open, hitting the wall, and then the squeaks of his bed. What a way to wake up, having your sister bounce on the bed.

"Damn, Rom. I'm gettin' up. Out," Tex grumbled. Still, I could tell he was smiling.

Low grinned at me like a fool. "I better go save the presents from Rommy until we're all out there." She quickly ran out of the room, dressed in jeans and a red Christmas top.

Christ. As I walked down the hall, I noticed my little bird went the extra mile without telling me about it. There were white powdered footprints on the floor running all down the hallway and into the living room.

Low came up to me as I entered, wrapped her arms around my waist and tightened her grip. I looked from a bouncing Rommy, who sat with so much excitement in front of the tree while she waited for her brother, to my woman, tagging my arm around her shoulders.

"Little bird, the footprints?" I asked in a whisper.

She beamed. "It looks like Santa got snow everywhere."

Fuck me. She was something special. I had a huge amount of special in my house and I'd do anything, fucking *anything*, to protect her and the kids. And later, when we were at the compound with all my brothers and their families sitting around chilling, I knew I'd do goddamn anything to protect them, as well. Just like I knew they'd do it for me.

Because Hawks was about safety, family, friends, and fucking hard. Living strong and finding peace. I'd found mine, and I wanted the brothers who hadn't found theirs to get the chance, too.

HAWKES MC: CAROLINE SPRINGS
CHARTER: BOOK 3

PROLOGUE

DIVE

Simone took my breath away the first time I laid eyes on her in the bar. I wanted nothing more than her sexy-as-hell legs wrapped around my waist and to be buried deep inside her. That night she granted me a taste. A kiss that blew my mind and nearly my load. From then on, I was addicted.

Then I went and fucked it all up when she wouldn't fall for my plays straight away. We went on a couple of dates, and my cock led my brain, not for the first time, so when she didn't put out for me after the third date, I saw it as her playing mind fucking games and considered her a tease.

Even if my brain, real brain not my knob, told me she wasn't like that, I still sought a drenched hole to sink into. When she found out, she told me to fuck off. Apparently, she'd known I was a player, so when we'd started out, she'd been giving me a chance to prove myself by dating her and staying loyal. I screwed it all up because of my dick.

When I realised I liked her a hell of a lot more than what I'd thought, it was too late. My mind seemed obsessed with her, so I let her lick her wounds for a month, and then I set out to make her mine. I had to convince her my dogging days were done.

I also prayed I could keep it in my pants until she was willing to spread her legs for me.

The only problem was I loved sex. I fucking craved it. I had to have it, if I could, for morning, lunch, and dinner. I wished the taste of pussy was on my tongue all day long. The feeling of getting off was spectacular. Hell, I looked forward to shooting my load out every time because the peaceful feeling of release was a high.

Sex was my drug, and I couldn't get enough.

How-fucking-ever, I had to be goddamn proud of myself. While I stalked Simone for a month, I managed for my hand to become best friends with my dick. Never had I used so much lube in my life because I didn't want to get rash burns from rubbing it off too many times.

Simone soon found out I was serious about her. She couldn't *not* see it since it stared her in the face every time she turned. I'd become her stalker. Everywhere she went, I was there with a wink, a smile, and some smart-arsed comment.

It went on for a good couple of months.

After her best friend Josie went through what she did with her dad and then with Pick nearly getting killed, I thought she'd give me the chance to comfort her and, in a way, instil myself in her heart where she couldn't dislodge me. It didn't work.

It wasn't until four months before Willow showed up in my best mate's life that I finally had a breakthrough with Simone.

The day would forever be cemented in my brain because it was the day I used my best line on my woman. She was standing in line in her favourite coffee place before her classes started. She looked tired, more than usual, but still fuckin' stunning. I walked in and up behind her. When I placed my chin on her shoulder, she tensed a moment until her chest raised in a deep inhale. She relaxed immediately, leaning back into me and waited for whatever I was going to say.

It'd been like that for the last month. Her body finally craved my touch. Both her smirk and giggle told me I was wearing her down. My charm was the shit, and fina-fucking-lly, it was working.

Little did I know my next words, for some stupid reason, would be what worked to get her back in my life and bed. I nipped at her earlobe before whispering, "If I got to my hands and knees, would you milk me like a cow?"

Her laughter was loud, free, and full of humour. She turned, wrapped her arms around my neck, and pulled me in for a dick-hardening kiss.

When she pulled back, I grinned like a fool. "If that was all it took, I would have said some other dumb shit a long time ago."

She giggled, patted my cheek, and said, "Everything you say is dumb shit. But I'm finding myself becoming addicted to it."

"Thank fuck, 'cause I've laid my best moves out just for you, woman."

She snorted. "Well, if those have been your best moves, I better show you how much I appreciate your idiocy."

I pouted and whimpered, "And *I* would appreciate you showing me just how much you adore whatever comes outta my mouth."

Her expression changed. My heart dipped when her carefree smile fled, replaced with a frown. She searched my face for something. I had no idea if she found it, but she said, "I don't just adore what comes out of your mouth, Kalen Brooks. I adore *you*. Thank you for showing me I'm worth something."

It was my turn; my smile vanished. "You always have been."

She smirked. "Just took you a while to see it."

Rolling my eyes, I then winked. "Never said I was the smartest outta the bunch."

She giggled. "Oh, I know that."

"Cheeky wench." I smacked her arse.

A throat cleared behind us. "You two going to move up and order, or stay in everyone's way and keep making us sick?"

Tensing, I looked over my shoulder and glared. "I'll do whatever the fuck I want since I got my woman back in my life. Just because you ain't gettin' any, don't be a dick about it."

The dude's hands came up in front of him. His eyes widened. "All good, keep doing what you're doing."

"I will," I snarled.

"I can't," Simone said. I looked to her as her lips touched mine, and then she stepped back. "I have to get to class anyway. You go, and I'll see you later."

Raising a brow, I asked, "My place? I'll cook."

Her little chuckle was sweet and caused my dick to grow harder. "How about I bring takeaway? I've heard about your cooking. I don't want food poisoning."

Hell, fuck Pick for catching me throwing my guts up after I ate bad shellfish. The bastard was quick to tell everyone and no doubt, his woman told Simone.

"As long as you come, I don't give a fuck what we eat."

She grinned cheekily. "Oh, I do hope to come."

Groaning, I kissed her hard once and walked out before I had my pants down trying to stick my dick in her in any way I could.

As I left the café, I seemed to have a new spring in my step. Fuck, if that was what being in love was about, I was all for it. Shit, I couldn't stop smiling like a tool. But hell, if anyone said anything, I'd tell them where to go.

I was happy.

Finally, fucking happy.

Since it was my day off, from there, I went straight home to clean the pigsty.

The garage Hawks owned off the compound was busy. Even though Pick and Billy had finally started after Josie's shit had gone down, it was still bustling with customers, new and old. Which explained why my house was filthy.

At around seven, Simone turned up with pizza. It was great to see her in my house, making herself at home because one day, I could see her moving in and all her girl shit laying around.

After we had eaten, we sat our arses down in the living room. I didn't have much in the house. It was a true man's place. It included the main things I needed: a TV, a couch, a bed, and a bathroom. But Simone didn't seem to care; she curled up beside me while we watched random stuff on the TV in between talking.

"You're staying the night," I ordered.

"Sounds like the perfect plan." She grinned.

For five months, things were fucking amazing.

We were in love.

We told each other that every night when she'd come by to stay.

Only time wasn't on our side. She was busy with uni, and I was busy with work. We were both tired, but every night she stayed, I made sure my woman knew how I felt about her.

Five months, I had her in my life before it went to shit. I'd known something was wrong when she hadn't wanted to tell anyone about us. No one knew of our relationship. She wanted to keep it a secret to see how things went. I understood because I'd been the one to fuck it up the first time. Still, she knew I was all in, but it appeared she wasn't for some reason.

It was a month after Willow turned up, and her thing with Dodge went down that shit changed. I was sure when Willow moved in, she knew someone was sneaking into the house and my bed. Fuck, it made me feel like a cheap whore, but I did it for Simone. I kept our relationship a secret for her, and then I got nothing. One night she didn't show, and I didn't know what had happened. If I'd done something.

I tried to fight for my woman. I rang her. I went to her place. I asked Josie; she didn't have a clue. I asked Nary, who'd moved in with her, but none of them knew what was going on. She'd been spending more time with her family than at the house with Nary. In the end, she even avoided Josie.

It went on for five months.

And then my life, my heart, every-fucking-thing went down the drain.

CHAPTER ONE

DIVE

My head was under the hood of a car in the Hawks garage when my phone rang. I ignored it and kept doing what I was doing, thinking they could leave a message because the client was going to be back later that day to pick up the piece-of-shit car. Then my thoughts drifted over to hurting Willow for even booking the car in the first place. However, she was a sucker for a sad case, and the old woman had talked Willow into taking her shit car in for a service. It needed more than a service; it needed to be put down.

My phone rang again.

Then again.

And again.

"Fuck," I cursed, wiping my hands on the rag from my back pocket as my heart took off in my chest. Hell, I probably should have answered it anyway in case it had something to do with the fuckhead Baxter, but all my brothers were at the garage working alongside me, so nothing bad could have happened.

My heart slowed.

Just as it started ringing again, I answered with, "Yo."

"Josie, no," Simone yelled in the background. Again, my heart sped up as I tensed, my jaw clenching in worry.

"Josie, what's goin' on?" I clipped roughly. Both Pick and Billy, Josie's men, stopped what they were doing and came towards me.

"Dive, y-you need to come to Simone's place, right now. She has something to tell you." Her voice was soft and quivered at the end.

Christ. If someone had hurt Simone, I'd stab the fucker.

"I'm there," I bit out, hung up, and thrust my phone in my back pocket of my jeans. Looking to the waiting men, I said, "Josie's fine, but she wants me to get to Simone's."

"We're comin', just in case," Pick said, throwing his

cleaning rag to the bench next to him. I knew not to argue with him or even Billy when it came to Josie.

We made our way out the front after letting Dodge know we were taking off. He nearly bitched that all of us couldn't go until I told him about the phone call. Instead, he nodded. Concern filled his eyes before he said gruffly, "Call if you need me."

We straddled our bikes, and they roared to life. The ride seemed to take longer than it usually would. My hands sweated the whole way; my heart thumped hard in my chest, and my teeth fucking hurt from clenching them along the way while I agonised over what in the hell could have happened. Finally, we pulled up to a stop out the front of Simone's apartment building. We were all off at the same time, and swiftly, we made our way in and up to the second floor. Just as I was about to bang on her door, it swung open. Josie stepped out, her eyes red from crying. Stepping right up to Pick, she buried her head into his chest as Billy stepped up behind her, his body stiff, and his eyes hard with unease.

"What the fuck is going on?" I growled.

"Dive?" Simone called from inside.

Josie turned her face to me and smiled sadly. That was when I knew it was something bad. She reached out her hand and gripped my wrist, giving it a squeeze. "Go easy on her," Josie pleaded.

With a stiff nod, I shook off her hold and stepped into

the living room. Billy closed the door after me, leaving them on the other side. It was then Simone walked in from the kitchen. With red-rimmed eyes, she offered me a small, shy smile. I gave her a chin lift, and that was when I looked down.

My eyes widened, and my jaw popped open. Shock froze me in place. "You're knocked up." Her stomach was huge, and she waddled as she took the last steps to the couch. Slowly, she lowered herself backwards and sat.

"Before you ask, you're the father." She cringed as my eyes darkened on her to a glare.

My body liquefied. Clenching my hands, my knees wobbled until I steadied myself. Anger flared inside of me instead. "And you chose to tell me like this?" I seethed through clenched teeth.

She looked to her stomach and rubbed a hand over it. "I'm sorry, Kalen."

My hands gripped my hair where I tugged on it. Then I threw my hands up in the air. I was pissed. I was fucking frustrated. None of it made sense. "Why did you disappear? Why would you do this to me when this is my kid? I could have been there for you through this. I could have helped you, supported you. But you ran, and it's never made sense because you knew I loved you. You knew I wanted us for-fuckin'-ever. Why in the fuck did you run?"

Tears ran freely from her eyes while her bottom lip

trembled, and I realised I hadn't listened to Josie and gone easy on her. How could I, when I'd just found out I was going to be a father from a woman so selfish, she'd cut me out of the first part of everything there was to experience? How could I when the woman I loved shut me out, cut me off, and had just shit down my throat?

"Would I be here if it weren't for Josie?"

She wiped her face and shook her head. "No."

Pain threatened to weigh me down. My stomach flipped and then dropped in misery. Gutted. I was absolutely gutted. "Why?"

She shrugged. "I didn't think you would want it."

I picked up the picture frame next to me and threw it to the wall. My hands then landed on my hips so I wouldn't grab anything else. She jumped when I roared, "How could you think that when I loved you with everything I have?"

The door behind me crashed open. "Brother?" Billy said.

"I'm fine," I snarled. "It's fine. Everything is *fucking* fine."

As I went to walk out the door in need to calm the hell down, Simone's pain-filled voice called, "Kalen, please. Please, I'm so sorry. I know I went about this the wrong way. But I promise I thought I was doing it to save you." Spinning to her, I watched her struggle to stand. It was hard not to go to her and help. I still loved her, which was why her deceit was harder to take. We'd made a child together, something so precious, but she threw away my feelings. I didn't count at all to her in this situation. Anger at her selfishness caused me to clamp my teeth together.

Of course I would have wanted to know. I'd want to be there every step of the way. I'd missed out on so much already: the first time she got to hear the heartbeat, the first picture of our child, the growth. Fuck, everything. I would have taken care of her. I would have helped. But I had no choice given to me and not only did it piss me way the fuck off, but it felt like my heart had been sliced open.

Her cry of pain brought my attention back to her, just as a puddle of wetness pooled down her legs to the floor.

"Shit," Billy bit out. "Josie," he yelled.

Pick was the first in the room. When Josie got through the door, I heard her gasp.

"No, no, no. It's too soon. Call an ambulance," Josie ordered as she ran to Simone's side. "Dive, get your arse over here and help her." My body jolted and my eyes went to Simone. Panic held her eyes wide and kept me captive.

Moving to her side, I gripped her arm and slid my other arm behind her back. "Come on, baby. Let's get you outside." All anger fled seeing Simone scared.

"Dive," she whispered. Her nails bit into my arm as a

contraction had her crying out again. Once it settled, she said, in a scared, soft voice, "It's too soon. He shouldn't be coming now. I don't want to…."

"The doctors will get it all sorted, baby. Could be,"—fuck, I didn't have a clue—"I don't know, a false alarm or something."

We started for the door when I heard Josie whisper, "Did you tell him?" Her voice was tight with sorrow. Simone shook her head, and Josie sighed. Her eyes met mine over Simone's head, and all I saw was pain.

What wasn't Simone telling me?

We'd made it down the stairs before another contraction nearly took her to the ground. The pain was obvious on her scrunched-up features, and I wished I could take it away from her. Even though she'd fucked up big time, my feelings never vanished. Hell, I even kept my dick in my pants since she'd been out of my life, in the hope she'd come back. Now I wouldn't leave her with a choice; she was having our kid. She was mine, and she'd better bloody accept it.

Billy stood out on the street ready to flag down the ambo. I was leaning against my ride with Simone between my legs leaning against me. Josie paced in front of us while Pick stood back watching his woman, his body tense. All of us wore a frown of worry, our brows drawn down in concern, and I knew I wasn't the only one feeling anxious, wishing help would hurry the hell up. Simone looked weak and tired. She'd lost weight even though she was pregnant. It was as if dark circles had been drawn under her eyes. Pale skin replaced what used to be a healthy glow, and she had no strength as she leaned against me. Her head rested in the crook of my neck until another contraction took hold. I grabbed her and held her up as she breathed through it, but every one she had seemed to drain her each time. More worry burned low in my belly as her panting breath worsened. Her eyes drooped lower and her cheeks seemed hollowed.

Thank fuck the sirens sounded off in the distance. It wouldn't be long until we had her at the hospital, and they'd be able to help her where I couldn't.

"They're coming, baby," I said and kissed her forehead. "We'll be okay."

"Dive," Simone whispered, her voice trembling.

"They're here," Billy announced. My shoulders sagged in relief. I gently guided Simone to stand and stood behind her as they pulled up. One woman and a guy jumped out of the vehicle and ran our way.

"What do we have here?" the woman asked.

"What in the fuck do you think?" I clipped out harshly. Did she know how to do her job?

"Casey," the guy ambo said. I watched the woman catch his eyes, and then he flicked his gaze to our

Harleys. She stiffened and walked back to the ambulance to grab out the gurney and wheeled it over.

"Dive, let them get Simone to the hospital," Josie said in a soothing voice. "They know what they're doing."

Glaring at them, I said, "I'm going with her."

"No," Simone yelled.

"Don't start, woman," I barked down at her as they helped her lay on the mattress.

"Please, I need you to bring my car. The keys are inside, and I'll need the car seat."

"Billy can take care of it," I ground the words out through clenched teeth.

"Dive," Josie started, laying her hand on my arm. "I'll go with her. We know you won't be far behind, and I promise I won't let anything happen to her."

Fuck. I didn't want to leave her, and I didn't understand why she wanted me out of her hair for the ride there. None of it made sense. Though I didn't want Simone worked up more than she was. Time was taking a toll on her. Finally, I nodded, and they bolted, with my woman on the gurney, to the ambulance. Before they were ready to take off, I ran to Simone's apartment, grabbed her keys, and tailed it to her car. Pick and Billy were already on their rides. I knew they'd follow me the whole way there.

In the rear-view mirror, I saw Nary pull up out front. Billy stayed back to let Nary know what was going down.

Betrayal clawed at my chest. Had she known Simone was pregnant with my kid and didn't tell me? Hell, I hoped not. I was ropable already, and I didn't want to take it out on Nary. She had enough going on.

My hands gripped the steering wheel tightly as I looked in the back seat at the small car seat strapped in. Christ, I was going to be a father. Me, a dad. My mind struggled to comprehend it. Also, a deep-rooted dread pounded through my veins; Simone was holding something back from me.

Was something wrong with our kid?

My chest ached at the thought.

Pulling up out the front of emergency, I jumped out and bolted for the doors. Pick was hot on my heels. As soon as the doors opened, I was at the counter demanding to be let through for my woman.

From there, everything went fast. Too fucking fast.

A nurse led me through to Simone's room. Josie was in there holding her hand. Two different doctors were rushing around hooking my woman up to machines while a nurse was between her legs checking out something down there.

"Everything all right?" I asked. All movement ceased for a second to take me in. Then the doctors looked at the nurse.

She sighed and nodded. "All looks good for the child. It's a bit early, but we'll take care of everything."

I gave her a chin lift as another nurse came in with some space-looking crib thingy. She smiled at me and said, "It's an incubator. Your child will have to stay in here for a little while until it's ready to go home."

Grunting out a reply, I then asked, "So, the kid is coming?" My head spun. Everything was happening so fast.

She smiled, but it was sad. "Yes, your child has had enough of waiting. It wants to come and now."

My feet took me to my woman's side before I even registered I'd moved. Josie, who stood on the other side, was crying. My knuckles were white with how hard my hands clenched at my sides. Something was going on I didn't know about. But just as I was about to demand answers, another contraction hit Simone. Her eyes closed. Her mouth pinched tightly, and she bared down.

My gut dropped at the sight of Simone in pain. I'd do anything to take it from her. *Fuck.* I ran a hand through my hair in frustration.

"Should she be pushing?" Josie asked in an alarmingly high voice. Panic reared inside of me.

A doctor pushed me aside and barked down at Simone, "No pushing, Simone. Please just let us do a C-section."

What in the fuck is goin' on?

She shook her head and licked her dry, cracked lips.

"T-there's no point. We all know this." She opened her eyes and called, "Dive."

The doctor stepped back, his face solemn, his eyes sad.

I stepped up, my mouth dipping down with worry. "Baby, what's going on?" I pleaded.

"G-get Pick or Billy in here for Josie, please."

My head jerked back. "Why?"

"No one else can come in. The room is already too full." The other doctor said before he stepped up to Josie's side and held his stethoscope to Simone's chest, listening to her heart.

Simone snorted. "What's one more, Doc?"

"Simone." The doctor sighed and shook his head.

"Please," she begged. "They'll need him."

"Who will need who?" I asked, confused at fuck.

My eyes stayed on my woman, even as Josie bent low and whispered something to her. I didn't see anyone leave the room, but I noticed when Pick came in. He immediately stood behind his woman.

Flexing my clenched jaw, I welcomed the grind of pain and the distraction it offered. The nurses and doctors busied themselves around the room while Josie stood and held Simone's hand tightly, but she curled her body into Pick. He wound his arms around her as her body shook with sobs.

Simone's hand in mine tightened, only just a little; her strength wasn't there. My eyes went back down to her. She smiled up at me, but I could see the strain on her face. She cleared her throat. "I'm so sorry." Tears fell from her eyes. "I love you. I always have, but I wanted to protect you from this and leave you with something to remember me by."

Fear gripped my heart and squeezed. "Wait, what? Baby, what do you mean? What are you talking about?"

Her chest heaved with a heavy breath; she opened her mouth to answer, but then her eyes widened, and her hand went slack. The machines went crazy, and Josie screamed, as I watched Simone smile before her eyes closed.

No. Christ, please no.

Cold. I was so fucking cold as I watched on powerless. My whole body shivered, my stomach churning at the sight of my woman lying motionless on the bed.

"Do something," I yelled, my voice thick with misery.

Doctors barked orders I didn't listen to. Pick pulled Josie back to let the doctors work while I leaned down and whispered, "Don't you die on me, baby. Don't leave me. Our kid needs you, needs his mother. And I need my woman. My life. Don't leave me, baby." My voice quivered. *Fuck. Fuck.* "Please," I begged her.

Her body jolted. I looked down to see a doctor slice open my woman's stomach. Seconds ticked by before I saw a baby pulled free. It was tiny, still and silent.

Fuck. Jesus, no, no, no.

I closed my eyes tight. I didn't want to see; all of it was fucking agony laced with more heartache.

"Sir," a nurse beside me murmured.

Ignoring her, I opened my eyes to Simone. It couldn't be over. Gripping my hair, I shook my head. I wanted to tear my fuckin' hair out, slit my wrists, or have someone beat me senseless so I didn't feel. I didn't want to feel. It hurt too much. Though, my body seemed to be already going through the process. A stabbing pain ripped through my chest, my stomach convulsing in agony. Still, my head, my mind wouldn't let it be the end, wouldn't accept it. "No," I whispered through clenched teeth.

People around me yelled and moved. They'd left Simone to work on the baby.

"She's gone. I'm sorry." The nurse touched my arm. I shook her off and pressed my forehead against my woman's.

"Please, come back to me, baby." My breath hitched. "Please."

"I'm sorry," the nurse said again.

My hand went to Simone's face, but it was cold. She was cold and still. No life left inside of her. My woman was gone. No longer would I see her smile, hear her laugh and feel her at my side.

Standing, I threw my head back and screamed my anguish, "No!" Tilting my head down, my eyes landed on

317

the nurse, and I ordered with a snarl, "Work on her. Make her live." I grabbed her arm and pulled her closer. "Fucking help her."

"Brother," Pick said, his usually hard voice was soft. He grabbed my wrist. "Let the nurse go."

"She needs to help my woman," I demanded, my eyes hard on my brother.

"Brother," he whispered, his eyes heavy with sorrow. "She's gone."

My eyes narrowed even more. "She's not."

Don't make it real. Don't take my life away from me. We can make us work. We're a family.

But they were so still. They weren't moving. My woman. My child. Unmoving and no breath in their bodies.

My chest heaved to fight for air.

"She is," Pick murmured.

He dropped my wrist when I let go of the nurse, who immediately stepped back. It was just as well because the next thing I grabbed was a stand. I picked it up and crashed it to the floor, over and over, screaming and cursing through the pain ripping into me. Through the reality crashing into my soul.

"Get him out," someone barked.

A hand wrapped around my throat, and I was pushed up and then out of the room, stumbling until my back was forced up against a wall with Pick in my face snapping, "Enough."

"Fuck you," I snarled. "Fuck you," I roared.

Ruckus arose around us. People yelled, ran, and things fell to the ground.

"I'm sorry," Pick offered.

Leaning forward, his hand tightened on my throat as Billy showed at his side, "Fuck. You," I growled. Anger was good. Better than sorrow.

Pick shook his head sadly. "She's gone, brother. Let it sink in. Take it on board and come back to the now because you need to fight for your kid."

"No." I shook my head, my eyes closing. "It wasn't moving. It wasn't crying. They fuckin' cry when they come out. It's... Fuck. Fuck me, motherfucking hell."

"It's not the end, brother. They're still in there fighting for him. You need to as well."

Unmanageable pain nearly took me to my knees, but Pick had me. He dropped his hand from my throat and held my chest against the wall.

"Fight for him," Pick whispered.

"She's gone." Despair formed inside of me.

"She is." Pick nodded.

"She's gone," I cried, opening my eyes as tears filled them.

"She has."

"Brother." Pain weaved itself through that one word,

desperate and with no chance of ever dulling. I banged my head back into the wall and snapped my eyes closed. I let it all seep in. The loss, the pain, the anguish.

I let it all in until I heard a baby's cry from the other room.

ACKNOWLEDGEMENTS

First and always, Becky and her team at Hot Tree Editing.

To my ladies in the Hawks MC Fan Group. The help you give me, I appreciate having it every day. Naming the characters wouldn't be the same without your input! Love ya all xx

TL Smith, you, girlfriend, have a gift to write dark scenes. Thank you for your help and your friendship!

My soul sister, Justine Littleton xxx

Lastly, but never least, my family. Your encouragement and love means everything to me.

ALSO BY LILA ROSE

Hawks MC: Ballarat Charter

Holding Out (FREE) Zara and Talon

Climbing Out: Griz and Deanna

Finding Out (novella) Killer and Ivy

Black Out: Blue and Clarinda

No Way Out: Stoke and Malinda

Coming Out (novella) Mattie and Julia

Hawks MC: Caroline Springs Charter

The Secret's Out: Pick, Billy and Josie

Hiding Out: Dodge and Willow

Down and Out: Dive and Mena

Living Without: Vicious and Nary

Walkout (novella) Dallas and Melissa

Hear Me Out: Beast and Knife

Breakout (novella) Handle and Della

Fallout: Fang and Poppy

Standalones related to the Hawks MC

Out of the Blue (Lan, Easton, and Parker's story)

Out Gamed (novella) (Nancy and Gamer's story)

Outplayed (novella) (Violet and Travis's story)

Romantic comedies

Making Changes

Making Sense

Fumbled Love

Trinity Love Series

Left to Chance

Love of Liberty (novella)

Paranormal

Death (with Justine Littleton)

In The Dark

CONNECT WITH LILA ROSE

Webpage: www.lilarosebooks.com

Facebook: http://bit.ly/2du0taO

Instagram: www.instagram.com/lilarose78/

Goodreads:

www.goodreads.com/author/show/7236200.Lila_Rose